PRAISE FOR

The Wedding Date

"A swoony rom-com brimming with humor and charm."

—*Entertainment Weekly*

"Guillory's debut is as enchanting as her characters—bright, bold, warm, and wonderful. Even better, there's a proposal to rival any commercial that Madison Avenue can deliver."

—*The Washington Post*

"This novel reads like a truly *contemporary* contemporary romance in that the hero and heroine grapple with issues anyone dating today will relate to."

—NPR

"What a charming, warm, sexy gem of a novel. I couldn't put *The Wedding Date* down. I love a good romance and this delivered from the first page to the last. . . . One of the best books I've read in a while."

—Roxane Gay, *New York Times* bestselling author

"*The Wedding Date* brims with personality. It's funny, deeply honest, and above all, truly swoony."

—Heather Cocks and Jessica Morgan,
bestselling authors of *The Royal We*

"[An] incredibly delicious meet-cute. . . . Guillory keeps this contemporary romance fresh with well-drawn multicultural characters navigating the perils of long-distance relationships."

—*Booklist*

The Wedding Party

JASMINE GUILLORY

JOVE
NEW YORK

A JOVE BOOK
Published by Berkley
An imprint of Penguin Random House LLC
1745 Broadway, New York, NY 10019

Copyright © 2019 by Jasmine Guillory
Readers Guide copyright © 2019 by Penguin Random House LLC
Penguin Random House supports copyright. Copyright fuels creativity, encourages
diverse voices, promotes free speech, and creates a vibrant culture. Thank you for buying
an authorized edition of this book and for complying with copyright laws by not
reproducing, scanning, or distributing any part of it in any form without permission.
You are supporting writers and allowing Penguin Random House to continue to
publish books for every reader.

A JOVE BOOK, BERKLEY, and the BERKLEY & B colophon
are registered trademarks of Penguin Random House LLC.

Library of Congress Cataloging-in-Publication Data

Names: Guillory, Jasmine, author.
Title: The wedding party / Jasmine Guillory.
Description: New York: Jove, 2019.
Identifiers: LCCN 2018057817| ISBN 9781984802194 (softcover) |
ISBN 9781984802200 (ebook)
Subjects: | BISAC: FICTION / Romance / Contemporary. | FICTION /
Contemporary Women. | GSAFD: Love stories.
Classification: LCC PS3607.U48553 W44 2019 | DDC 813/.6—dc23
LC record available at https://lccn.loc.gov/2018057817

First Edition: July 2019

Printed in the United States of America
1   3   5   7   9   10   8   6   4   2

Cover design and illustration by Vikki Chu
Book design by Kristin del Rosario

To my sister,
Sasha Guillory,
who always listens to my dreams.

ACKNOWLEDGMENTS

I am grateful from the bottom of my heart for so many people for all their help, advice, cheerleading, and support. You've all played a role in bringing this book to life, and I can't thank you enough.

Team Berkley: you are all a dream come true. Cindy Hwang, you're not just a fantastic editor, but you believe in me more than I believe in myself. Jessica Brock and Fareeda Bullert, I'm happy every day I get to work with you. Angela Kim, Kristine Swartz, Erin Galloway, Craig Burke, and Jin Yu, you've all gone above and beyond for me in every way possible. Megha Jain, Marianne Grace, Kayley Hoffman, and Vikki Chu, thanks so much for everything you do for my books. And a huge thanks to Jaci Updike, Lauren Monaco, Andy Dudley, and the incredible Penguin Random House sales team across the country.

Holly Root, you are the best agent any writer could ask for. I don't know what I would have done these past few years without you by my side, and I don't even want to think about it. And thank you to Alice Lawson for everything you've done for me and my books. Thank you both for answering my many (many) questions, and being incredible partners in my career.

Reese Witherspoon and the entire Hello Sunshine team, thank you so much for everything you've done for my books, and especially for introducing them to so many enthusiastic readers.

Writers and those in the publishing world are some of the most generous people I've ever encountered. Amy Spalding and Akilah Brown, you're two of the first people I ever talked to about writing, and your support then and throughout these past few years is a big part of what got me here. Thank you to Roxane Gay, Heather Cocks, Jessica Morgan, Robin Benway, Tayari Jones, Ruby Lang, Alexis Coe, Esmé Weijun Wang, Sara Zarr, Nicole Chung, Jami Attenberg, Liz Lopatto, Rainbow Rowell, Daniel Ortberg, Nicole Cliffe, Laura Turner, Caille Millner, Stephanie Lucianovic, Samantha Powell, Melissa Baumgart, Kayla Cagan, Lyz Lenz, Maret Orliss, Margaret Willison, and Rachel Fershleiser for all your support, advice, enthusiasm, and reassurance. I'm so grateful for all of you.

I have the best friends in the entire world. Simi Patnaik and Nicole Clouse, I love you both so much. Janet Goode, I'm happy every day that I have your friendship. Jill Vizas, I'm so happy that you've been a constant in my life for over thirty years. A huge thanks to Melissa Sladden, Jina Kim, Julian Davis Mortenson, Nathan Cortez, Lisa McIntire, Nanita Cranford, Joy Alferness, Sarah Mackey, Maggie Levine, Sara Kate Wilkinson, Kate Leos, Lyette Mercier, Kyle Wong, Ryan Gallagher, Sarah Tiedeman, Veronica Ades, and Toby Rugger for your friendship and love.

Wellesley College and all of her alumnae: I'm grateful every day I have you in my corner.

Special thanks to Matt Kagan, Sybil Grant, and Annette Majerowicz. Everything I got right about comms work is because of you; we'll call everything I got wrong poetic license.

Librarians and booksellers: you're the best people! Thank you for the love you have for my books; your enthusiasm has meant so much.

And to my family: I am so grateful for your support and love throughout the many ups and downs. Thanks to my huge extended family on all sides and extra thanks to all my cousins, who are always there for me.

Mom, Dad, and Sasha, I love you all so much.

Thank you to all my readers. I'm overjoyed at how you've embraced my books, and I hope you love this one, too.

Chapter One

~⁓⁓~

MADDIE FOREST DIDN'T WANT TO GO TO THIS BIRTHDAY PARTY. SHE didn't like parties in the first place—they were always too loud, there were always annoying people who she had to pretend to be nice to, and there were never enough snacks. But she especially didn't want to go to Theo Stephens's party. It was likely to be as boring, self-important, and pedantic as the guest of honor.

But, unfortunately, one of Theo's best friends was her best friend, Alexa, and Alexa had asked Maddie to come with her to the party. Alexa's brief fling with some doctor in L.A. had just ended badly, and Maddie could tell she was still upset about it. So instead of being either snug at home in a caftan watching *House Hunters* and eating delivery pizza, or out somewhere with Alexa, drinking wine and eating fancy pizza, she was looking for parking in one of the worst neighborhoods in San Francisco in which to find parking.

"Don't worry, we don't have to stay all night," Alexa said as they circled the block. "I know you'd rather be watching HGTV, but I couldn't skip Theo's birthday and I wasn't in the mood to come alone."

Alexa must have been desperate to have her there, because she'd told Maddie if she came, she would wear whatever Maddie wanted. There were few things Maddie loved more than when she got to style conservative Alexa in something edgy and force her to branch out.

"I'll protect you from the bros. Just give me the nod whenever you want to take off," Maddie said.

"Not all of Theo's friends are bros!" Alexa said. "Not even most of them. There are just a few who rub me the wrong way. His brother should be there tonight—he's kind of a bro, but also hilarious and Theo's opposite. You'll like him. Anyway, thanks for coming. I know this isn't really your thing."

Maddie sped up as she spotted a parking space down the street.

"You'll pay me back for this next time I need a buddy. Just don't make me wear a shift dress and a cardigan that time, please."

Alexa looked down at herself as Maddie pulled into the parking spot.

"Speaking of, are you sure about this outfit? I have way too much cleavage with this dress."

Maddie turned off the car. Too much cleavage? Please. Alexa had been corrupted by her conservative work wardrobe, and now she thought even the hint of a breast was shocking in public, especially if she was around people who knew she was the chief of staff to the mayor. Her dress had *barely* any cleavage, come on.

Well. Okay. That wasn't quite true. But it was barely any cleavage in comparison to other dresses Maddie could have put her in.

"I'm very sure. I'm a professional, remember? That dress has just the right amount of cleavage for a Saturday night out at a bar." She checked her makeup in her car mirror. Yes, she'd put the perfect amount of highlighter on her brown skin; just enough so she looked like she'd been at the beach earlier that day, but not so much that she looked like C-3PO.

She got out of the car and linked arms with Alexa.

"And stop tugging at that dress. You look fantastic. Let's go dazzle these men."

When they walked into the bar, Maddie surveyed the crowd. Lots of jeans and hoodies, as she'd suspected. She shook her head and followed Alexa to the back of the bar, where the party presumably was. Oh, yep, there was Theo. The one good thing about Theo: you could always count on him to dress well. He had on well-fitting dark jeans and a soft blue button-down. He greeted Alexa with a big hug.

"You made it!"

"Happy birthday! I wouldn't have missed it for the world," Alexa said as she hugged him back.

Theo pulled back from Alexa and saw Maddie, and the grin dropped from his face.

"Maddie." He nodded at her. "Thanks for coming."

"Theo." She nodded back. Ugh, she guessed she had to say it. "Happy birthday."

He raised his eyebrows and smirked at her.

"Thanks. I'm delighted you're here."

She and Theo both knew he was as delighted to have her here as she was to be here.

She'd first met Theo three years before, at Alexa's birthday party. Theo had recently started as the mayor's communications director, and when Maddie had seen both how cute he was and his excellent pin-striped shirt, she'd thought maybe there might finally be a spark between her and one of Alexa's nerdy friends.

She could not have been more wrong.

After a few minutes of chat about what kind of pizza and beer they should order, she'd asked him where he'd been before coming to the mayor's office.

Theo had sat up a little straighter.

"Well, after I left *Harvard*," he'd started. Ugh, of course he was that guy. He went on to talk for ten straight minutes about himself.

Finally, he'd climbed out of his own asshole and asked her where she went to college. When she'd said she'd started at the local community college and then moved on to UCLA, he responded with, "Good for you!" in the most condescending way possible. Then he asked what she did. When she told him she was in the process of starting her own personal styling business, he'd asked, "Why would anyone pay you to help them get dressed?"

She'd looked at him and smiled.

"You know, I couldn't decide how you'd react to that. I was torn between condescending to me about my career, or mansplaining my job to me. Considering the rest of our conversation, it was touch and go which one it would be, but you landed on the first. Congratulations, I guess, on being so predictable."

While he tried to find a comeback, she'd moved to the other side of the table to talk to someone else. She didn't often let herself be that bitchy anymore, but few things infuriated her more than when people looked down on her job.

They'd barely spoken to each other since that night, even though they were both frequently in the same room because of Alexa. Why she was so close to Theo, Maddie would never understand.

Maddie shrugged. She didn't care about Theo or any of his

ill-dressed friends; she was just here to help her best friend recover from that Drew guy she'd clearly liked a lot more than she was willing to admit.

"Who wants a drink?" Theo asked.

Alexa's hand shot in the air.

"I'm not as quick on the draw as Hermione over here, but I want one, too," Maddie said. If she was going to be here, she might as well get a free drink out of this.

Theo put his arm around Alexa and started walking toward the bar, leaving Maddie to follow them.

"Come with me. The bartender is supposed to be serving my friends first, but we'll see if that actually works."

Five minutes later, both she and Alexa had gin and tonics in their hands. Thank God they did, because Alexa forced her to circulate around the party.

"Come on, there's good networking here! See, I told you not all of Theo's friends are bros; there are lots of women here. I bet you a drink you can pick up a client or two at this party. Did you bring your business cards?"

Maddie rolled her eyes at her best friend as she pulled her card case out of her jacket pocket.

"You trained me well. Of course I brought them."

She followed Alexa around the room and watched her network.

"Four weddings to go to in the next month? Oh God, I've been there!" Alexa said to the girlfriend of some friend of Theo's. "Thank God I had Maddie—I had no idea what to wear to any of those weddings, and now with Instagram, you can't wear the same dress to all four weddings or people will think you only own one dress. Maddie helped me find outfits and negotiate all of the weird dress codes people come up with."

"Oh my God, the dress codes!" the woman said. "What does 'beach chic' mean? Or 'farm formal'? Those are just two of the annoying dress codes for these weddings, and I have no idea what these people want from me. Just tell me if I need to wear a cocktail dress or if I can wear a sundress! Heels or cute sandals or comfortable sandals? I don't know!" The woman turned to Maddie. "So what is it you do? Is she right that you know what these dress codes mean?"

Maddie launched into her elevator pitch.

"I'm a stylist, which means I help people find outfits for all sorts of events, whether it's work or weddings or anything in between. And yes, I've successfully dressed clients for those exact dress codes and ones that sounded even wackier."

Alexa grinned at Maddie. See, *this* was when having a wing woman was key. Who cared about having one to help out with men? It was for this kind of stuff where having Alexa by her side and pumping her up was most important. Alexa walked off to join Theo, while Maddie went in for the kill.

Ten minutes later, Maddie presented Alexa with a gin martini.

"We have an appointment next week," she said. "Thanks for that."

Alexa grinned back at her.

Just then, a tall white guy in a button-down shirt, who was way too attractive for his own good, came up to their group. Oh God, yet another bro.

"Alexa?"

Wait a minute. From the look on Alexa's face, this wasn't just yet another bro. Why did she have that look on her face for some guy that Maddie didn't recognize?

"Drew? What are you doing here?"

This was Drew? No wonder Alexa had been so upset when their thing had fizzled out.

Maddie looked from Alexa to Drew. It was her turn to be a wing woman. She plucked Alexa's martini out of her hand, grabbed Theo by the arm, and pulled him over to the other side of the bar.

"Who the hell is that, and why did you . . . Oh!" Theo stared at Alexa and Drew, who had moved into the far corner of the bar. "That guy she went to the wedding with?"

At least Theo caught on quickly.

"Yeah, it's definitely that guy," Maddie said.

"What's he doing here?" Theo asked.

Maddie sipped Alexa's abandoned martini.

"I have no idea, but he sure seemed happy to see her."

Theo turned to her.

"Do you think she's okay over there? Do we need to go rescue her?"

The one good thing Maddie could say about Theo was she knew he was firmly on Team Alexa.

Maddie looked over to the corner of the bar. Alexa did not look like she wanted or needed rescuing. At least, for now.

"She's okay. She knows we're here if she needs us."

Neither of them moved. They obviously had to stay close by. Just in case Alexa needed them. But they couldn't keep staring at Alexa and Drew; that was creepy. They both turned away from the corner of the room at the same time and looked at each other. Maddie tried to think of something to say.

"So, Maddie," Theo said, "watching any good TV lately?"

She spent a moment trying to decide if she should give him the real answer and let him make fun of her, or list all the boring and stressful prestige TV shows she knew a pretentious guy like Theo would be into, just so she didn't have to deal. Sure, she wouldn't be able to have a conversation about any of those shows about terrible men doing terrible things in very poorly lit rooms, but men usually didn't care about having an actual conversation about their favorite TV shows; they just wanted you to listen to them talk about them.

Hell with it. She didn't care enough about Theo's opinion of her to lie to him.

"I watch a lot of *House Hunters* these days, actually."

He laughed. Served her right for actually engaging in conversation with Theo.

"I love *House Hunters,*" he said. Wait, what? "I'm kind of obsessed with it. The people infuriate me, and look, I know the whole thing is fake, but I don't care!"

That was a surprise.

"You? Watching *House Hunters*? You don't spend all your time watching C-SPAN or documentaries or all of those shows about drug dealers or whatever?"

He shook his head.

"I deal with enough depressing and stressful stuff at work." He took a sip of his drink and shrugged. "Okay, fine, I have been known to watch a documentary or two in my time, but . . ."

Maddie pointed at him.

"I knew it!"

He shook his head and put his hand on her shoulder.

"*But,* as I was saying, I only do that when I'm in a really bad mood and want to lean into it. Otherwise, it's lots of house shopping and renovating shows. I find them so soothing."

Well, that was something she never would have expected to find out tonight.

"There you are!" A black guy in jeans, a black T-shirt, and very cool sneakers bounded over to them. "Happy birthday, dude."

"Oh, so my little brother finally shows up," Theo said as he smacked hands with his brother. "How many hours late are you this time?"

"Hours?" The brother looked at Maddie for support. "Back me up on this, beautiful woman I've never met before—I'm, like, barely an hour late."

Maddie grinned despite herself. Theo's brother had definitely gotten the lion's share of the family charm.

"Well . . . as much as I want to be on your side here, brother of Theo whose name I don't know, from what I was told, the party started at eight, and it's now almost ten, so . . ."

"That's ridiculous. No party starts at eight. No brother of mine would have a party that started at eight. You must be mistaken."

He reached out and shook her hand.

"And I'm Benjamin Stephens, but my friends all call me Ben, and I hope you and I will be friends."

Theo sighed.

"Maddie, this is my brother, Ben. He's shameless. Please feel free to ignore or snub or smack him whenever he says something worthy of one of those things. Ben, this is Maddie. She's Alexa's friend. Please don't embarrass me more than you already have."

Ben slapped his brother on the back and grinned at Maddie.

"Anything for you on your birthday. Speaking of, what are you drinking? I'll get you another."

Ben turned and looked over at the bar.

"Oh, wow, they have some great bourbon here!" He made a beeline for the bar without waiting to hear Theo's answer.

Theo opened his mouth to shout after him, then shook his head and turned back to Maddie.

"Well, that's my brother. I swear he's not always like that." Theo shook his head. "He's usually worse."

Maddie looked at Theo's brother, now talking animatedly to the bartender.

"He seems like a lot of fun . . . in small doses."

Theo laughed.

"He's a lot of fun in big doses, too; it's just that I usually need to sleep for three days after a night of drinking with him. That time we went to Vegas together . . ." Theo let out a long breath. "I think I didn't leave my apartment for a solid week afterward."

Maddie was just about to ask another question when Theo's eyes widened and he nudged her. She looked around, just in time to see Alexa and Drew walking toward them, holding hands. She turned back to Theo and widened her eyes at him and nudged him back.

Theo and Maddie shared a grin as Alexa introduced both of them to Drew and his friend Carlos, who was also randomly in San Francisco. *She absolutely didn't need rescuing*, their eyes said to each other. Theo had definitely never shared a joke with Maddie before.

Alexa was beaming. Oh, wow, she had it bad for this guy. Theo narrowed his eyes as he looked at Drew. Alexa had never told him exactly what happened at the end there, but Drew had better not hurt her. Right now, though, he looked very happy to be reunited with Alexa, so Theo would reserve judgment on him for now.

Maybe he'd get Maddie another drink. Would that make her smile at him again? Just then, his brother joined the group.

"You didn't tell me what drink you wanted, so I just got you bourbon," he said. Great timing, Ben.

Theo grabbed the drink from his brother and took a sip. His brother was forgiven; this was really good bourbon. And he probably didn't need to push it with Maddie—one smile was enough.

For some reason, Maddie had hated him basically on sight. Okay, he was pretty sure part of the reason was the stupid way he'd asked her about her job the first time they'd met. He hadn't meant to sound like such a jerk. Fine, he *had* sounded like a jerk, but she hadn't even let him back up and explain what he'd meant and had basically called him a pompous asshole. Whatever, he and Maddie would have never gotten along anyway. She was the cool, hot, party type, and he was the kind of guy everyone thought watched C-SPAN in his spare time.

He glanced up at his brother, talking animatedly to Maddie. She was smiling at him. Of course she was. Ben always managed to charm everyone.

He pulled his phone out of his pocket. Sure, it was Saturday night, but he could just check his work email for a second.

"Theo!"

He turned to see who was shouting his name and grinned to see two old friends near the door. He slid his phone back in his pocket.

"Alexa, yell at my brother if he gets annoying. I have to go say hi to some people."

He caught up with his friends Julian and Lindsey over by the bar. A few minutes into their conversation, Maddie walked by, presumably on the way to the bathroom. He reached out and touched her shoulder.

"Oh, it's you," was all she said when she stopped.

It was very irritating that Maddie was the only person he could talk to about this Alexa thing, but she was just going to have to deal with it.

"Yeah, it's me. Want to bet how long it'll be before they make some excuse and take off? I give it less than an hour."

She tossed her head and laughed. Why did it feel like every man in the bar turned to look at her when she did that? Yes, she looked incredible in that hot pink dress; even he could admit that. But he got the feeling she was laughing at, not with, him.

"I'd never take that bet." Yep, she was laughing at him. "I'd be surprised if they were still here in thirty minutes, though Alexa's tendency toward unnecessary politeness might force her to stay longer than she wants to."

He pulled out his phone and turned on the stopwatch.

"For science." He grinned at her. Amazingly, she grinned back before she walked away.

He shook off thoughts of Maddie and turned back to his friends.

In exactly forty-one minutes, Alexa came over to him.

"So, um . . ." She was definitely blushing. "I think we're going to take off."

He did everything possible to hold back a laugh.

"You and Maddie are leaving early? Okay, well, thanks for coming, and . . ."

She smacked his arm, and he finally let himself laugh.

"You're such a fucking asshole. No, not me and Maddie."

He leaned in for a hug.

"He'd better be nice to you. See you Monday."

When Alexa and Drew walked out the door, Theo looked around the bar for Maddie. She was in a group with Julian and

Lindsey, but she was looking right at him, and they grinned at each other. After a second or so, Maddie looked away from him and back at Lindsey. Okay, well, he guessed that was the one day in five years Maddie would be nice to him. Now that Alexa was gone, he figured she'd leave any minute.

But every time Theo glanced around the bar for a glimpse of hot pink, she was still there. After an hour or so, Theo saw Ben walk over to her group. He wandered over, too, just to make sure his brother wasn't causing any trouble.

"Hey, man!" Ben said. "I was just saying to these guys that we should go dancing. I know this great place in SoMa. Let's go!"

Yep, Ben was trying to cause trouble, all right.

"Have a fantastic time, and give me a call tomorrow to tell me all about it," he said.

Ben turned to Maddie.

"Maddie!" Ben said. "We're all talking about going dancing. Want to come?"

She shook her head.

"Thanks for the invite, but I have work to do tomorrow. I have to go. Theo, happy birthday."

She didn't lean in for a hug, so he didn't, either.

"Thanks, and thanks for coming. I saw you talking to Lindsey and Julian. Did you get another possible client?"

She nodded.

"I think so. And also maybe your friend Fiona."

"Oh good, Lindsey and Fiona are both great. Glad this may have been profitable for you." What a weird and businesslike thing to say at the end of a party. What was wrong with him? "See you around." No wonder she thought he was uptight; even with a little too much bourbon tonight, he sounded so stilted around her.

She smirked at him and turned to walk out, when he thought of something.

"Wait. Did you drive here?"

She turned back to him.

"Yeah, I'm just a few blocks away."

He checked his pockets for his phone and keys.

"Let me walk you to your car."

She shook her head.

"No, you don't have to do that. I'm fine to walk by myself. I don't want to drag you away from your party," she said.

He hesitated. He wanted to insist, but he couldn't tell if she said that because she didn't want him to feel like he had to walk her to her car, or if she said it because she was sick of him and really didn't want him to walk with her. But the Mission could get weird on weekend nights, with too many marauding bands of bros. Well, he'd ask one more time and then let it go.

"Honestly, it's no trouble. You're not dragging me anywhere. Plus, it gives me an excuse to disappear when Ben is hatching his plan to move to a second location, which is always a bad idea."

She shrugged and turned to the door.

"Suit yourself."

He waved to Ben and followed Maddie out the door. He was glad the party was over. He'd had fun, and he was even sort of glad Ben had harassed him into having one. But his ideal birthday would be spent at home on his couch with a good movie on TV and a large pizza on his coffee table.

The cool San Francisco night air was refreshing after the stuffy, beer-scented heat of the bar, and he breathed it in as he walked with her down Valencia. They walked in silence for a block or two, until they turned onto one of the quieter streets.

Okay, now the cool San Francisco night air was just flat-out cold. He hunched his shoulders against the wind.

"Did you have a good birthday party?" she asked, just when he thought she wasn't going to speak to him the entire walk.

"I did. I got coerced into having the party in the first place; I don't know if you've noticed, but I'm not a huge party guy." She laughed and he joined in. "But it was fun to see so many people who came out. Maybe I'll do it again in another ten or so years."

She laughed again.

"And I'm glad Alexa ran into that guy, though I'm still not quite sure what I think about him."

Maddie nodded.

"I'm not sure what I think about him, either, but I did appreciate the way he was looking at Alexa all night like he'd won an amazing prize."

That was a really good way to put it.

"You're right. Okay, that makes me feel a little better about him."

She turned to him and raised her eyebrows.

"Wait, did you really tell me that I was right? I'm stunned." They walked by a streetlight that showed him the smile on her face. He smiled back.

"I have a lot of faults, but I'm good at acknowledging when other people are right."

She stopped next to a black hatchback and gestured to it.

"This is me. Thanks for walking me to my car. Um, have a good night."

He nodded at her and stepped back onto the sidewalk.

"You, too."

While she got into the car and started it, he leaned against the

street-cleaning sign and pulled out his phone. He had no intention
of going back to the bar—Ben would just harass him into going
dancing, and Theo had reached his party limit about an hour ago.
Ben had known him all his life; he was used to Theo disappearing
from parties when he'd had enough. Even his own parties.

He opened an app to get a ride back to Berkeley. Ugh, there
was a five-minute wait for a ride. Hopefully no one thought he
looked threatening hanging out in this residential neighborhood
for the next five minutes, waiting.

"What are you doing? Why are you still standing there?" Maddie had started to pull away and was now shouting at him out the
window of her car.

"Waiting for a ride home," he shouted back. "Someone's coming in"—he checked his phone—"now it's six minutes? Why do
these apps have such problems with time?"

"You're not going back to your party?" She was looking at him
like he was some sort of alien, which made sense. Maddie was
probably used to all those life-of-the-party kinds of guys who he'd
always seen as foreign to him.

He shook his head.

"The party is mostly over. I told you, Ben's trying to get people
to go dancing, and I'm not in the mood."

She closed her eyes for a minute, probably trying to conceive of
how someone like him existed. Another car pulled up alongside
her car, and the driver made that *Are you coming out?* motion. Maddie nodded at her and turned back to him.

"Get in."

Wait, what? Was she going to take him back to the bar, or . . .

"Come on, someone wants this spot. Get in! I'll take you home."

Well hell, if she wanted to save him a thirty-five-dollar ride home from San Francisco to Berkeley, he wasn't going to say no. He quickly canceled his ride request and opened her passenger door.

"Thanks, Maddie, I appre—"

"No need to thank me. It's fine. I'm going the same direction as you are, and it's cold outside. I saw you shivering while we were walking to the car. Why don't men wear jackets?"

She glared at him as she leaned forward and turned the heat on in her car.

"I do wear jackets! Sometimes. It was so warm when I was getting dressed today, and it felt ridiculous to put something warmer on when I was walking to BART to come out here this evening." The warm air coming out of her car heaters felt really good right now. "Though, that's definitely one of my faults—I've lived in the Bay Area for a long time; I should know it's always at least ten degrees cooler in San Francisco than it is in the East Bay, and it gets really cold at night, but I never prepare for it."

Why was he still talking about the weather? He shut his mouth and settled into the passenger seat.

He glanced in her direction. She certainly didn't look happy to have him in her car. She was right that they were going in the same direction, but this was the first time he and Maddie had ever been alone together, and she really didn't seem to be enjoying the situation.

He didn't know what to talk about with her, or if he should talk at all. They'd been getting along well tonight, strangely, but he didn't want to push his luck.

"I'm surprised you watch *House Hunters*," he said. "I would have thought you'd watch *Project Runway* or all of those fashion-y shows."

Here he was, pushing his luck.

She shrugged.

"Oh, I watch it mostly because everyone expects me to have seen all of the episodes. But it feels like work, not relaxation." She sighed. "You know what the most relaxing show of all time is?"

He sat up straight and turned to face her.

"No, tell me."

The peaceful smile spread across her face.

"*The Great British Baking Show*. It's the best."

Unfortunately, this time he couldn't chime in about his love of the show.

"I've never watched it, but people have told me that. What do you love about it?"

They merged onto the Bay Bridge, along with many other cars. Thank God he'd come up with something to talk about; they'd be here for a while. He relaxed into her passenger seat.

"Well, it's a competition show—in Britain it's called *The Great British Bake Off*. I don't know why it has a different name here."

He turned to her.

"I know this! It's because of Pillsbury. It has a trademark for the term 'Bake-Off' in America, so they had to change the name."

She nodded.

"That sounds like the kind of thing you would know." Yep, he'd pushed his luck just a little too hard. Was it his fault he loved trivia like that?

"Anyway, I like it because even though it is a competition show, the contestants are so kind and gentle with one another. It's such a soothing show."

He nodded.

"Sounds good. I'll have to watch it."

Silence descended on the car again, but this time he didn't try to fill it. They burst out from the tunnel on the lower deck of the bridge, and he saw the white tower of the Bay Bridge glowing in the darkness. He loved this part about coming home from San Francisco at night.

"Why didn't you want to go dancing with your brother?" she asked him.

He laughed. If she only knew either him or Ben better, she'd never ask that.

"I wasn't in the mood."

She turned to him with one of those annoying grins she always sent his way.

"Oh, I get it. You can't dance. It's okay, not everyone is blessed with dancing ability. It's nothing to be ashamed of."

Oh hell no. He would not let this stand.

"I can *too* dance," he said. Maybe a little too loudly.

She chuckled.

"Sure you can. It's okay, you don't have to prove anything to me."

He shook his head.

"I know I don't—I don't need to prove anything to anyone—but I'm a fucking great dancer."

She nodded.

"Mmmhmm." She gestured to the freeway signs up ahead. "What exit?"

For some reason, her attitude was really getting to him.

"University. I'm near the North Berkeley BART station. And you can *mmmhmm* however much you want, but I speak the truth."

She changed lanes to follow his directions. He tried not to watch her expression too much. He didn't want to look like he was staring at her. But when a smile hovered around her lips, he found himself smiling back. Why? He had no idea.

He pointed at his building. Finally.

"This is me. Thanks for the ride. Remember: I can outdance you any day."

She pulled up in front, and he opened his car door and jumped out. Thank God he was home. He needed to go inside and sober up.

As he walked up the pathway to his building, he heard another car door slam, and he looked behind him to see Maddie standing on the sidewalk.

"You really didn't think I was going to let you end this conversation without me making you prove your alleged dancing prowess, did you?"

Chapter Two

MADDIE HADN'T PLANNED ON CALLING HIS BLUFF. SHE'D KNOWN THEO was bullshitting her in the car about how he was supposedly such a great dancer, but it was his birthday, so she was going to let him have this one. But he had to throw that shot in at the end, and she wasn't going to let him get away with it.

She followed him into his apartment and ignored his groans and pleas for mercy as she looked around. This place was so spotless and well decorated it looked like he'd had a magazine shoot earlier that day. Granted, she could identify most of the furniture as IKEA, but it still all looked way better here than any IKEA furniture she'd ever had. Big navy blue immaculate couch, cozy-looking chair to the side of it in warm caramel, wood coffee table with perfectly lined-up magazines, packed-full bookshelves she was sure were organized first by genre and then alphabetically. Yes, this apartment made sense for the stick-up-his-ass Theo she knew and loathed.

"I drove you home. It's the price of the drive," she said, interrupting his whine that it was his birthday and he was tired. "I'm not leaving until I see some dancing." She waved to the middle of the living room floor.

He shook his head and sighed.

"Okay, fine, I'll do it, but—I know I'm going to regret this tomorrow—I'm getting another drink first. Maybe then I'll forget this happened. You want one?" He didn't wait for an answer but turned to walk down the hallway.

He had to have another drink before he tried to dance. Oh, this was going to be so fucking funny. She couldn't wait. She grinned as she followed him to the back of his apartment.

"Wow, that's incredible." She stopped when she walked into the kitchen and stared at his bar cart.

He picked up a bottle of bourbon from it and two glasses.

"I love this thing. I found it at a garage sale nearby—the wheels worked, but it was totally scuffed and beaten up. I bought it immediately, then spent months researching how to fix it up, and then probably a month on and off sanding it and staining it. It didn't even cost all that much to fix it up, but now I spend far too much money on cocktail accessories and good alcohol, since I feel like the bar cart deserves it."

She ran her finger up and down the dark brown wood.

"I'm impressed. You did a great job." She picked up the cocktail shaker. "You probably got those fancy ice cube trays to make the good ice like they have at all those trendy bars." She looked up at his carefully blank face. "You did!"

He walked over to the freezer and took out an ice cube tray.

"I did." He set the glasses on the counter. "Want to sample the good ice? What's your cocktail of choice?"

She took a step back and considered the bottles of liquor he had sitting on the bar cart.

"You pick. You're the expert here."

He walked over to her to survey the choices on the bar cart. When he stood next to her, she could feel his body heat. She almost took a step back, but he selected a bottle and walked away before she could.

"I'll make you an old-fashioned. I like this bourbon. It's not my favorite one—that I reserve for sipping neat—but it's a great one for a classic cocktail. Do you like cherries?"

She nodded.

"Good, I have excellent ones here." He dropped this and that into their glasses as he talked. "Alexa got them for me for Christmas last year."

Maddie took her drink from Theo. She really shouldn't be drinking right now. She was going to have to drive home in just a few minutes, as soon as she made him dance for her. She took a sip anyway.

"These are good, but I liked the old neon red ones," she said.

Theo came around and leaned against Maddie's side of the island. He was close to her again like he had been before. No, maybe closer. His arm was propped next to her, just barely brushing against her waist.

She should move away. Why was she standing this close to Theo anyway? Why was she in his apartment? Why was she drinking his bourbon and listening to him talk about cherries? Why had she even stayed at his birthday party for so long? She should have been at home in her own bed at least three hours ago.

She stood upright.

"You're stalling. It's dancing time." She pulled her phone out of her pocket. "What song are we doing here? Madonna? Prince? Gaga? I want to see all your best moves." She held back a giggle.

He shook his head and picked up his drink.

"We'll do this in the living room, and I'm in charge of the music."

She followed him back to the living room and watched him push his coffee table up against the wall and roll his rug back. So he was really going to try to do this. Incredible.

He glanced up at her as she stood by the doorway.

"Thanks for the help."

She nodded and sipped her drink.

"It seemed like you had everything well in hand. I didn't want to get in the way."

He shook his head without saying anything and walked over to the record player in the corner of the room.

Of course he had a record player. He was just the kind of pretentious guy who would have one. He bent down to the shelf below it and pulled out a few albums. She couldn't remember the last time she'd seen a guy touch something that lovingly.

"Okay." He took another sip of his drink. "Sit down."

She obeyed him and took the seat at the far edge of his couch. He waited for her to sit down before he turned the music on.

She heard the opening strains of "Bye Bye Bye" and laughed out loud. This was what Theo was going to try to do?

He stood still for the opening stanza of the song, and just stared back at her with a faint smile on his face. Then, all of a sudden, he jumped right into it. His hips thrusted, his feet leapt, his arms flew, and she was mesmerized. He did it so well, and so unlike the Theo she thought she knew, that she laughed out loud again, but this time in wonder. He kicked, moved, and spun like he did this every day, all with a provocative look on his face, one she'd never seen before.

My God. He hadn't been fucking with her. He really could dance.

She put her drink down on the floor so she could concentrate on this performance. When he unbuttoned his oxford shirt and threw it across the room, she tossed imaginary dollar bills at him. He shook his—now that she thought about it, really good—butt at her, and she laughed out loud. In her wildest dreams, she never would have thought boring, pedantic, mild-mannered Theo could dance like a black Channing Tatum.

When he finished, with one last punch in the air, she cheered and clapped. He had a smug grin on his face, like he knew she didn't think he could do it, like he was thrilled to dance just for her, like he was victorious. Fine, he'd earned that smug look, this time.

She never thought she'd clap for anything Theo did, but this had been a surprising night in many ways. He bowed to her, then reached out his hand.

"Now you have to dance with me."

She let him pull her off the couch.

"Who said I have to dance with you?"

He kept hold of her hand.

"Those are the rules. Argue with the people who made the rules, not me."

She thought about arguing, but she knew it would just be for the sake of arguing. For some reason, she had no idea why, she really wanted to dance with Theo right now. She didn't question it and just let herself slide into his arms.

"Holy shit," she said. "I can't believe Alexa never told me you could do that."

He grinned.

"Alexa doesn't know. A guy has to have some secrets, after all."

She shook her head.

"I admit it," she said. "You can definitely outdance me. That was amazing."

He looked away from her and laughed. And she thought maybe even blushed a little.

"Thanks. My mom was a single parent and worked a lot, and Ben and I got in the habit of teaching ourselves all sorts of dances… I kind of never stopped. Yes, I know, I'm a big dork."

She had no idea he'd been raised by a single mom. She almost told him she had, too, but he kept talking.

"My brother's probably off at a club somewhere impressing a whole room of people, but that shows you the difference between the two of us in a nutshell. Ben likes to be the center of attention. I just like dancing."

Then he dipped her almost to the floor, which made her laugh so hard she couldn't talk for a while.

"Wait." She looked around the room. "You pushed the table out of the way and rolled the rug up like you do that all the time, because you do! You have regular dance breaks, don't you?"

He gave her a sheepish smile.

"Got to stay in shape. There's nothing like some NSYNC or Prince"—he winked at her—"or Beyonce for getting the butterflies out of your stomach before a big day at work."

She shook her head.

"Remind me to try that the next time I have an important client meeting."

The song changed, and he pulled her closer. She let herself cling to him; his soft T-shirt against her hand, the warmth of his skin underneath heating her up.

"I'll remind you. Now, let's try something fun."

He plucked her hand from around his neck and held it in his, and then at the beat of the music, spun her around. This time she didn't hesitate to follow his lead. When they were done, she held on tight to him.

"You could have warned me!"

He took both of her hands and stepped back, still dancing.

"But where's the fun in that?" He let go of one of her hands and spun her around, again and again, until she collapsed against him dizzy and laughing.

When he bent down to kiss her, she didn't hesitate there, either. It was like a fire had been lit inside both of them. His hands were in her hair, her arms were wrapped around his body, and they were kissing each other like it was the oxygen they needed in order to survive. The music played around them; they were both hot and sweaty and couldn't stop touching each other.

Theo had always been so buttoned-up, so measured, so conservative, and if she'd ever thought about what kind of kisser he'd be, she'd probably imagined that he'd be tentative, and slow, and awkward. That couldn't be further from the truth. She didn't know who the hell this guy was, but he wasn't the Theo she'd known for years. And holy shit, was *this* Theo hot. His hand was already up under her dress, and his other arm had locked her against his body. She reached down to cup that butt she'd admired just a few moments ago.

He pulled away from her with a groan. Why was he stopping?

He pushed her down onto his couch and bit her shoulder. She wrapped her legs around him, and he pulled her into another long, hard, deep kiss.

"Holy shit, Maddie," he said. Her sentiments exactly. He traced the hard outline of her nipples through her dress with his thumb, and she shivered. "Oh, you like that? I thought you would."

They kept kissing and touching, and as they moved against each other, the already short skirt of her dress shimmied up and up her thighs until it was like she wasn't wearing a skirt at all. His big, warm hand on her thigh made her tremble. He got closer and closer to her thong, but he didn't make any move to touch it, or pull it off. She felt like she was crying out for his touch there, like she'd never wanted anything so much.

Just when she thought she couldn't take it anymore, and would move his hands there herself, he sat up and reached for her hands again. She let him pull her off the couch and lead her down the hallway to his bedroom.

He stopped at the doorway and dropped her hands.

"Are you sure this is a good idea?" he asked her.

She rolled her eyes.

"No, of course it's not. What a stupid question," she said. "I thought you were supposed to be one of the smart ones."

Then she pulled off her dress and threw it on the floor.

"Any more stupid questions?"

He shook his head.

"Not a one."

Theo woke the next morning and turned over to see Maddie curled up next to him.

Maddie Forest.

Curled up next to him.

In his bed.

Naked.

It hadn't been a dream. Or even just a very vivid fantasy. He and Maddie had spent half the night having fucking incredible sex.

How in God's name had *that* happened? He knew he was a good dancer, and he also knew that women really liked that, but if he'd known that his dancing would have gotten Maddie in his bed, he would have . . . Well, hell, he had no idea what he would have done differently for the past few years, but it would have been something.

If anyone had tried to tell him the day before that he'd do something like kiss Maddie, he would have laughed until he cried. But they'd been dancing, and the music had been playing, and they'd been laughing, and she was in his arms, and he'd seen that look on her face, that look that women sometimes gave you when they wanted you to kiss them. Where they'd look at your lips and lick their own and then look back up at you with a smile in their eyes. So he'd kissed her like his life depended on it, and joy of joys, she'd kissed him back.

She stirred as he looked at her, and then opened her eyes with an expression of horror on her face.

"Good morning," he said.

She shook her head and sat up. He put on his glasses to get a better look. He'd seen Maddie a lot in the past few years, and no matter what she wore, she was hot with clothes on, but that didn't compare at all to how she looked without clothes on.

She turned to look at him and pulled the covers up to her shoulders. He tried to wipe the smile off his face, but he didn't think he quite accomplished it.

"I'm pretty sure we already did the first-time-seeing-each-other-naked part of this story," he said.

She put her face in her hands.

"That doesn't matter. Last night I was . . . Well, I don't know what was wrong with me last night. I wasn't even drunk, or even close to it. I just completely lost my mind." She glared at him. "As did you, I might add."

He sat up and nodded.

"You've got that right."

He got out of bed to pull some sweatpants on. When he turned around, Maddie quickly turned her head away, and he hid a smile. Who was checking who out now, hmm?

"I'm going to make some coffee."

He walked out of the room, stepping carefully over Maddie's dress in the doorway, and into the kitchen.

As much as he wanted to do this again . . . and again . . . and again, having a fling with Maddie seemed like a disaster waiting to happen. Plus, he would bet money that no part of Maddie wanted any kind of fling with him, given that look on her face when she'd woken up this morning.

A few minutes later, he heard Maddie walking into the kitchen.

"How do you take your coffee?" he asked her without turning around. Then he made the mistake of turning around.

Her dress was wrinkled, and her hair was messy, and she had makeup smeared around her eyes, and she possibly looked even hotter than she had the night before.

Damn it.

Maybe the disaster would be worth it.

"No sugar, but plenty of milk," she said. He stared at her for a second before he remembered what she was responding to.

"One second and I'll get you the milk."

He slowly poured boiling water into the cone and filter he'd set up over a mug and handed it to her, and he did the same with a second mug, before he reached into the fridge for the milk.

She poured a bunch of milk into her coffee and stirred it for a long time before she finally looked up at him.

"You have to promise me something."

Well, shit, this could be anything.

"What is it?" he asked her, before he took a sip of his own coffee. Damn, he'd forgotten to put milk in his.

"First, we're agreed that we both lost our minds last night and this can never happen again, right?"

He hadn't quite gotten there, but okay.

He looked away from her and poured too much milk in his coffee.

"Obviously. Wait, was that the thing I had to promise? That doesn't seem like so much of a promise, as an—"

"No, I wasn't finished. You have to promise not to tell Alexa. She'd be thrilled; it would be a nightmare. This never happened."

He couldn't let that go.

"Which part of it never happened? The part where I almost pulled your clothes off on my couch and you wanted me to? Or the part where you threw your clothes off as soon as you saw my bed? Or the part where I pushed you back on my bed and knelt down, and . . ."

She banged her empty coffee mug down on the counter, and he laughed.

"See, this is why I don't like you," she said. "Oh God, this was such a mistake. What the hell was I thinking?"

He picked up his coffee mug. He tried to stop smiling but couldn't help it.

"Thanks for the birthday sex, Maddie. Relax. This will never happen again, and Alexa will never find out."

She glared at him.

"You would be the type of guy to tell me to relax. Not at all surprising, but disappointing all the same."

Before he could respond, she turned and walked down the hallway. Seconds later, he heard his front door slam.

He looked down at his too-milky coffee and sighed. He'd handled that one well.

Chapter Three

Six weeks later

THEO SCANNED THE CROWD AT THE CITY COUNCIL MEETING, ONE HE
and Alexa had been working toward for months. And of course,
the first person he saw was Maddie, front and center. He stifled a
groan. He'd spent the past six weeks carefully making sure he
wasn't in the same vicinity as Maddie, and now he'd have to sit
there and stare at her all night.

Why the fuck did Alexa have to have such supportive friends?

He tried hard not to look at her throughout the city council
meeting, but it wasn't easy. It wasn't like he'd fallen in love with her
that night, or any bullshit like that—Maddie was the last kind of
girl he wanted to date. All she cared about were clothes and celeb-
rities, from what he could tell; the things he cared about—politics,
books, music—didn't seem to matter to her. Hell, they didn't even
like each other.

But the sex. Oh God. He'd thought about that night, on aver-
age, twenty times a day for the past six weeks. A lot more than that

for the first two weeks, actually. He couldn't help it at first—he had bruises all over his arms from where she'd held on to him. And each one of those bruises made him think about the way her face looked when she'd touched him, the filthy things she'd whispered in his ear, the way she'd reached for him over and over again, how he'd never wanted the night to end.

It wasn't like it could ever happen again; even if the morning after hadn't gone so badly, he knew that was off the table. But oh God, if only it could.

He picked up his pen and took frantic notes, just so he would look somewhere other than at Maddie.

Finally, it was time for the key part of the meeting: the program for at-risk teenagers Alexa had been working on for months. When Alexa's sister, Olivia, got up to speak, he was terrified for a moment. Had he been right to get Olivia to fly across the country to do this? He looked around the room to see how people were responding to her speech. Everyone was rapt, including the city councilmen. Thank God.

But as he looked over the audience, he and Maddie locked eyes, until she finally looked away.

The program passed easily, and he distracted himself from Maddie by silently celebrating with Alexa. As soon as the meeting was officially over, he pulled Alexa in for a big hug.

"You did it!" he said.

She squeezed him tightly.

"We all did it. Thank you for everything, but especially for whatever you did to conspire with my sister to get her here."

The mayor came over to congratulate them, and there was a flurry of handshakes and hugs from city council members and

other staffers. Just as he was about to gather up everyone to head
to the bar to celebrate, he heard Alexa say, "Drew?"

Theo turned and saw the doctor who had shown up the night
of his birthday party. He'd thought that guy and Alexa had broken
up for good a few weeks ago, but here he was, standing in front of
Alexa with a hopeful and scared look on his face.

"Um, Olivia?" Theo said under his breath. "I think we should
all get the hell out of here."

"Alexa always said you were one of the smart ones." Olivia
slung her overnight bag on her shoulder. "Maddie? You joining us
for drinks? I have a feeling we'll have a few things to celebrate tonight."

Right, of course Maddie would come, too.

Theo buried himself in his phone on the walk to the bar. He
returned a few celebratory emails from allies and sent out the press
release he'd had ready to go, about how gratified the mayor was to
see that the city council prioritized the marginalized children of
Berkeley. But the whole time, he was aware of Maddie, the sound
of her voice, the ripple of her laughter, the sway of her body as she
walked ahead of him. He tried not to eavesdrop on her conversation with Olivia, but he couldn't help it. They were talking about
Maddie's new dress. Obviously.

Why the fuck did Maddie have to be in that thin, clingy dress,
anyway? It might be July, but it was July in Berkeley. It was too cold
tonight. She should be in an oversize sweat suit. Something
warmer. Something that would make him stop remembering what
she looked like without anything on at all.

He needed to just pretend Maddie wasn't here. Oh God, but he
couldn't ignore her all night—what a jackass move that would be.

He had to say something to her, but he had no idea what to say. He tried to put that out of his mind as he walked into the bar.

"First round is on the mayor," he said. He pulled the crumpled bills the mayor had given him out of his pocket and handed them to the bartender.

"Good job, boss," his assistant, Peter, said. Theo grinned and fist-bumped him.

"Thanks, but the real heroes are the Monroe sisters. But really, thanks for everything you've done on this over the past few months."

He made his rounds with everyone else from the office, to thank them for their hard work, and they all had that same gleeful, almost high look on their faces he could feel on his own. Working in politics had some terrible lows, but every victory was so sweet.

Everyone made it to the table after a while, and Olivia sat down next to him, with Maddie on the opposite side of her. Good, this way he couldn't even see her.

"Thanks for giving me the push to make it to this," Olivia said, clinking her glass with his.

"Thanks for doing it," he said. "I'm so glad you managed to get here."

"Me too. I wouldn't have missed seeing that look on my sister's face when the city council voted for the world." She laughed. "Or the look on her face when she saw Drew standing behind me, actually."

"How's life in the big city?" he asked Olivia. "Getting sick of New York yet and ready to move home to California?"

She gave him a twisted smile.

"Actually, yes, but don't tell my sister that. She would get way too excited and think I was heading home immediately. But yeah, I've been missing California more and more these days, which is why I've managed to do a business trip up here or to L.A. at least every few months. And it's getting harder to go back to New York every time. No imminent plans to move back, but . . . we'll see."

He felt his phone buzz in his pocket and pulled it out to see news alerts; a few reporters had their stories already up.

"Hold that thought," he said to Olivia. He scanned the stories, and only that one guy who had it in for the mayor said anything negative; everyone else thought the program sounded great. Just as he checked in on Twitter, he got a tap on his shoulder.

"We getting good press?"

He looked up to see Alexa's euphoric face. And Drew standing behind her smiling just as big.

"You bet we are." Theo stood up and gave her a huge hug. "You did it, Lex."

She squeezed him hard and let go.

"*We* did it." She laughed. "Don't think that I'm trying to be modest here—it sure as hell was my idea and it never would have happened without me—but I needed everyone here and more to make it happen."

He gave her another quick hug and glanced at Drew.

"Sit down, we've got a lot to celebrate."

Drew pulled up extra seats for him and Alexa, and everyone scooted around and rearranged themselves to give them space at the table.

And somehow, as all of this happened, Theo found himself sitting next to Maddie. Of course.

Why had Olivia chosen just the wrong moment to go get another drink? If she'd been sitting there when they all moved around,

Maddie could have just made sure Olivia was between her and Theo. Or if Maddie had thought quickly enough, she would have gotten up then and moved over to talk to Drew. But no, Olivia came back right when everyone was scooching around to make room for Alexa and Drew, and there was nothing Maddie could do to avoid sitting next to Theo without making it obvious.

It was probably better it happened this way—they couldn't avoid each other forever. They might as well get the awkward thing over with now, so that the next time they saw each other at a party, they could go back to cheerfully ignoring each other like they had for years.

It had been six weeks, and she still couldn't believe she'd slept with Theo Stephens. If she hadn't been sore for days afterward, she would have tried her best to just chalk it up to a fever dream.

Why did the sex have to be that good? Why did even that first kiss have to be so good? If Theo had been a shitty kisser, there was at least a ninety percent chance she would have taken a step back, said, "You know, Theo, we both know this is a bad idea, don't we? Happy birthday, and thanks for the dance," and walked out of his apartment.

But noooo. Her whole body had hurt for days, because of the way he'd pushed her legs apart, and . . . No, stop it, Madeleine. She could not sit here right next to him and fantasize about that *again*. She needed to get ahold of herself and remember this was just Theo. Boring, full-of-himself, pedantic Theo. That night had been some wild aberration.

"Hey," he said.

She turned toward him, and his smile was neither the sexy grin from that night, nor the smirk from the next morning. It was nervous.

"Hey," she said back.

"Thanks for coming tonight. I know Alexa was glad to have the support."

Yeah, Maddie knew that, too, since Alexa had been her best friend for more than twenty years. What was he even doing, thanking her in that condescending way? Did he think she would have missed this?

Her face must have shown her thoughts, because the smile dropped from his face.

"I didn't mean . . . I mean, obviously you were going to come. I just meant . . ." He sighed. "Sorry. I was trying not to make it awkward, but I'm not great at that. I should have texted you the next day, just to, I mean, I don't want to be that asshole, but I didn't have your number, and I obviously couldn't ask Alexa for it, but . . ."

As delightful as it was to see Theo stumble like this, she needed to put this guy out of his misery. She smiled and put her hand on his arm.

"It's okay, don't worry about it. And thanks for everything you've done for Alexa tonight, especially getting Olivia here. I know that meant a lot to her."

Now he smiled that same goofy smile she'd seen on his face a few times at his birthday party.

"That's so nice of you to say, thank you."

Why was he so strangely attractive when he smiled like that?

Ugh, what had gotten into her? Why was she suddenly finding Theo attractive? A man dances for you ONE TIME and you just want to take his clothes off every time you see him after that?

Maybe it was just something in the air tonight, what with whatever had happened with Alexa and Drew back in the city council chambers. Or maybe it was that Theo's clothes tonight were excellent, even better than usual. She'd never seen him in a suit before, and his gray suit was immaculate. His tie, a blue one with a leafy green pattern on it, was loose at his throat. His hair was shorter than it had been the night of his birthday. He must have gotten a haircut for the city council meeting. She hated that she found that so charming.

Good Lord, this was absurd. It was just because she'd been too busy over the past few months to go out with anyone else, so her brain was stuck on the last guy she'd slept with, who happened to be sitting next to her. All she needed to do was get out of here and text one of the dudes in her phone and by the next morning she'd never think this way about Theo again.

At least they'd both successfully managed to not tell Alexa about what happened. Maddie hadn't told either Alexa or her mom, the two people who she told basically everything. It was weird to have a secret like this from both of them.

Someone at the other end of the table called Theo's name, so he turned further toward her to shout back at them. Perfect. If only he'd gotten up to move back there, everything would be fine. Time to think about something else.

Maddie beckoned to Alexa, who leaned in behind Theo.

"I've been very patient," Maddie said, "but if you don't give me at least the CliffsNotes version of this Drew thing right this second, I'm going to start throwing things. I hope you realize that."

Alexa laughed, her eyes shining.

"I do realize that." She glanced around and lowered her voice. "He loves me, I love him, he's moving to Berkeley. How's that for the CliffsNotes version?"

"Ahhhhh!" Maddie almost screamed but realized just in time they were surrounded by Alexa's coworkers. So instead she squeezed both of her hands tightly and screamed under her breath.

She only realized one hand was still on Theo's arm when he sat up straight, almost knocking Alexa in the head, and making both Alexa and Maddie laugh. Maddie patted his likely bruised arm and moved her hand back onto her lap.

"Sorry about that. It was unintentional," Maddie said in response to his raised eyebrows. He grinned at her and went back to his conversation.

She should probably move away from him. She could push her chair back, go sit next to Alexa, and get more of the details of the Drew story.

But it was comfortable to sit next to him. To have his leg, in his perfectly cut gray wool pants, pressing gently against hers. It wasn't about him, not at all. It was just nice to feel a warm body next to hers on this chilly summer night, to feel the warmth of him through her impractically thin cotton dress. If she'd just dressed more warmly for the city council meeting, she would get up to move. But she loved this dress, and tonight she'd chosen vanity over warmth. Theo was clearly warm enough that he'd taken off his suit jacket and rolled up the sleeves of his shirt. She looked away from his forearms and back to Alexa.

The party went on until the bar closed. As they all shuffled out, Maddie turned to Olivia.

"Hey, you can sleep in my guest room tonight. My place is kind of a mess, but you can just push all that out of the way."

Alexa spun around.

"Absolutely not. My sister is staying at my house."

"Okay, but Lexie . . ." Olivia said. "There's someone else here tonight to see you. Don't you think you want some privacy?"

Alexa shook her head.

"Drew's going to be around for a while. Olivia lives all the way in New York, I never get to see her enough, and she came out all this way to surprise me!"

Maddie and Olivia looked at each other, and then at Drew, who just shrugged.

"Drew indeed will be here for a while," he said.

Maddie smiled at them holding hands and beaming at each other and sighed. It had been a long time since anyone had looked at her like that. Since she'd looked at anyone like that.

As the others walked toward their parked cars, Theo turned to go in the opposite direction.

"Okay, I'm this way. Good night, everyone!"

Alexa stepped back when he tried to hug her and frowned at him.

"Are you trying to walk home? You're trying to walk home, aren't you?"

He sighed and looked up to the heavens. He was hoping to get away with this tonight.

"She does this to me all the time," he said to the other three. "Yes, I'm trying to walk home. I live a mile away, I have perfectly fine legs, I can walk home."

"Yes, I do this to you all the time, and who always wins this fight? I do. I have a perfectly fine car. I'll drive you home, along with the rest of this crew."

Drew dangled her keys from his fingers.

"You mean I'll drive him home, right? Or did you forget you handed me your keys when you ordered that third drink?"

Alexa shrugged.

"WE will drive you home, how about that? No need to walk when my car is right here. And you live more than a mile away—remember how I measured it that time?"

Theo shook his head.

"How could I forget?"

"I'll drive him home," Maddie said. "You three have had a big night. This is when you delegate some things to your friend who also has a car right here."

Alexa grinned at Maddie and smirked at Theo.

"How did you survive growing up with this one as a little sister?" Theo asked Olivia.

She laughed.

"It was a struggle. Drew, do you know what you're in for?"

When Drew didn't answer, the other three looked back to see Drew and Alexa kissing on the sidewalk.

"Ewww, come on, my eyes!" Olivia yelled.

Theo was still laughing when he got into Maddie's car.

As soon as he fastened his seat belt, it hit him. How the hell did he end up in Maddie's car again? After he'd almost melted down just sitting next to her at the bar, he'd planned to avoid being in close quarters with her ever again.

And now they were alone in her car, heading down University Avenue in an awkward silence. At least this ride would be a lot shorter than the last one.

He should make conversation.

"So, Alexa and Drew, huh?"

Maddie laughed.

"Just what I was thinking." She paused for a while. "She looked really happy."

Theo nodded.

"She did. I'm really happy for her. And I liked Drew better tonight than I did the night of my birthday." He made himself smile. "Which is good, I guess, because it seems like he's going to be around for a while."

He and Alexa had been so close for the past few years, they'd often finished each other's sentences. She felt like the sister he'd never had: she always insisted on giving him rides home; he'd bought her a ladder so he could more easily change the light bulbs on her high ceilings. Now that Drew was going to be here, he would need to adjust to Alexa having a guy around who wasn't him.

"Yeah," Maddie said. He wondered if she'd heard what he'd left unsaid. "He seems like he really loves her." She glanced toward him with her eyes narrowed. "Don't worry: if he doesn't, I'll know."

He lifted his hand to high-five her.

"He's moving here—you heard that, right?"

He nodded.

"Yeah."

"Yeah." Maddie sighed. "I am *so* happy for her—I'm not just saying that—but . . ."

"Same here," Theo said. "It's going to change things."

Maddie flipped a U-turn and pulled up in front of his building.

"Yeah. It's going to change things. I wouldn't take this away from Alexa for the world, but it'll require some adjustment. I hate change. Anyway, I feel like an asshole now."

Theo put his hand on her arm.

"Don't. Or, I mean, do, but know I feel like an asshole, too. I don't like change, either."

Maddie turned off the car.

"Well, at least I'm in good company."

Theo grinned at her.

"I can't decide if that's a compliment or an insult."

She pushed her hair out of her face.

"I'm not going to be the one to clear it up for you."

They grinned at each other, until she looked away.

"Anyway, thanks for the ride home," he said. "Even though you clearly had no choice in the matter."

She shrugged.

"I could have made Drew do it. Congratulations again about tonight."

"Thanks." He pulled her in for a quick hug and half expected her to recoil to the other side of the car. But instead, she wrapped her arms around him and held on tight. They sat like that for a while, not talking, not moving, just breathing in unison.

When she rested her head on his shoulder, he was scared to move or breathe, in case she pushed him away. Finally, he moved his fingers into her hair. She sighed, and he could feel her breath on his neck. He dropped a light kiss on her hair, and waited. After what felt like hours, he felt her lips on his neck.

Don't rush, Theo. Don't freak her out. Go slow.

He gently pushed her hair back and kissed her hairline. Then her forehead.

She sat up slowly, and they looked in each other's eyes for a long time.

He had no idea who moved first, but suddenly they were kissing so hard it almost hurt.

"Inside. Now," he said in her ear.

In response, she opened her car door.

The next morning, Maddie opened her eyes in Theo's bed and shook her head.

"We were NOT going to do this again," she said to her pillow.

He chuckled in her ear, and his arm tightened around her waist.

"We didn't do it on purpose," he said. "It was an emotional night, we lost our minds, maybe someone put fairy dust or something in our drinks. That's our story, and we're sticking to it."

She couldn't bring herself to regret the night before, at least not right now when she was so cozy and satisfied. She was certain that would come later.

"Mmm, good, as long as we have a story." She should probably get up to leave. She should definitely get up to leave. But instead, she sank deeper into the bed and pulled Theo's arm closer against her. He took the hint. His fingers moved up higher on her torso and cupped her breast.

"How . . . how long does that fairy dust last, anyway?" she asked him.

He stroked her nipples, and she sighed. He draped his leg over hers.

"Mmm, I would say twelve hours." He kissed her neck, and she turned over onto her back to give him more access. He smiled down at her. "So that gives us about two more hours."

She moved her hands up and down his back.

"We'd better not waste a minute, then."

A while later, when Maddie woke up again, she kept her eyes closed. What the fuck was wrong with her? Was there some sort of force field around Theo's apartment that led straight to his bed?

Was there an invisible sign when you turned onto his street that said in big letters BAD DECISION CENTRAL? How had she ended up in his bed again?

And why was she still there? They'd had morning sex, for the love of God!

She needed to pull the plug on this immediately. She forced herself out of bed.

When she came back from the bathroom, Theo was in the kitchen. Making coffee, she assumed. She pulled her clothes on and went to the doorway of the kitchen.

"Um, is there enough coffee for me?" she asked.

Why did she ask that? She should have just snuck out the door while he was making coffee. Now she was stuck here.

He gestured to the two cups waiting by the kettle. He was shirtless, with those gray sweatpants on again. Did he have anything on underneath them? No, Maddie, no, she was not going to let herself think about that.

"Plenty of milk, no sugar, right?"

She nodded. "Right. Wait, don't you have to go to work?"

He picked up his phone and waved it at her.

"I sent ten emails while you were in the bathroom. I have to make it to the office eventually, but I have time for coffee first."

The kettle whistled, and he made coffee for both of them, then handed her the milk from the refrigerator. She poured some in her cup and passed the milk back to him.

It was weird: any other time if she'd woken up in a guy's bed after a night of really good sex—or honestly, even moderately good sex—and was now in his kitchen drinking coffee with him, she'd be hoping he'd bring up when he was going to see her again. She'd certainly figure out a chill way to make sure he had her number. And now it was the opposite—she was trying to figure out a chill way to make sure he knew this was never going to happen again, despite what it had seemed like in his bed this morning . . . and last night . . . and that night six weeks ago.

But he beat her to the punch.

"Look, Maddie," he said. "This was really fun, but we both know—"

"That we can't do this again." She nodded vigorously at him. "We absolutely both do know that. It was the fairy dust, remember?"

He smiled and took another sip of coffee.

"It was." He wrapped both of his hands around his mug. "Okay, great. I just didn't want it to be weird. I mean, next time we ran into each other."

She shook her head.

"No, it's fine. We'll be fine. Don't worry about it." She drank from her mug, barely tasting the coffee. "What time is it?"

He looked down at his phone.

"Almost eight thirty."

She gulped down the rest of her coffee and set her mug on the counter.

"I have to go. I have a client coming by at ten thirty, and I need to look presentable by then."

He looked her over as he raised his mug to his lips. She could tell he was smiling even with his mouth hidden.

"You look great to me."

She ignored the warm feeling that spread over her.

"Mmm, yes, high praise from the half-naked guy over here." She changed the subject. "Oh, do you have any idea where my purse is? I didn't see it in your bedroom. I didn't leave it in the car, did I?"

He thought for a second, and a sly smile broke out across his face.

"I think you may have dropped it by the front door?"

"Oh." Right. Yes. When they'd first walked into his apartment the night before, he'd pushed her up against the door and pulled down her panties and . . . Right. She must have dropped her purse then. No wonder she couldn't find her panties in his bedroom, either. "That, um, makes sense."

He grinned at her, and she blushed and looked away.

"Here, I'll walk you to the door." He set down his coffee cup and they walked to his front door. She scooped up her hot pink underwear from the floor by the door, and put it in her purse, abandoned in the corner.

"Okay, good luck with work today. See you around," she said.

He opened his front door for her.

"You, too."

Maddie got in her car, still blushing as she remembered exactly how her pink underwear had ended up in the hallway. She'd never expected Theo to be quite so . . . forceful. It was too bad that all of that was wrapped up in someone as pedantic and annoying as Theo.

Why did he have to be so condescending in the kitchen this morning anyway? "This was really fun," like he was letting her down easy. The gall of him. He'd been eager less than an hour before to have sex with her again, and then he handed her a cup of coffee and sent her on her way like her time had run out? How the hell had she ever let herself sleep with someone who thought he was so much better than her? She deserved better than him!

Men. Why hadn't women invented a world without them yet?

Chapter Four

Ten months later

THEO KNOCKED ON ALEXA'S DOOR, WAITED FOR A FEW SECONDS AS HE listened to the music and laughter inside, and then pulled it open. The engagement party was in full swing. He walked in and waved to a handful of his coworkers as he looked around for Alexa or Drew. Or Maddie.

He knew she was going to be there tonight. Maybe tonight would be the night she would seem just annoying and bitchy and full of herself again. Instead of all those things and also the hottest woman he'd ever seen.

He'd spent, conservatively, at least an hour a day for the past ten months kicking himself for letting her leave his apartment that morning like that. Why had he even said that thing about how they both knew it couldn't happen again? They both didn't know that! He didn't know that! He'd be thrilled for it to happen again, even though, yes, it was a bad idea for so many reasons. But no matter how bad of an idea it was, he couldn't get her out of his head.

It's not like—he got to this point every time he thought about that morning—if he hadn't said something, Maddie would have been all in. She didn't like him! She'd made that clear repeatedly! He needed to get over this.

"Theo!" There was Alexa, talking to her mom in the living room.

"Congratulations again." He handed her the bottle of champagne he'd brought and hugged her. "You know how happy I am for you."

She hugged him back.

"I do. Mom, you remember Theo, don't you?"

Her mom hugged him, too.

"Of course I do. I always sort of hoped . . . well, never mind that now. Good to see you again, Theo!"

Alexa shook her head and walked away. She beckoned him to follow her.

"Come to the kitchen with me. I'll get this in ice and show you where all the snacks are."

He looked over at the cheese plate on the coffee table and the charcuterie platter at the table over by the TV.

"More snacks than those?"

Alexa laughed.

"Oh, those are just the starter snacks. Come on."

He followed Alexa into the kitchen, where a tall Latino guy wearing an apron was taking something out of the oven.

"Drew, slide the cookie sheet that's in the fridge into the oven while I put these on a platter." He turned when they walked in. "Alexa, are you sure about marrying this guy? He's useless in the kitchen, you know."

She stuck the bottle of champagne into a big metal tub filled with ice.

"I know, I know, but at least he takes direction well. But then, neither of us is a real cook like you." Alexa turned to Theo. "Theo, you remember Carlos, right? He was there with Drew the night of your birthday party last year? Carlos's engagement present to us was to make a bunch of our favorite snacks for tonight. Thank God, because if either Drew or I had tried to make pigs in a blanket and baked Brie and gougères, this would be a disaster."

That was an excellent engagement present. He'd only brought champagne and general anxiety. Theo picked up one of the pigs in a blanket and popped it in his mouth.

"Thank God I got here on the early side. I wouldn't want to miss any of this food."

Drew grinned at him while he handed Carlos some tongs.

"I told Alexa to warn you, man. Carlos over here has many hidden talents." Drew glanced at Carlos and his smile got bigger. "As a matter of fact, you might have seen him on TV recently. Did you see that JumboTron proposal at Dodger Stadium? The one where the girl said no?"

Carlos turned between Theo and Drew, a tiny pastry puff between his tongs.

"That was NOT me. I was not the proposer, anyway. I just happened to be sitting behind the couple, that's all."

Drew smirked.

"Oh yeah, sure, that's all."

There was definitely a story there, but he might have to wait to get it from Alexa on Monday morning.

"Where are the other platters you said you had?" Carlos asked Drew.

Alexa handed Theo a bottle of beer and poured more champagne in her glass.

"Theo and I'll get them. I left them in the closet in the guest room, along with the rest of the extra party stuff. We'll be right back."

She led him down the hallway and into the guest room.

"Hey, um, Theo. While I have you alone here, there's something I wanted to ask you."

She had a weird look on her face. Was this about work? Did he have a typo in that press release he sent out on Friday? Now he was anxious about something other than Maddie.

"Go for it," he said.

"It's just, um, I was thinking about the wedding. I haven't done a lot of planning so far, of course, since we just got engaged last week. But there are a few things that I already know, and one of those is who I want to be there for me at the wedding. Theo, would you be my bridesman?"

He laughed and wrapped her up in a bear hug.

"First, that's the most hilarious title I've ever had, and I've had some weird titles in my day. And second, of course I will. I'd be honored."

She rested her head on his shoulder.

"Well, I'm honored that you'll do this for me," she said, in a voice he'd never heard from her before. He pulled away.

"Don't you dare cry, Alexa. Your mom will murder me if you walk back into the party with tears on your face."

She picked up a package of napkins and tore it open.

"It's okay, I've been doing this all the time lately." She dabbed at her face. "Luckily, they've all been good tears. Now let's get those platters back to the kitchen before Carlos kills us."

He knew as soon as he walked back into the party that Maddie was in the room. Why he was so hyperaware of a woman he barely knew, he had no idea. Was it her perfume? No, it was impossible to smell it from here, not with all of these people around. But sure enough, when he set his pigs in a blanket–filled platter down and looked around the room, he saw her. Her back was to him, but he knew it was her. Her green sleeveless dress skimmed over her body and clung to all of the places he most wanted to . . . He snapped his head back around. What the hell was he doing, lusting so obviously over a woman who wanted nothing to do with him? He needed another beer.

He walked back into the kitchen to find one. Carlos was taking yet another tray out of the oven. Oh good, here was something he could do.

"Need help with that?" Theo asked as he opened the fridge. "Drew's stuck in the other room chatting with some of Alexa's cousins."

Carlos laughed.

"From what I've heard about her family, that may take all night. Yeah, sure, I could use a hand. I could also use another beer, if you want to grab me one."

Theo pulled two beers out of the fridge and opened both of them.

"Here you go. Tell me what to do."

Soon, Carlos had him occupied rolling tiny cocktail weenies up in triangles of puff pastry. This was way better than standing around in the other room trying not to stare at Maddie.

"Oh, and don't forget, just a little dot of Dijon mustard before you roll," he said to Theo.

People came in and out of the kitchen as he and Carlos worked, but always just to grab another plate of food or something else to drink, wave at them, and leave again. Why had he never tried hiding in a kitchen during a party before? You got to be around the party, but not, like, right in the middle of it, do something at least semihelpful, and not get stuck in prying conversations. Win-win.

Carlos handed him a chip dipped in guacamole.

"Taste this. Does it need salt? I think it needs salt."

Theo popped it into his mouth.

"Just a little. And maybe some more jalapeño?"

Carlos pointed at him.

"You're right. Yes, that's it." He touched up the guacamole with his back turned to Theo. "So, did you and Alexa ever date?"

Theo almost choked on his beer, and Carlos turned around.

"Oh, sorry, I thought you'd probably be used to that question."

Theo swallowed and shook his head. He just hadn't expected the groom's best friend to ask him that at the engagement party, but then it was his own fault for hiding in the kitchen away from Maddie.

"Oh, I am, you just surprised me, that's all. We've both gotten that question a lot. But no, never, even though it seemed like the whole world was trying to get us to date each other for years. Including Alexa's mom, which she reminded us of when I walked in. We've just been really good friends from basically day one."

A burst of laughter preceded Alexa's entrance into the kitchen. This time with Maddie. Perfect.

"Hey, that's where you are!" Alexa said. "Carlos, I like that you're putting all the men to work. You can come up here and take over my kitchen anytime. He has you making more pigs in a blanket, huh?"

He made eye contact with Maddie just for a second before she looked away. Why did she look better every time he saw her? This time her hair was curly and brushed against her shoulders whenever she turned her head. It made him think of that first morning when he'd woken up and looked at her lying there on his pillow, her hair spread everywhere, the sheet barely covering her. It made him want to . . . What was wrong with him? He looked down at his . . . weenies? Really? Oh my God, this was a nightmare.

"He was all by himself in here. I had to do something," Theo said. He tried to smile like everything was normal, and he didn't desperately want to push Maddie down onto the nearest surface, pull her panties down like last time, and—

"I'm just glad I got extra of all the ingredients." Carlos took the now-full cookie sheet away from Theo, slid it into the oven, and put an empty cookie sheet down in front of him. "I prepped a bunch of these this afternoon, but all your people have eaten these up like this is the first real food they've had for weeks. And I thought it was people in L.A. who were all on the juice cleanses."

Alexa and Maddie both grabbed bottles of champagne out of the cooler.

"Oh no, people in the Bay Area are like that, too, unfortunately," Maddie said. "But that's not why the people here are eating so much. It's just that Alexa's friends all really like food."

They made eye contact again, and this time, she didn't look away. They looked at each other for what felt like forever, while Alexa teased Carlos about some girl.

"And see, I was going to try to introduce you to someone up here to try to lure you to the Bay Area, but it seems like you're taken now."

"I'm not taken! I never should have told you about Nik; it's not like that. Don't you have things to do? Take your food and go away and leave the kitchen to the men."

"Come on, Mads, let's let the boys do their thing," Alexa said, right before she popped a pig in a blanket in her mouth.

Maddie picked up the guacamole and chips tray.

"This will get demolished in about ten minutes. I'm warning you now. Theo, I hope you're getting good at making those things. Go faster."

She looked right at him and smiled, damn her. She knew the effect she had on him, and now she was just fucking with him.

He smiled back at her.

"I'm good at everything."

Ooh, he got her to blush.

Theo let out a deep breath as he watched Maddie walk out of the kitchen.

Carlos looked at him and grinned.

"What's the story *there*?"

Theo looked back down at the puff pastry.

"I don't know what you mean."

Carlos shook his head.

"Okay, man. If that's the way you're going to play it. I didn't see a thing."

Maddie set the food down in the living room and escaped as soon as she could to the bathroom. She needed to stay away from him. Fine, yes, okay, she'd worn this dress tonight because she knew it looked fantastic on her and she wanted him to see her looking so great, but she hadn't really thought about what it would do to her when he looked at her like that.

It made her want him to rip her panties off again, that's what it did to her.

Damn it.

If he was so definite that they shouldn't sleep together again, why the hell did he look at her like that? It wasn't fair. No one should be able to reject a woman and then stare at her like he wanted to eat her up like one of the appetizers.

No, she was making too big a deal of seeing him again. This was going to be fine. They hadn't seen each other in a while; of course they'd both maybe think about things, but she'd go back out there and the rest of the party would be normal and they wouldn't interact at all and they wouldn't have to see each other again for months. Maybe even years!

She needed another glass of champagne, that's what she needed. She checked her makeup in the mirror, washed her hands, and ventured out of the bathroom.

She spent the next hour eating the delicious snacks that kept coming out of the kitchen, drinking champagne, and lightly flirting with two of Drew's doctor friends (who were dating each other, which made the conversation very low pressure). Alexa was all over the place, talking to her friends and family. It was nice to see her so happy. Maddie had been a little suspicious of Drew in the beginning—a pretty boy doctor from Los Angeles, of all places, was no one's idea of a stable guy for their best friend—but he made Alexa so happy that he'd won her over.

Finally, Alexa walked up to their group with a bottle of champagne.

"Refill? My mom insists on doing a toast, so everyone needs some champagne now to be prepared."

Maddie held out her glass for Alexa to fill.

"So, Alexa, have you jumped into wedding planning yet?" Drew's friend Adam asked. "Do we have a date?"

Alexa laughed and shook her head.

"Oh God no. I have a few spreadsheets other people sent me of how they did it, but just looking at them made my eyes glaze over. All I know so far is that my sister is my maid of honor, and Maddie here and my friend Theo—you guys have met him, the guy in glasses over there—are both in the wedding party. Work has been too crazy these past few weeks for me to think about anything else, but I'm sure it'll come. I'm relying on Maddie to help out a lot with the whole dress situation."

Did she say Theo was also in the wedding party? The same Theo? Yes, it had to be; she pointed at him.

"Theo's in the wedding party, too?" She hoped her voice didn't sound as alarmed as she felt.

"Oh yeah, didn't I tell you?" Alexa beckoned Drew over. "I asked him tonight. He's going to be a bridesman, which is a very silly-sounding word, but then so many wedding-related words are ridiculous."

So much for that thing about not seeing him for months or more. She'd be seeing him constantly now. For, like, the next year. She pasted a smile on her face.

Clink clink clink.

Oh thank God, the toasts. Something else to occupy everyone.

While Alexa's dad made the guests laugh and cry, Maddie wondered why it had never occurred to her that Alexa would ask Theo to be in the wedding. It made perfect sense: he was one of her closest friends; they saw each other all day every day; and Theo was one of the few people who had heard about Drew from the beginning. It was probably just that he was a guy, and she was used to weddings with strict gender divides for the bridal party. In general, despite how much she loved dresses and high heels, she was not big on gender roles—she could use her own power tools and change her own tires, thank you very much—but in this one tiny, specific case, she wished Alexa had been a hell of a lot more traditional.

Whatever. She was a big girl. She could deal with this.

"To Alexa and Drew!" Alexa's dad shouted.

"To Alexa and Drew!" Maddie and everyone else shouted back as they clinked glasses.

For the rest of the party, she tried to avoid looking at Theo, which meant that she looked at him far too often. Once or twice she caught him looking at her, which made her feel both victorious and furious. How dare he keep looking at her like that? How long could this go on?

People finally started to trickle away well after midnight, and Maddie collected some of the abandoned bottles all over the house and brought them into the kitchen.

Everyone who was left at the party helped to clean up, despite Alexa's efforts.

"You guys, really. You don't have to do this. Drew and I can figure all this out tomorrow. You're our guests."

Theo nodded.

"Sure, Lex. No problem. I'll go home in a second. Just tell me where to put all these platters first."

Alexa sighed and pointed at the cabinet next to the back door.

Alexa's cousin Leann bumped the music back up, and the cleaning party turned into an impromptu dance party, with everyone laughing and twirling around the living room and the hallway.

Drew grabbed Alexa and dipped her to the floor, as she shrieked and laughed, and everyone around them clapped. Without even meaning to, Maddie glanced at Theo, and he had the same smile on his face she felt on her own. He met her eyes and she looked away.

Maddie gathered up some of the gifts people had brought for Alexa and Drew—despite their "No gifts necessary!" note on the invitation—and took them into the guest bedroom. Maddie brought everything in a wine bag into the closet, since she knew that was where Alexa and Drew stored all of their wine. Maddie kept trying to get Alexa to just buy a wine refrigerator, but she claimed she didn't need to, when that closet was so cold as it was.

Maddie set the bottles on their sides on a shelf and shivered. Okay, Alexa had a point: it was freezing in there.

She heard the door creak open and closed behind her and turned.

"Oh! Hi, Theo, I was just putting the wine . . ." Her voice trailed away as he got closer and closer to her.

"What are you doing?" she whispered, when he was so close they were almost touching. She shivered again.

"Are you cold?" He rubbed his hand up and down her bare upper arm. "Looks like you have goose bumps."

"I, um . . . It's chilly in here."

Theo ran his fingers through her hair, and she closed her eyes. That felt so good, she wanted him to go on forever.

She forced herself to open her eyes.

"What happened to 'We can't do this again'?" she asked him.

He didn't stop touching her.

"That was a very stupid thing for me to say," he said.

She shook her head.

"No, it wasn't." Now both of his hands were in her hair, and he was bending down toward her. "We both know this is a bad idea. We shouldn't do this."

He paused, his lips just inches from hers.

"Tell me to stop, then."

He waited, his fingers brushing across her cheek. She opened her mouth, but she couldn't say it.

"That's what I thought," he said.

He kissed her, and at the touch of his lips, she wrapped her arms around him and pulled him close. He smiled against her lips and kissed her hard. It had been months since they'd touched each other, but it was like no time at all had passed. Their lips fit together, their bodies fit together, like they were lost puzzle pieces just waiting for each other.

He pushed her up against the wall, and she moaned into his mouth. His hand traced up her body, from her knee to her hip to her waist to her breast. She couldn't believe how good it felt.

"Come home with me," he said in her ear. "You know how good it'll be."

She nodded as she kissed his jaw, his neck.

"I know. But . . . there's Alexa. We can't . . ."

He put his finger under her chin.

"We won't. She won't know anything. Don't worry about it."

He kissed her again, and she was lost in the kiss for a long time before she pulled back.

"But, Theo, this doesn't make sense. We don't even like each other."

He laughed as he traced her ear with his finger.

"What does that matter? Did it matter the last time? Or the time before that?"

He had a point there.

"Okay." She pulled away and smoothed her hair and dress. "Let me go back out there and, um, get my jacket and bag."

He nodded.

"I'll meet you in the living room in a few minutes."

Maddie knew if she let herself think about how stupid this was, she wouldn't let herself do it. So she just wasn't going to think about it.

She plucked her bag and jacket up from the pile on the guest room bed, checked herself in the mirror to make sure it wasn't obvious that she'd just been making out with someone in a closet, and went out into the living room.

"More champagne, Mads?" Alexa asked. "Or one of the last pigs in a blanket?"

Maddie scooped up a pig in a blanket but shook her head to the champagne.

"I think I've hit my limit for the night. Unless you need anything else, I should probably take off."

Alexa jumped up to give her a hug.

"Thanks for everything! Are you sure you're okay to drive?"

Alexa didn't notice anything when she hugged her, did she? No, she was way too tipsy and happy to think anything was off now. This was fine.

"Oh, I got a ride from Lisa, but to get home I was just going to call a . . ."

"I can give you a ride home, Maddie. I owe you one."

She knew if she tried to meet Theo's eyes her face would betray her, so she looked somewhere over his shoulder.

"Oh, it's late, Theo. You don't have to do that."

He took her coat from her.

"I insist. Good night, Alexa. Congratulations again."

Theo hugged Alexa and they both waved to Drew before they escaped from the house.

Chapter Five

THEO HELD HIS BREATH AS HE WALKED WITH MADDIE DOWN THE
street to his car. He couldn't believe his luck. It felt like at any moment she'd run back to the house, get a ride from someone else, flag
down a passing car—anything to not go home with him. But she
walked next to him, so close, but not quite touching him, until they
got to his car.

Once they got in his car, they looked at each other and laughed.

"You don't think she noticed anything, do you?" Maddie asked
him.

Theo shook his head. Alexa'd had way too much champagne,
and had been too excited about everything else going on, to pay
attention to the two of them.

"No chance. You know Alexa; she just wants to make sure
everyone gets home safely."

He turned on the car and made a left turn onto Alcatraz Avenue on the way to his place. My God, she looked incredible in that

dress. He couldn't wait to get it off her. Thank goodness his apartment was just a few minutes away.

As they walked up his front steps, he took her arm. He couldn't wait to touch her, but reaching for her hand felt too intimate for what they were.

"Oh, look at you being gallant," Maddie said.

Theo shrugged.

"Those heels you're wearing are very high. I didn't want you to trip. Just think of what would happen if you fell and broke something outside of my building. That would be a public relations nightmare, and my whole job is to prevent those."

Maddie laughed and leaned against him.

He unlocked the door and ushered her in, and shut the door behind her.

Once they were inside his apartment, where they'd been twice before, they stopped and looked at each other expectantly. Finally, he broke the silence and leaned forward to kiss her. This time he held back, and kissed her slowly, gently.

He pulled back, and they smiled at each other. She reached for him again, and he shook his head. He stooped down and took off first one of her gold sandals, and then the other. He held on to one of her feet, and used his thumb to knead the arch of her foot.

"Those shoes look like they hurt," he said.

She shook her head, her eyes closed.

"Mmm, I'm used to them. But that feels nice."

He set her foot down on the floor and picked up the other foot.

"I thought it might."

After a few minutes, he stood back up and took her hand.

"Come with me."

She followed him without a word.

They walked into his bedroom, and he took her purse off her shoulder and set it on the floor.

"Last time, and the time before, we rushed through things," he said, as he unbuttoned his shirt. "And it was great. Really great. But tonight, I want to take my time with you. We have all night."

Maddie's eyes followed his fingers as they went down his body. She started to reach for him and stopped.

"We do," she said.

He threw his shirt onto the floor and pulled his undershirt off in one quick motion.

"That doesn't mean you can't help me," he said.

Her hands were on his belt within a second. She slid his belt out of the loops, caressing the leather, so close to touching his skin, but just managing to avoid it. She unbuckled the belt, step by gradual step, until he felt like he was going to die if he didn't get this belt off him and her hands on him immediately. Whose fucking idea was this 'we have all night' nonsense anyway?

Finally, she threw his belt on the floor and popped open the button on his jeans. She moved her fingers up and down the zipper, right over his growing bulge. His breath came faster and faster. She unzipped his jeans with one quick motion and pushed them down over his ass.

He kicked off his shoes and pulled his jeans all the way off, until he was standing in just his boxer briefs. She reached for them, but he stopped her.

"Wait. Turn around."

He'd noticed the zipper up the back of her dress early in the night. That zipper had been tantalizing him for hours.

He gathered her hair in his fist and kissed the nape of her neck. He dropped kisses down her neck, all the way until the top of the zipper. He pulled it down slowly and moved his hands and lips down her body as each inch of skin was exposed, until the zipper was all the way at the bottom.

He stood back up and hooked the straps of the dress over his fingers to pull them off her shoulders, and the dress dropped to the floor. She turned around to face him and smiled.

"My God." He took a step back to look at her. She had on a strapless black bra and a lacy black thong, and it took everything in him to not rip them off her body and throw her on his bed. But he'd promised her he'd take it slow this time.

"You're incredible," he said.

She grinned and pulled him toward her.

"Just for that, good things will come your way tonight."

They kissed and kissed and kissed, their hands roaming over each other's bodies, their lips following their hands. He listened to her sighs and moans and breaths to teach him what she liked, what she wanted more of, where she wanted to be touched the most.

He walked with her, still kissing her, until her legs bumped up against the bed.

"Lie down," he said.

She obeyed him and was soon flat on her back on his bed, looking up at him. Her lips were swollen and her hair surrounded her face. She was the most incredible thing he'd ever seen.

He hooked his thumbs in her lacy underwear and, inch by inch, pulled it off her body. He dropped it on the floor, then knelt between her open legs.

"I seem to remember you liked this," he said as he pushed her legs open wider and bent his head down.

"Mmm, people change, you know." She propped a pillow

under her head and smiled down at him. "Things might be different now."

He paused, his fingers on her inner thigh.

"Is that a challenge I hear?"

She shrugged.

"I'm just saying, who knows if I still—"

She gasped at his next movement, and for the next few moments the only sounds she made were unintelligible.

When her spasms subsided, he crawled up her body.

"Wait, I couldn't hear that," he said in her ear. "Did you just say, 'Theo, you're very good at that'?"

She grinned.

"Theo, you're very good at that. But then, I think you already know that."

He kissed her cheek and nodded.

"I do, but that doesn't mean I don't like to hear it."

He turned on his side and grabbed a condom out of his bedside table.

She pulled off her bra and propped herself up on her elbows.

He stopped to stare at her boobs. My God, they were perfect. He quickly finished rolling the condom on, and then reached for a nipple.

"Do you know how much I wanted to do this all night?" he asked her. "You and that dress . . . Every time I saw you from across the room, all I wanted was to touch you here . . . and kiss you here . . . Did you know that? Did you wear that dress just to drive me crazy?"

She nodded.

"Absolutely."

He was so surprised he sat back.

"Really? You did?"

She nodded again.

"I did. After last time, I thought . . . I mean the way things ended, it felt like you hadn't really . . ."

He shook his head and put his hand back on her breast.

"Oh God no. You thought last time I said we shouldn't do this again because I didn't want to do it again? Good God, it was the opposite." He moved his hands back down her body. "I said that because I wanted to do it again and again and again, and I knew if I got another chance, I might not be able to stop."

She closed her eyes and opened her legs wider.

"Mmm, well, we can talk about that later. But you know how you said we were going to go slow tonight?"

He moved on top of her again and bent down to kiss her.

"Yeah, what about it?"

She opened her eyes and looked into his.

"Can we speed it up a little? Because I want you inside me right now."

Holy shit, well, when she put it that way.

He pulled up her knees and pushed himself inside of her up to the hilt.

Maddie grinned into Theo's chest when his breathing got closer to normal. How did sex with him just keep getting better? It made no sense.

He dropped a kiss on her shoulder and stood up.

"You want some water?" She nodded and went off to the bathroom while he was in the kitchen.

He came back into the bedroom with glasses of water for both of them. She turned on the bedside lamp, and he turned off the overhead light.

"I like your sheets," she said as she slid in between them.

He got in next to her and pulled her against them.

"I like you in between my sheets, so that's perfect."

She put her finger over his lips.

"Shhhh, the sex was so good, don't ruin it."

He laughed and turned off the light.

In the morning she woke up with her head on his chest and his arm around her. How the hell had she gotten herself into this situation yet again? And she was going to have to see him all the time now, for, like, the next year or more, depending on when Alexa and Drew's wedding was, and try to keep her hands off him. This was going to be torture.

"Are you awake?" she whispered.

"Yes," he whispered back. His fingers moved slowly over her hair, and she sighed. Damn it.

She sat up.

"We have to talk."

He shook his head and didn't move.

"Why did you have to say that? Those are the worst four words in the English language. It's too early in the morning for 'we have to talk.' You can't 'we have to talk' me before I've even started the coffee. That's not fair. Come back here."

He pulled her back down onto his chest, and she didn't resist.

"Sorry, I know, I know." She tried to relax against him, but she couldn't. "But Alexa said last night that she asked you to be in the wedding."

His fingers traced a pattern on her shoulder.

"She did. I'm going to be a bridesman! Wild, right?"

Oh my God, what was wrong with men? He was so cheerful and relaxed about this.

"I'm also in the wedding."

She felt him nod his head.

"I assumed you were. And?"

She couldn't take it anymore and sat back up.

"And? And that means that we're going to be around each other all the time for the next—I don't know how long! Doing wedding events and helping her with clothes or whatever and all the stuff with the wedding, and it's clear that even though you irritate the hell out of me, and I assume I bug you, we can't keep our hands off each other. What are we going to do?"

He sighed and sat up.

"I think we should stop fighting it. Stop pretending to ourselves—and to each other—that we're not going to end up in bed together every single time we see each other, because I think we both know now that it's going to happen."

She threw up her arms. Why was he acting like this was such a simple and obvious solution?

"But why does it have to happen? We saw each other at Alexa's parties for years and nothing like this happened until last summer!"

He folded his arms behind his head and lay back down.

"Why can't you get a champagne cork back in a bottle once you've popped it? That's how it was before; this is obviously how it is now. Are you really going to tell me it's not true?"

She really wanted to tell him it wasn't true, especially when he had that smug look on his face, but she couldn't do it.

"I guess not, but . . ."

He got out of bed and pulled sweatpants out of a drawer.

"If you're going to make me talk about this, we have to do it in the kitchen while I make coffee. Come on." He threw her an oversize hoodie. "It's cold in there."

Maddie grumbled as she followed him into the kitchen. Was this why Alexa was friends with someone as annoying as Theo? Because he had the same obsession with coffee as she did? Maddie drank coffee every morning and all, but come on.

She stood in the corner of his freezing kitchen, her arms wrapped around herself, the hoodie covering her from shoulders to butt, and watched him fill up and turn on his electric kettle, grind and measure coffee, and then set up little cones full of ground coffee on top of mugs. This was the third time she'd been here for coffee in the morning, but the first time she'd really paid attention to the complicated way he made coffee. She'd been so distracted the other times, she hadn't even realized he started by boiling water instead of just pushing a button on a coffee maker like a normal person.

"Oh God. You're one of those annoying coffee people." Maybe better than the annoying beer people, but only slightly. "A normal coffee maker is a lot faster, you know."

He nodded without turning around.

"I know. I like it better this way."

She watched him make the slowest coffee in all of California.

"I can't believe I slept with someone who boils water every damn morning to make their coffee."

He looked up from pouring the water.

"Actually, it's not boiled; I heat the water to exactly two hundred five degrees in order to get the best—"

"You should stop talking now if you really want to have sex with me ever again."

He shut his mouth and set a full mug in front of her. She opened the fridge for the milk while he poured the water over his own coffee grounds.

"Okay." He poured milk into his own coffee and turned to face her. "Where were we? Oh, right, you couldn't deny that we're going to end up in bed together every time we see each other now."

She grunted in frustration at her coffee mug. The problem was, he was right. She glared at him.

"How does someone who heats his water to exactly two hundred or whatever put milk in his coffee? Don't all you annoying coffee people take it black?"

He looked down at his mug. Was that a blush she saw?

"I drank it black for a long time before I let myself admit I like it so much better with milk and gave myself permission to stop punishing myself." She grinned, and he looked up at her and grinned back. "But stop changing the subject! We were talking about you and me and the likelihood this is going to keep happening over and over again, remember?"

She remembered.

"Okay, fine! I admit it! It's going to keep happening again! But we need some ground rules if we're going to do this."

He picked up his coffee mug and walked back into the bedroom. She followed.

"I like rules. Hit me with them."

"Okay." She took a sip of coffee and got back in bed. It tasted just like the stuff she made in her coffee maker, except hers was not quite as bitter. "Rule one: no one can tell Alexa."

He set his coffee on his bedside table and got in bed next to her.

"Hasn't that always been the rule? Did you think I was going to burst into Alexa's office Monday morning and say, 'Lex, guess what? I'm sleeping with your best friend!'?"

She pictured the look on Alexa's face if he did that and had to grin.

"If we're going to make rules, we might as well spell all of them out," she said.

He leaned against the headboard and picked up his mug.

"Good point. What's rule two?"

"This ends with the wedding. Maybe by then we'll have gotten it out of our systems, and we can go back to ignoring each other."

He nodded.

"I can accept that. Anything else?"

"Rule three: no dates, just this."

He tilted his head and smiled at her.

"What does 'this' mean?"

He knew what she meant. She gestured at the bed.

"This."

He put his mug down, and in one quick motion pulled her on top of him.

"You mean this?" He kissed her. She relaxed against his body and kissed him back. She moved her fingers up and down his bare chest. Damn it, why did this have to be so good?

"Mmm, yes, I mean this."

He nodded as his hands unzipped the hoodie.

"Okay, just checking: do we also get to do *this* in the hallway, or on the couch, or even in the kitchen, or are we restricted to just my bed?"

She shook her head and tried to concentrate on something other than the touch of his skin, his body underneath hers.

"We can do *this* anywhere we want."

"Mmm." He pulled her legs along either side of his so she was straddling him. "I like the sound of that." He bent down and licked the tip of her nipple. "All these rules sound good to me. Anything else?"

"Just . . . one more." She brushed her hand over his hair. "Rule four: we only see each other when we've been with Alexa. We're doing this because we have to, not because we want to." She let out a moan as he sucked her nipple into his mouth.

He rolled her over so she was now underneath him and pulled back. Oh God, why did he stop?

"You get four rules, I get one: no sleeping with anyone else," he said. "I don't like sharing."

Maddie grinned at him.

He leaned down to kiss her but she pulled away.

"One more question," she said.

"Hit me," he said.

She gave him a mischievous look.

"Next time, will you dance to 'Pony'?"

He sat back and grinned.

"That depends on what I get in return."

Maddie pulled him back down to her.

"I'm an only child. I'm not a big fan of sharing myself."

They didn't talk about rules or anything else for a long while.

Chapter Six

MONDAY MORNING, THEO GOT INTO WORK EARLIER THAN USUAL. IT
was the week before Memorial Day weekend, and he knew from
experience there would be at least a crisis a day from Monday to
Thursday, until everything went dead on Friday. He sort of loved
weeks like this.

He sat down at his desk, still with the grin on his face that had
been there since Sunday morning. He couldn't quite believe his
luck. He half expected that next time he'd see Maddie and suggest
she come back to his place, she'd shudder and tell him that she'd
been feverish or concussed or otherwise out of her mind when she'd
agreed to their deal. He needed to find a way to see her as soon as
possible, just to make sure this whole thing was real.

He spent the first hour at work cleaning out his email box and
getting himself back down to inbox zero. He always felt off and
disorganized if there were any emails in his inbox at all, and last
Friday had been so busy that he'd left the office with twenty in

there. He'd planned to deal with that on Sunday, but Maddie hadn't left his house until midafternoon, and at that point, he'd been in no frame of mind to deal with work.

Alexa poked her head into his office and he jumped. Oh God, had thoughts of Maddie been on his face? She was usually so good at reading him; please let her not be able to see right through him right now.

"Morning," she said. "Ready for the week? Boss in yet?"

He shook his head.

"I don't think so. How are you? Have you recovered from your engagement party yet?"

He certainly hadn't recovered from her engagement party; hopefully she wouldn't figure that out, or else Maddie would kill him.

She grinned and held up her large thermos of coffee.

"Barely. Thank God you guys stayed to help clean up on Saturday night, because yesterday Drew and I basically spent all day on the couch eating leftovers and praying our hangovers would go away. Mine is gone now, but it still feels like it could come back at any second, so I got a large breakfast sandwich on my way in and am trying to drink as much water and coffee as humanly possible."

He laughed. All he wanted was for her to not ask him too many questions about if he had fun at the party. Unfortunately, Alexa saw through him like almost no one else. When Maddie had said they had to keep this a secret from her, he thought it was no big deal—he'd kept the secret from her the other times, hadn't he? But now he remembered that both other times he'd slept with Maddie, he and Alexa had had something else major to talk about the following Monday—both of which involved Drew showing up out of the blue, come to think of it. Now there weren't any distractions on her side, she might see right through him and ask more questions about why he had this look on his face, and he might accidentally spill everything to her.

"I cracked up when I got your text yesterday," he said.

She'd sent a text to him, Maddie, and Olivia the day before, with a picture of the recycling bin full of empty beer, champagne, and tequila bottles, captioned, "Sign of a good party, or sign of an enormous hangover?" He and Maddie had gotten it and laughed at it while she was still at his house. He had been very grateful to Alexa for that text: now he finally had Maddie's number. The problem was, now he didn't know when to use it.

"I still don't quite know why we decided to open those last few bottles of champagne after midnight," Alexa said.

"Go eat your breakfast and drink your coffee so you make it through today," he said. Thank God she walked away without asking any difficult questions.

The mayor walked into their meeting a few hours later with a big grin on his face. Theo looked over at Alexa, who was looking back at him. They both knew this could either be great news, or "great" news that made their jobs nightmares for the next few days or weeks.

"Great news!" the mayor said. Theo looked down at his notepad so he wouldn't look over at Alexa and laugh. "This isn't public yet, but the ballot initiative for universal pre-K in California qualified for the November election!"

The whole room cheered. Okay, that was actual great news.

"And, since I'm one of the cosponsors of the initiative, I'll be working a lot with the governor, a number of other mayors, and other elected officials around the state to get this passed. It's going to be a tough road to November, but with a team like you working hard with me on this, we can do anything!"

Ah yes, the rare great news and "great" news, all in one.

The mayor beckoned Alexa and Theo to walk with him to his office after the meeting.

"I would have talked to you two about the initiative before the staff meeting, but the governor's office called right before I walked in. But as you both know, this initiative is my baby."

Theo and Alexa nodded. The mayor had been advocating for universal pre-K for years, and he'd worked closely with the organization that had drafted the measure for the ballot.

"Therefore, I want to be heavily involved in this campaign." He turned to Theo. "The campaign itself will do the heavy lifting, but this still means a lot of extra work for you, because the goal is as much press—good press—as we can get. And obviously you'll have to work a lot with the governor's press office and all the other elected officials around the state."

Theo nodded. Universal pre-K was an issue close to his heart, too. And a campaign like this would help both the mayor (who Theo knew had higher political ambitions) and Theo (who did, too) raise their profiles statewide. Especially if they managed to get the campaign to agree to have at least one major event here in Berkeley.

That is, it would help Theo raise his profile statewide if he did a good job. He knew that with one misstep, everything could come tumbling down.

"Can't wait," he said to his boss.

The mayor rubbed his hands together.

"Me neither."

Maddie stared at the piles of clothes around her bedroom. One of her clients today was Maya Leslie, the sports reporter for a local news station, and she always liked to make a special effort to look poised and put together when she saw Maya. She felt like TV people expected it.

Maddie had loved giving fashion advice all her life, and sometimes she still couldn't believe this was her actual job. Her first job in the stylist world had been a fluke; she'd been a college student in L.A. and a part-time barista, and one of her regular customers was Amelia Powell, an up-and-coming stylist. One Friday morning she came in desperate for caffeine and sympathy; her assistants all had the flu, and she had to get three clients ready and fitted for awards shows that weekend. Maddie had said, "I'm free this weekend, and I know how to sew." She'd worked with Amelia all that weekend, and then on and off for years. She'd eventually moved back to the Bay Area for a more practical—and more steady—job, but she'd missed the fun and hustle of styling. A few years before, Amelia had begged her to come to L.A. for another awards show weekend to help out, and Maddie had taken the opportunity to ask for her advice about starting her own styling business. Six months later, she had her first three clients, and Maya had been one of them.

One of the many reasons Maddie loved working with Maya was that with Maya, she could be her naturally bossy self. For some of her clients, she had to be supportive and encouraging and persuasive when she worked with them, instead of demanding. She could be supportive and encouraging; she was happy to do it—it was just that hand-holding and cajoling took more out of her. It was much easier to just order people to put jumpsuits on.

Why was it taking her so long to decide what to wear today? She knew her wardrobe well enough that she could make these decisions in a snap.

Oh, right, because she'd seen her green dress on top of the pile
of dry cleaning in the far corner of her room. The dress she'd put
on that pile yesterday after she'd gotten home, well into the afternoon, from Theo's house. After a very good night . . . and day.
Damn it, what had she gotten herself into?

She reached for her second-favorite jeans; they weren't quite
worn in enough to be comfortable, but they looked fantastic on her.
Her button-down white silk blouse, miracle of miracles, was still
pressed and hanging in her closet, so she pulled on a nude camisole
and carefully buttoned up the blouse. Now, time for a good lots-of-
makeup "no makeup" look.

She stared at herself in the mirror as she put concealer on under
her eyes. What the hell had she agreed to the day before? Theo
had somehow convinced her they had no choice but to keep sleeping together. How had she gone along with that?

She brushed on just enough bronzer and blush to give herself a
glow. To be fair to Theo—which she loathed doing—she'd done a
hell of a lot more than go along with it. She'd definitely been an
active participant in everything they'd done that night . . . and the
next morning . . . and afternoon.

But she'd spouted those rules off to him like she'd been thinking
about them for months. Like she'd been planning this! When that
couldn't be further from the truth. The last thing she'd wanted was
to be forced to spend a lot of time with Theo in the run-up to Alexa's wedding. And God knew how long that would be. Alexa and
Drew didn't seem to have any urgency about picking a wedding
date, so she was likely going to have to keep seeing him for well
over a year.

And then, of course, every time she saw him, she was going to
have to have sex with him.

Multiple times.

As she patted on nude eye shadow, she saw the smug look on her face in the mirror. She tried to stop smiling, but it was impossible.

She reached for her mascara. At least her rules made it so he wouldn't start thinking she wanted to see him all the time. No dates, and only after they'd been with Alexa. Since Alexa was still at the beginning of all this wedding planning stuff, Maddie might not see him for months.

She swiped on a second coat of mascara. How much time did she have? She checked her phone: ten minutes before her first client. Ugh, why did she keep getting disappointed whenever she checked her phone and she didn't have a text? He had her number now, after Alexa's half-drunken group text. But she didn't even *want* Theo to text her! Was she just conditioned to think that if she slept with a dude, he had to text her the next day, even when they had a perfectly rational agreement that precluded the necessity—or even the possibility—of a day-after text?

This was the fault of the fucking patriarchy.

She swiped on some red lipstick, admired her fresh blowout in the mirror, stuffed a few things in her tote bag, and left her bedroom to walk out her back door and into the tiny cottage that housed her studio. There she had appointments and fittings with her clients and did any simple alterations, though she frequently also toted trunks full of clothes and shoes to clients' homes and offices all around the Bay Area.

She had two quick clients that morning, and just enough time to refresh her lipstick before Maya knocked on her door.

"Maddie!" Maya air-kissed the vicinity of Maddie's cheek and walked in the door. "I'm so sorry I'm late. We had a little crisis at the office."

Maddie smiled at Maya's outfit, one of the best she'd put together for her last quarter.

"Oh, it's no problem. I have some great stuff for you this time; it's all on the rack."

Maya made a beeline to the rack. She flipped through the clothes, moving quickly past some and lingering at others. The ones she paused at, Maddie grabbed and moved to the end of the rack. One of the reasons Maddie loved working with Maya is that she was so decisive. But she was also willing to take a risk now and then. It made her fun to dress.

"I'm already excited to try all of this on." Maya looked at a boldly patterned shift dress. "I'm not positive how this will work on TV, but I think I love it, so let's try it anyway."

Maddie arranged the forty or so garments Maya had chosen at the end of the rack, first by type, and then by color.

Maya stepped out of her clothes and into the first dress, a black pin-striped cap sleeve shift dress that Maddie had thought would be a slam dunk. It was.

"I love this. I want it in every color it comes in." She turned around for Maddie to unzip her. "So this is fun: they're thinking about doing a show at the station where women who have been homeless, or in rehab, stuff like that, learn how to dress for success. Isn't that a great idea?" Maya pulled on a color-blocked dress and smiled at herself in the mirror.

Maddie handed her a blazer to put over it.

"That is a great idea. I hope they get it right."

Maddie knew well how badly most of the world treated poor and struggling women, especially if they were women of color. There were a lot of ways to get a show like that wrong.

Maya pulled on the jumpsuit Maddie handed her.

"I don't know about this one, Maddie. What do you think? This pink is great on me, but can I pull off a jumpsuit? On air?"

Maddie had her arguments all ready.

"You absolutely can. First, look at this one: the fit on you is fantastic, it's blousy in just the right kind of way, and as you said, the color is perfect on you. And it's no problem to wear it on air— the color will pop, the neckline will work with any kind of necklace, you can throw a blazer over it and look super professional, and you're behind a desk anyway. And if you stand up, hell, you just look cool."

Maya grinned at herself in the mirror and shrugged.

"Okay, fine, you've convinced me. I notice you didn't say anything about what a pain it's going to be to go to the bathroom while wearing this, but I guess we're both just taking that as a given and moving on."

Maya pulled off the jumpsuit and reached for Maddie's next option.

"Back to the show—I think it could be great," she said to Maddie. "They'll just have to have the right host for it; someone who is good at styling but is also great on camera. That'll be a challenge."

She slipped on a bright red skirt with a kick pleat and stepped into the leopard print heels Maddie handed her.

"Okay, you're officially brilliant. I was doubtful about both of these, but they're great on me, and these shoes are way more comfortable than I thought they'd be."

Maddie gave her a black ruffled top from the reject pile.

"I know you already said no to this, but I don't care. It works with that whole outfit. Just try it on."

Maya looked at herself in the mirror and slowly shook her head.

"See, this is why I love you. You badger me into wearing clothes that look incredible on me." She looked down the rack of clothes. "*And* you found all this stuff, and it was all here ready for me. I could have spent a day shopping and not found this many good clothes."

Maddie grinned as she hung up the clothes. Compliments from her clients were always welcome.

"Shopping has always been one of my best skills. People"— people like Theo—"always tried to act like that was a stupid thing to be good at, but once I realized I could do it for a living, I didn't care what they had to say anymore."

Maya tried on the next outfit.

"We all have to lean in to our skills and passions—one of the best things I've realized in my thirties," Maddie said.

Maya turned to her with a smile.

"All of that is exactly why I told the producers I knew the perfect person to host the show."

Maddie stared at her for way too long before she realized where Maya was going with this.

"Me? You want me to do it?" Maddie shook her head. "Thanks for the compliment, but I don't think—"

Maya's grin was very wide.

"You'd be amazing at it! You're so good at this anyway; it'll just give you a bigger platform to be good. And you'll help so many people!"

"All of that's true, but, Maya . . ."

Maya didn't let her finish.

"You're going to say you're not sure about being on camera, but I bet you're great on camera. Just look at you!"

Maddie couldn't help but be flattered.

"You've beaten down all my arguments, so fine, I'll think about it, but . . ."

Maya grinned.

"Fantastic. I already told them about you and that I'd see you today. You should get a call from them very soon. Do you have a headshot? If so, send it to me. Also, I love this dress, but don't you think it needs to be like half an inch shorter?"

Maddie laughed and knelt down to pin the hem of the dress.

Chapter Seven

THEO GOT HOME FROM WORK LATE THURSDAY NIGHT, AND AFTER shedding his bag and shoes at his front door, he investigated the contents of his fridge. Bleh, three different plastic containers of too-old leftovers, a carton of eggs, and half of a brown avocado. He'd meant to go to the store on Sunday, but between Maddie being there most of the day and his need for a nap once she'd left, he hadn't made it there. And this week had been so busy because of the pre-K campaign, so he hadn't gotten there. He probably had something or other in his freezer, but it was probably freezer burned by this point. He had two chocolate chip cookies from the bakery across the street from his office in his bag, but that was dessert, not dinner. He picked up the phone and ordered a pizza.

He went into his bedroom to change into sweatpants, and when he tossed the handful of change from his pockets onto his dresser, something gold and shiny fell onto the floor. Where the hell had that come from? He bent down to pick it up and twisted it in the air. A delicate dangly gold earring. He flashed back to that moment he'd kissed Maddie in Alexa's closet and saw that same gold earring.

Was the other one here, too? He looked on the dresser and saw it right there on the corner. He put the two earrings together in the old ashtray a kid from his volunteer program had made for him and sat down on his bed to think.

What was his move here? He hadn't heard from her since she'd left his house on Sunday afternoon, he had no idea when he was going to see her again, but he should at least tell her she'd left her earrings at his house, right?

If he did it now, would she think he was trying to get back into her pants?

He *was* trying to get back into her pants, obviously; he just didn't know if this would increase or decrease the likelihood of that happening.

Hell with it. He had to break the ice sometime. He picked up his phone.

Hey Maddie, it's Theo. Hope you had a good week. Just fyi, I have those long gold earrings of yours. Let me know if you need them.

There. No big deal, he just had her earrings; he wasn't violating any of her rules or anything, just giving her some information. Ball was in her court now.

He dropped his phone and pulled an old T-shirt on. Should he have said, "Come by and get them anytime"? Eh, baby steps.

He grabbed a beer out of his fridge, went back down the hall to his living room, and turned on the basketball game. He probably should work on the press release that needed to go out Tuesday, but he'd been working nonstop all day, and he wanted to sit on the couch and yell at sports for a while to give the work part of his brain a break.

His phone buzzed, and he snatched it off the coffee table.

You watching this game?

Ben.

Yeah, why?

Knowing Ben, it could be anything between "I just won $1,000 on Curry's last shot" to "My ad agency has a commercial in the next break. Watch it!"

I got a last minute ticket from someone at the agency 10th row, look for me on TV

Yeah, that sounded right.

Asshole

He set his DVR to record.

His doorbell rang—pizza, thank God. He handed over cash and plunked the pizza box down on his coffee table.

Just as he picked up a slice of pizza, his phone buzzed once more. If it was Ben again . . .

Thanks for letting me know. Getting drinks with Alexa now btw

Not Ben. He took a bite of pizza and leaned back against the couch cushions.

Ohhh, does that mean I need to be circumspect about what I text in case she sees your phone?

This was going to be fun.

Maddie saw Theo's text flash onto her phone and put her forearm on top of it.

"So are you going to do it?" Alexa asked.

Was she a mind reader? How did Alexa know she was thinking about whether she should stop by Theo's place later? Just to get the earrings. She wore those earrings all the time and needed them for the weekend.

"Do what?"

"Apply for the job at the station? The thing we were just talking about?" Alexa picked up Maddie's glass and peered into it. "How much tequila is in that margarita?"

Maddie took her glass back.

"Ha-ha, very funny. Sorry, I lost my train of thought. It's been a long week." Getting paranoid there, Madeleine. "I think so. It's a great way to raise my profile, that's for sure. And I really could help people who need my skills. I'm just not sure if I'll be good on TV."

Maddie had been thinking about the job at the station all week, and the more she thought about it, the more excited she felt. She'd already heard from the producer, who said he'd be in touch with more details in a few weeks. She'd talked to her mom about it, and her mom had told her to make a pro/con list, like she always told her to do for any major—or sometimes minor—decision. But she knew her mom loved the idea; she was a social worker, and she knew how much of a barrier the right clothes could be, especially for poor women. Plus, she and Maddie both knew how hard life was as a woman who didn't know all of the unwritten clothing rules that seem to come up everywhere you go.

Maddie had always wanted to be able to do something to give back—that was part of the whole reason she'd started this business in the first place. But she'd been concentrating so much over the past few years on getting her business established, she hadn't had any time. Now here was something that could both help her business *and* help people.

Her phone buzzed, and she glanced down at it.

Because I could mention something about when I noticed those earrings on Saturday night. I saw one of them just brushing your right shoulder, and it made me want to put my lips just there. And then later, when we were in the closet, I did it.

He needed to stop this. Just thinking about when he'd kissed her like that in the closet made her shiver.

"Are you kidding me? You'll be great on TV!" Alexa said. She had to stop thinking about Theo around Alexa. "You have the right look for it, and you've styled so many people for TV appearances that you know all the clothes that will work."

Maddie nodded.

"Oh, I'm not worried if I can *look* good on TV—that part I have down. It's if I can *be* good on TV. I feel like they want a certain type for that kind of show—bitchy but helpful, snooty but with a heart of gold, et cetera. And look, I can BE a bitch, but—"

Alexa burst out laughing.

"Oh, really? You can? I had no idea."

Maddie elbowed her.

"Shut up. My *point* is that I just don't know if that's the right way to go for this kind of thing? Or am I overthinking it?"

Alexa was still laughing.

"You're definitely overthinking it, at least for now. Right now, just wait to see what happens. You can figure out your TV persona later."

Her phone buzzed again.

And then later that night, you were naked on my bed but the only thing you had on were those earrings. When did you eventually take them off?

She remembered that, too, damn him. What was he doing? He knew she was there with Alexa!

Alexa's phone buzzed and she picked it up. Oh thank God, now Maddie could reach for her phone, too.

You're killing me here. I took them off before we fell asleep, I can't sleep with those on

His text came within seconds.

You sure can fuck with them on though

She pretended her laugh was a cough. Luckily, Alexa was busy texting.

"Sorry about this. Olivia is in L.A. for work and had a restaurant question. Just one second."

Theo! Are you trying to give us away? I barely managed to not laugh out loud there

She drained the rest of her margarita.

I'll stop as soon as you tell me to stop

"Okay, sorry." Alexa put her phone down. "I'm excited you're doing this. Keep me posted as soon as you hear from them."

Maddie pulled her attention away from her phone.

"I will. I'm not getting my hopes up; they could already have someone in mind that Maya doesn't know about, or the show could just be a pipe dream."

You know, now that you mention it, I don't remember seeing them on you in the morning. I should have realized you didn't have them on then. I was watching you pretty closely when you climbed on top of me. I guess I was distracted by other things.

She crossed her legs. Damn this man for making her so heated. She hated that he was doing this to her.

Maybe sometime you could come by my office when the coast is clear and lock the door, and we could do all of that and more on top of my desk

She pictured that in her mind and shivered. All she could think about was climbing on top of him again as soon as possible. She texted back.

I'm going to get back at you for this

The bartender stopped in front of them.

"Ladies, another round?"

Alexa shook her head.

"I shouldn't. Drew should be home soon. But Maddie, go ahead. I have time to hang out for a little while longer."

Maddie pushed her glass away.

"No, I've got a busy day tomorrow."

As weird as it was to keep a secret like this from Alexa, it was actually kind of nice to have a fun secret, something interesting going on in her life. Especially right now, when it felt like Alexa was falling away from her. Not that she didn't like Drew, or wasn't happy for Alexa; that wasn't it. But for twenty years it had been Maddie and Alexa all the time for everything, and now it was Alexa and Drew. He was her default now, and Maddie didn't have one anymore.

When Maddie got to her car, she pulled out her phone again. She had another text.

I'm at home tonight, if you're nearby and need those earrings

She could just stop by and get the earrings; she didn't have to sleep with him.

I'll be there in 10 minutes

Was she coming over to get the earrings, or was she coming over to "get the earrings"? He had no idea.

Should he change? He looked down at what he was wearing. No, that would make it seem like he thought this was a booty call, and even if that's what it turned out to be, he didn't want her to think that was on purpose.

Even though it was.

The earrings were still on his dresser. Should he bring them into the living room?

What a stupid question.

When the doorbell rang, he walked back down the hall to the front door.

"Hey," he said when he opened the door. She looked fucking incredible. As usual. "Come on in."

Without waiting for a response, he turned and went into the living room.

"You hungry? I have this whole pizza. Well . . . most of it."

He sat down in the middle of the couch.

"Starving, now that you mention it. What kind of pizza?"

She sat down next to him. She hadn't brought up the earrings yet. This seemed like a good sign.

"Pepperoni, mushroom, and roasted garlic. Is that acceptable?"

She made a face but flipped open the pizza box and picked up a slice.

"All those things but the roasted garlic is fine. That's a little much for a pizza, don't you think?"

He laughed.

"Everyone makes fun of me for how much I love roasted garlic on pizza. Sorry about that."

He picked up his slice, and she looked down at his plate, then back up at him. "Oh, aren't we fancy, eating pizza on a *plate*."

He handed her a napkin.

"Some of us are civilized, Maddie. Stick around. Maybe you'll learn a little something."

She waved the pizza slice at him.

"Speaking of being civilized, what were you thinking sending me those texts when you knew Alexa was right there?"

He had to grin.

"I couldn't resist. It was funny, you have to admit."

Was she trying to hold back a grin? He couldn't tell, but he thought so.

"It was not funny! Alexa and I were talking about work and wedding stuff, and I kept getting distracted by you."

Hmm, that was a very good sign.

"What distracted you the most?" he asked, as he brushed her hair back from her face. "Was it just my texts? Was it remembering what we did last weekend?" He put his hand on her knee. "Or was it thinking about what we could do later on tonight?"

He kissed her earlobe, then trailed kisses down her neck as he pushed her back onto the couch. She dropped her slice of pizza back into the box.

"No option for all the above?" she asked him, and pulled him down against her.

Their kiss was hot and fast and needy. Was it obvious that he'd been thinking about her all week? Right now he didn't care.

He pushed up her shirt and rolled her nipples between his fingers, the way he knew she liked it. She moaned and tossed her head back against his couch cushions. That sound sparked something in him. He wanted to hear it more. Longer. Louder. He slipped his hand under her skirt. She opened her knees for him and he leaned over to kiss her lips.

"You were so ready for me, weren't you?" he said against her mouth. She nodded and opened wider. He slid one finger inside, and then two. "Were you ready like this, when you were sitting there at the bar, getting my texts? Tell me the truth."

She opened her eyes and smiled at him.

"Why do you think I got here so fast?"

He pulled her panties off and pushed up her skirt.

"Let's see if we can get you somewhere else fast, too."

He ducked his head under her skirt, and from her cries and moans a few moments later, he determined that he'd accomplished his goal.

He stood up, pulled a condom out of his pocket, and let his sweatpants drop to the floor.

"Do you normally carry condoms around in your pockets while you're alone in your house?" she asked him, with a very contented smile on her face.

He looked at the condom in his hand with pretend shock on his face.

"Well, I never! How did this get in my pocket? It must have been the condom fairy."

She rolled her eyes and shimmied her skirt off.

"The condom fairy? Is that like the tooth fairy, but for condoms?"

He nodded.

"Exactly! I've heard people talk about the condom fairy, but I always thought she was a myth. I guess everyone was right when they said that if I just needed a condom enough, she would come to me." He ripped open the wrapper. "Since she blessed us with her presence today, it would be an insult to not make use of her gift, don't you think?"

He watched her watch him roll the condom on. He liked it when she stared at him like that.

"I, for one, could never spit in the face of the condom fairy like that," she said, as he knelt above her on the couch.

"Mmm, me neither," he said.

They didn't talk for a while after that.

Finally, Maddie sat up and reached for her half-eaten piece of pizza.

"Well. I didn't expect my Thursday to end like that, but I can't pretend I'm not glad it did."

She definitely couldn't pretend she didn't know what was going to happen as soon as she walked into his apartment. If she was being honest with herself, she knew what was going to happen as soon as she saw his first text.

She didn't have to tell *him* that, though.

Theo rolled off the couch and stood up.

"Save me some pizza, rule breaker."

He walked down the hallway to the bathroom. Maddie sat up straight as she finished the slice.

Fuck. He was right. She was the one who had listed their rules in the first place, and not a week into this agreement, here she was at his place on a Thursday night, a night when the two of them had very much not just been with Alexa.

Technically, they'd both broken the rule, but a) she'd been the one to make the damn rule in the first place, and b) she'd also been the one to come over on a very thin excuse.

Just as he walked back into the room with a glass of water in each hand, she had a brain wave.

"We didn't break the rule!" She took the water he handed to her and set it down on top of a magazine. "I was with Alexa tonight, wasn't I? There we go, no rule breaking."

Theo narrowed his eyes at her.

"Hmm." He took a sip of water and set his own glass down. "I seem to remember that when you came up with this rule, the point was . . ." He shook his head. "What am I saying? I take it back. Sure, you're right, you're absolutely right."

She frowned as he leaned back against the couch cushions with a big grin on his face. Wait, why was he so ready to tell her she was right? That didn't seem like the Theo she'd known and loathed for years.

"Are you making fun of me?" She stood up and pulled her skirt back on.

"Absolutely not." He shook his head. "I think what you say makes a lot of sense. I submit to your superior reading of the rule. After all, you were the one who made up the rules in the first place, so your word is law here."

She stood with her hands on her hips staring at him, but he just smiled back at her.

"I'll be right back." She went to the bathroom, still puzzling over why he looked like he'd just gotten an advantage over her. Maybe that was how he always looked after sex? No, she remembered the other times. That definitely wasn't it.

It was only when she was washing her hands that she realized.

"You think . . . you think that because you work with Alexa and
see her every day . . . you think that means . . ." She yelled her way
back into the living room. His smile was even more smug now.

"I knew you'd get there eventually," he said. "Look, you're the
one who made the rule. I bow to your interpretation of it, that's all."

She shook her head.

"That's not what I meant! I just meant that I, personally, didn't
break the rule tonight! But that doesn't mean that . . ." Yeah, no.
She couldn't even finish that sentence with a straight face. She
didn't even try.

"Okay, fine, I guess it means that." She sat back down on the
couch and grabbed another slice of pizza. "But this isn't booty call
central here. I have a busy few months coming up, and I might be
in the running for a new job. I can't have you texting me at all
hours of the day and night."

Theo laughed and picked up his beer.

"Yes, ma'am. What's the new job? I thought you were set on
working for yourself."

She nodded and tucked her feet up on the couch.

"I am. I'm not giving that up, don't worry." She regretted
bringing this up. She didn't really want to hear what he had to say
about the show, but now she'd brought it up, she had to tell him.
"One of my clients works for channel seven, and this week she told
me about a new show they're thinking about doing, a kind of
update-your-fashion show for people who have been through a lot,
and they need a host. She thought of me."

He sat up straight.

"That's awesome! You'd be great at that."

Huh. She hadn't thought that would be his reaction.

"Thanks, I think. That's what Alexa said, too. I'm worried it'll take a lot of time away from my business, which will always be my priority."

He nodded.

"I can see that, but I also think that this kind of thing can be a great advertisement for you and your work. I'm not saying I know anything about fashion or this kind of work—"

Theo? Admitting he didn't know something? That was a first.

"I see that look on your face. I know, me, admitting ignorance, you never thought you'd see the day, et cetera. Anyway, what I do know is P.R., and this is the kind of thing that will send you a ton of clients. Especially if you're great at it, which you would be."

Maddie reached for another slice of pizza and mulled over what Theo had just said. Had he . . . complimented her? About something that wasn't sex? He probably hadn't done it on purpose.

"That's a good point. I'm waiting to hear the details from the station manager, so . . ." She was going to say, *I'll keep you posted*, but that sounded weird. Why would she keep Theo posted about something like this? No matter how interested he'd seemed tonight, he didn't really care about this. She just let her sentence trail off instead.

He reached out, and for a second she thought he was going to put his arm around her, but he dropped it on the cushion between them.

"Great. Well, I hope you get good news soon."

They looked at each other and smiled. This felt weird. Why were they being so nice to each other? She looked away and reached for her phone.

"Actually, I should go. It's getting late, and I have a client coming early tomorrow morning, so . . ."

He stood up when she did.

"Yeah, it is getting late."

She bent down and picked up her underwear from the floor and tucked it in her purse, making a mental note as she did so to remember to take it out of her purse as soon as she got home tonight so she didn't accidentally fling it across the room tomorrow while she dug for her wallet, like she'd done the last time.

They walked together to the front door, and he opened it for her.

"Good luck with the job," he said.

He was still being so weirdly nice. She didn't even know how to respond to it.

"Thanks," was all she said. She turned to walk out the door.

"Oh! Wait a second."

He ran down the hallway into his bedroom. Mmm, she was really glad he hadn't bothered to put his shirt back on after they'd had sex. Watching him run like this was excellent. If only he hadn't put his pants on.

He came running back out a few seconds later.

"Here." He dropped something into her hand. "Your earrings? I figured I could give them back to you, now that you don't need an excuse to come over."

She turned her back on him and walked to the car without a word. His laughter followed her the whole way, but she only allowed herself to smile when she was safely in her car.

Chapter Eight

THEO GLANCED AT HIS PHONE BEFORE LEAVING WORK A FEW WEEKS later. He'd hoped to see a text from Maddie but wasn't surprised that he didn't. He'd already seen her once this week, and once the week before. The first time, he'd texted her asking if she'd had any updates from that job, and she'd said the station manager had emailed her to set up a preliminary interview. He'd told her to come over so they could celebrate. Amazingly, that had worked.

And then he'd texted her two days ago when he and the mayor had spent all day in Sacramento in a good but exhausting planning meeting for the pre-K ballot initiative. He'd asked her if she was in the mood for some pizza and/or to let off some pent-up energy, and she'd shown up at his place holding a pizza and wearing some fucking incredible lingerie.

So it was probably too soon for him to hear from her, and it was definitely too soon for him to text her again. But he still wanted to.

He did, though, have a text from his little brother.

Meet me for a drink or three, you know where I am

Theo sighed. He loved Ben, but he was also exhausting.

Dude, it's been a long week. Heading home to sit on the
couch and drink beer and do nothing

How likely was that to get Ben off his back? Not at all. He
didn't even mention to Ben he'd probably do some work while he
was sitting on the couch; he knew that would make things even
worse.

Ben texted him again before Theo had even left the building.

Oh hell no you're not that old. You can come sit on a
barstool and do nothing just as well and maybe smile at
some pretty girls while you're doing it. It's always "been a
long week" for you

Ugh. He had a point. Theo stopped outside of City Hall, trying
to decide whether to turn left to walk home, or right to walk to BART
to meet Ben in San Francisco.

"Bye, Theo." The mayor's secretary walked by him on the way to
her car. "Heading home to relax on the couch? Have a great weekend. Don't do too much work."

Oh God, was he that predictable? Did the whole building know
that he was that guy who went home on Friday nights to sit on the
couch and get *work* done?

Okay fine, on my way

By the time Theo got to Ben's favorite bar, he was already regretting this. There were too many people around, everyone seemed either drunk or high already, and they all kept looking at him and his blue button-down shirt and gray suit pants like he was a narc. Was it his fault that everyone in San Francisco thought wearing khakis and a hoodie was dressing up?

"You're buying," he said as he pulled out the stool next to his brother.

"Already got the first round, asshole," Ben said, gesturing at the glass of bourbon sitting in front of him.

Theo picked up the drink.

"Thanks. I guess I needed this more than I thought."

"Keep 'em coming!" Ben waved at the bartender, who grinned at him. Ben always managed to charm teachers, babysitters, and bartenders alike into doing whatever he wanted. Theo didn't know how he did it.

Ben turned back to Theo.

"What's going on? Why is my normally mild-mannered big brother so irritable today?"

Theo shook his head.

"No big deal, it's just that work is stressful right now. I have to deal with a bunch of people from all across the state on a major campaign, and I'm just trying not to fuck it up."

Ben laughed.

"You? Fuck something up? I can't even picture that happening."

Theo took a sip of his drink.

"I know what you're going to say. We don't have to discuss Ben's theories about Theo's psyche tonight."

Ben grinned.

"Oh, you *are* grumpy tonight! Okay, tell your little brother all about it. What are you working on?"

Theo rolled his eyes.

"Now that you asked: the mayor has thrown himself into this ballot initiative campaign, and I'm the main person supporting him. Don't get me wrong, I'm thrilled to be doing it; I believe in the campaign, it's great experience, and it increases my profile with other politicians around the state. But it's also a lot of pressure."

He was suddenly glad he'd met his brother for a drink—crowds, drunk people, and Ben teasing him notwithstanding. Ben was one of the only people who he could vent to like this. He could talk to Ben about how much stress he was under without feeling like Ben was looking down on him, or thought less of him for letting the pressure get to him.

Another drink landed in front of him without him even having to ask for it. There were definitely some advantages to going to his little brother's favorite bar.

"What's the campaign for?" Ben plucked the maraschino cherry out of Theo's drink and ate it. He'd been doing that since they were kids. "The mayor doesn't run for reelection until next year, does he?"

Theo always assumed Ben didn't listen to a single thing he said about his job, and then he would say stuff like this that proved he'd been actually paying attention.

"You're right; he doesn't. This is a campaign for a statewide ballot initiative for universal pre-kindergarten in California. The mayor is a big supporter of it, as are the governor and a bunch of other elected officials around the state, so everyone wants to make a big push for it to win."

Ben picked up a handful of cocktail nuts and tossed them in his mouth.

"Does that mean you're dealing with a bunch of massive egos and trying to keep them all satisfied about the plans and the amount of attention they'll get?"

Theo lifted his glass to his brother.

"Bingo. That's exactly what I'm doing, and what the next five or so months are going to be like."

Ben nodded and drained his glass.

"Well, at least this is something you care about. Did you tell Mom about this? She'll be thrilled."

Theo grinned. He *had* told his mom, and she *had* been thrilled.

"Yeah, she's all over it. Wants to volunteer to help out and everything. Wait, did she tell you she's going to Hawaii with Aunt Leslie in September?"

Ben nodded.

"Yeah, I talked to her the other day. She's so excited about it."

Theo reached for the cocktail nuts.

"I'm jealous. After the week I've had, a Hawaiian vacation sounds like a dream."

Ben drained his glass.

"Well, you know what would make you feel better? If you got laid. One of the girls I work with was asking about you—Caitlin, she came to your birthday party last year, remember?"

Ah yes, just as he started taking his brother seriously, he would come out with something like that.

"No, I don't remember her, and anyway, I'm doing okay without your setups, but thanks."

Unfortunately, he had a feeling getting laid *would* make him feel better tonight, but that was more complicated than he wanted to get into.

"Oh, she's hot—long black hair, really funny, great—"

Theo held up a hand to stop his brother.

"Oh my God, Ben, no thanks. If she's so great, why don't you date her?"

Ben shook his head.

"I have a strict no-women-I-work-with policy. I may be an asshole, but I don't want to be that asshole."

Theo cast his memory back to all of the varied women Ben had told him about.

"Is this a new policy? Because what about that girl you ran into during that earthquake drill at work that time?"

Ben shook his head.

"Nope, we didn't work for the same company. She was three floors up." He shrugged. "And she's another reason why this is a good policy—we didn't even work at the same company, and it was a nightmare after we broke up. I had to keep taking the stairs after that time I ran into her in the elevator and she yelled at me the whole way up."

Theo laughed.

"Oh yeah, I remember that. Poor woman."

Ben paused, his drink halfway to his mouth.

"Poor woman? Poor Ben! I worked on the seventh floor! That was a lot of stairs to climb up and down if I wanted to run out to grab coffee."

Theo finished his drink, still laughing.

"Anyway, no, I don't want to date your coworker. Things are complicated enough in my life right now as it is."

Ben's head snapped toward him.

"Complicated how? Other than work, I mean. There's more to life than work, Theodore. Like, what were you doing last Friday night? At home getting work done, I bet."

Last Friday night flashed through Theo's head. That had been when Maddie had come over to celebrate getting a preliminary interview. She hadn't left until a very good start to the next morning. He couldn't keep the smirk off his face.

"Wait just a minute." Ben pointed at him, his mouth wide open. "WAIT a minute. What is that look? Who is it? Why are you keeping this from your little brother?"

Theo knew he shouldn't tell Ben. He would never be able to keep this to himself.

"No one. I don't know what you're talking about."

Ben poked him in the chest.

"Stop lying to me. You know I know you're lying. Tell me. Who is she? Where did you meet her? Why didn't you tell me before when I was going on and on about Caitlin?"

Theo knew he should hold out, but a) he'd had too much bourbon at this point, and b) he was honestly dying to tell someone.

"Okay, fine, but you have to promise me you won't tell anyone."

Ben looked at him sideways.

"Why? Why is it such a secret? Is she famous or something?"

Theo shook his head.

"Just promise."

Ben shrugged impatiently.

"Fine, fine, I promise, now tell me."

Theo grinned.

"It's Maddie. Alexa's friend. You met her at my birthday party last year."

Ben slammed his hand down on the bar. Everyone turned to stare, of course.

"The hot one? That Maddie? The one who I tried to get to go out with me and who was so mean when she blew me off it made her even hotter? That Maddie?"

Why did his brother have to be like this? Theo put his head in his hands.

Ben poked him in the side.

"Seriously. That Maddie?"

Theo nodded and sat up.

"Yes, that Maddie, but can you please shut the fuck up about it? It's a secret, and I clearly never should have told you, but now that you know, can you just pretend that you don't and we can both move on?"

Ben shook his head silently.

"Wow. I'm impressed." He grinned at Theo and took the cherry out of his drink. "But wait. Why is it a secret?"

Theo shrugged.

"Neither of us wants Alexa to know; it would make everything even more complicated. You know how Alexa is; she'd be thrilled, which would make it really awkward when this thing eventually blows up. Maddie doesn't even like me, so the whole thing won't last that long, but . . ." But the sex was great, so he didn't care.

Ben snapped his head around.

"No, don't stop talking. You were about to say something interesting there."

Theo grinned and waved at the bartender for another drink.

An hour and a half later, Theo felt his phone buzz in his pocket as he walked out of the BART station in Berkeley.

You home? I had a very annoying day. Can we sit on your
couch and make fun of all of the people on house hunters
and then take our clothes off?

Oh thank God. He texted Maddie back.

Absolutely. Walking home from BART now, should be home
in ten min. I also had an annoying day, and I'll warn you, was
just in sf drinking with my annoying little brother, so I'm
drunk and hungry and ready to do all those things

I'll pick up pizza on the way. Be there in 30 min

Well, this was turning out to be a much better Friday night than
he'd anticipated.

Thursday night, Maddie was right at the beginning of her nightly
dish-washing routine when her phone rang. Washing her dishes
every night was the only real habit she'd ever managed to keep on
the housekeeping front. And it was only because a few years before,
her cousin had bet her that she couldn't wash her dishes every day
for a month. Out of sheer competitiveness, Maddie had done it,
and the habit had stuck.

She pulled her phone out of her pocket and hit speaker.

"Hey, Mom. You're on speaker. I'm washing dishes."

"Hey, girl," her mom said. "Why are you always washing
dishes when I call you?"

Maddie scrubbed out her coffeepot and set it upside down on
her dish drainer.

"Because you always call me when I'm washing dishes! How was your day?"

Her mom laughed.

"Oh my God. Did I tell you about all the dick pics?"

Well, that was something she didn't expect to hear from her mom.

"Um, NO. Who is . . ."

Her mom laughed harder.

"No, no, not to me. Some jerk was sending unsolicited dick pics to one of the patients." Her mom was a social worker at a local hospital. "She asked me for advice, and I told her to just block his number, but her friend had a better idea, and they spent like twenty minutes finding other, and um . . . much bigger pictures on the Internet, and then texted all of them to him. Maddie, I had to go into the hallway, I was laughing so hard."

Maddie and her mom both went off into peals of laughter. Maddie had forever been impressed that her mom almost always managed to find something humorous in her difficult job. She'd gone to school at night to get her social work degree when Maddie was growing up, and had been doing this work for almost twenty years now. At this point, nothing could faze her.

"What happened next? Did he text her back?"

Her mom was still chuckling.

"Yes! He said 'Why would I want to see all of that?' And then she said, 'Why would I want to see your little thing?' And *then* she blocked him. It was amazing."

Maddie described her relationship with her mom by saying they were like the black versions of Lorelai and Rory Gilmore, except without the rich Gilmores to fall back on. Granted, her mom hadn't been as young as Lorelai when she'd had Maddie, but the single mom–only child bond thing was still very accurate. Vivian had worked hard all of Maddie's life to make sure she had every possible opportunity.

"How was your day?" her mom asked once they'd stopped laughing. "Any fun clients? Didn't you have that chef today?"

"Yeah, the chef was today. She was great. Super nervous at first, but she ended up really liking the stuff I found for her for the photo shoot." Maddie turned off the water and dried her hands. "So the station manager called today again about that TV show."

Her mom cheered.

"Yes! What did he say? Are they ready to hire you immediately? I knew this job would be perfect for you. It's like they came up with it with you in mind! When I think about all the ways you helped me prepare for job interviews when you were just a teenager, it still amazes me. You learned to sew and everything! You'll be so good at this."

Her mom had been Maddie's first styling client, sort of. She'd been turned down for a string of secretary jobs while Maddie was in middle school, and Maddie had told her mom it was because her clothes were all old and ugly. She still felt terrible about how awful she'd been to her mom as a teenager. But eventually Maddie'd gotten her head out of her ass and helped her mom find new interview outfits she could afford.

Her mom got the next job she interviewed for.

"Slow down, they haven't even seen me in person yet!" Maddie said. "I'm going in next week to talk to him, but he made it clear that this is the first round of a long process. He did tell me more about the job—they want it to be an afternoon show, one of the ones that come on between when the soaps end and the news begins. I think they're still figuring out some stuff about it, but Maya sang my praises, so he seemed excited to talk to me."

Maddie had been excited to talk to him, too, though she had played it cool. She was trying hard not to get her hopes up, but that was hard with the way her mom talked about this job like it was already hers.

"I can't wait! My baby is going to be on TV. I'm going to tell the whole world to watch your show. Just think of how much the women will learn from you! People need someone like you to help get them where they want to go; clothes are so important, even though everyone tries to pretend they're not."

Maddie shook her head and dried off the inside of the coffeepot so it would be ready for the next morning.

"Slow down, Mom. Not that I don't agree with you, but I haven't even met with them yet. I'll keep you posted, though."

"Mmmhmm." Maddie knew her mom hadn't paid attention to a single word she'd said. The fantasy of her daughter on television—even just local television—would sustain her for weeks. "What about boys? Anybody I need to know about?"

Maddie talked to her mom about almost everything, but she hadn't told her about Theo. She'd told her mom about a number of guys in the past, and even introduced her to a few when they got serious enough. But it seemed pointless to tell her about Theo. This wasn't that kind of relationship. They didn't even like each other!

Granted, she'd thought about telling her, almost every time she'd talked to her mom in the last month, especially since she couldn't tell Alexa, the person she did tell everything to. Sometimes she felt like she'd burst if she couldn't share this joke—that she was sleeping with Theo Stephens, of all people!—with someone. Or tell someone how nice it was to be sleeping with a guy who didn't seem to want or need all of the other bullshit men always wanted from her—parties, meeting their friends, all the big showy stuff she always dreaded. All she and Theo did was eat takeout on his couch, watch TV, and have great sex. It was heaven.

It was too good. There was no way they could keep going on like this. Hell, she was certain their thing wouldn't even last until the wedding, but she'd ride it out as long as she could. She just had to pray she could trust Theo not to tell Alexa.

So, therefore, she absolutely couldn't tell her mom.

"No, Mom. There's no one you need to know about."

Would her mom give up? She was betting no.

"What about that Theo, Alexa's friend? You've mentioned him a few times recently. Is there anything . . ."

Shit. This is what happened when you talked to your mom too much. You accidentally kept mentioning the guy you were keeping a secret from everyone.

"Oh God no, Theo and I have nothing in common. We're just both in Alexa's wedding party, and you know Alexa. There's all sorts of planning that needs to be done already."

Maddie mentally apologized to Alexa for maligning her that way. So far, they'd barely discussed the wedding, other than a few conversations about location.

Her mom sighed.

"You haven't met anyone else interesting, huh?"

"Where would I find the time to meet a boy?" Maddie asked her. "Plus, I've given up on men—they all think I'm going to be some party girl when they start dating me, because of how I look and dress, but then they get to know me and discover I have a personality and ambitions and am actually kind of a homebody, and they freak out. I thought about changing the way I look and dress to make it clear who I am, but fuck that. I like the way I look and I like my clothes. I don't want to change that for a man."

Her mom laughed.

"I'm with you there."

Maddie grinned.

"Speaking of, mom, how's *your* love life going?"

Her mom huffed.

"Madeleine. We are talking about you right now, not me!"

Maddie laughed. Her mom hated when she tried to get information about her dating life out of her, even though she pried into Maddie's constantly.

Watch, she'd change the subject back to Maddie now.

"Anyway. Maybe you'll meet someone good at Alexa's wedding. Drew must have some smart doctor friends."

Maddie smiled to herself. Alexa certainly had some smart— and talented—friends herself.

"The wedding's not for a long time," she said.

Chapter Nine

"I'M SO GLAD I TALKED YOU INTO THESE CHAIRS." MADDIE LAY BACK IN
one of Alexa's backyard lounge chairs and sighed in contentment.
Alexa was in the chair next to her, separated by a table just big
enough for their bowls of chips and salsa and cans of fizzy water.
Their original plan had been to go shopping that day, but the Bay
Area was experiencing one of its rare spells of over-eighty-degree
weather, so Alexa had called an audible and they'd changed their
plans to a day of sun and relaxation. Maddie had come over with
chips and salsa in her bag, and her bikini on underneath a caftan,
to find Alexa filling up the kiddie pool in her backyard. They'd
been in the lounge chairs ever since.

Maddie looked at their cans of fizzy water and frowned. They
were missing something.

"You know what we need," Alexa said. "Margaritas. That's
what we need."

It was useful to have a best friend who could read your mind at times like this.

"Hard agree," Maddie said. "Isn't this why you have a man around now? So he can make us fruity cocktails on short notice?"

Alexa nodded.

"That is certainly one of the reasons, but unfortunately, the man I keep around is working all afternoon. Do you think I can call him at the hospital and tell him it's a margarita emergency and he'll come running? Should I try it?"

Maddie shook her head.

"I'm guessing it won't work, unfortunately. Though if I know Drew well enough by now, you should do it, just to make him laugh."

Maddie looked over at their quickly depleting supply of chips and salsa. Come to think of it, they could also use some guacamole, and maybe even some queso if they were going to keep up their strength.

"I don't know how we're going to make it, Lex," she said. "Sunshine and snacks and even a kiddie pool, but no margaritas?"

"I have rosé," Alexa said half-heartedly.

Maddie shrugged.

"We can live with rosé, I guess. Is it cold?"

Alexa shook her head.

"No, I'm sorry. I'm a failure. Why didn't I think to put rosé in the fridge last night?"

Maddie gasped dramatically.

"I can't even believe you. Not to mention that these are the last two cans of fizzy water. Does someone have to go to the *store*?"

Alexa sat up and reached for her phone.

"I have an idea." She fired off a text. God only knew who she was texting, but Alexa had connections everywhere, so Maddie didn't even ask.

A few minutes later, Alexa's phone buzzed.

"Excellent," she said. "Theo's on his way. He's going to make us margaritas."

Maddie snapped her head around.

"Theo? He's coming here?"

Alexa lay back in her lounge chair and nodded.

"Yes! He makes amazing cocktails—you have no idea."

Oh, she had an idea, all right.

Alexa sat up and turned to her.

"It's okay that he comes over, right? I know you two have had your differences, but I figured you'd be a fan of delicious margaritas that come straight to this backyard."

Maddie had never told Alexa exactly what Theo had said to her that first time they'd met, other than to say she thought he was a pompous jerk. It wasn't so much that she'd wanted to protect Theo; to the contrary, she just hadn't wanted Alexa to get furious at a coworker on her behalf. She knew how much Alexa loved her job, and she hadn't wanted to get in the way of that.

And now, well, there were so many more layers to her relationship with Theo that would make this awkward.

"Sure, it's no problem," she said. "The margaritas had better be as good as you say, though."

Plus, she very well might enjoy seeing Theo see her in this bikini.

"Tell him to stop at the store and get us some guacamole while he's at it."

Alexa laughed and grabbed another chip.

"Theo would never stop at the store to buy us guacamole. He

would go there to get avocados and then painstakingly make the guacamole in my kitchen. I adore him, but he's a bit of a perfectionist that way."

Hmm, Theo certainly was a perfectionist in other ways that mattered, too . . .

Maddie hid her smile from her friend.

When Alexa went inside to the bathroom, Maddie took the opportunity to pull out her phone. She was pretty sure she'd have a text.

Yep, she was right.

> Playing with fire, are we?

She laughed at Theo's text and texted him back.

> It was Alexa's idea! She said I had no idea what amazing
> cocktails you make. I almost died

She and Theo hadn't been together around Alexa since the engagement party. Well, it would be good practice for whenever all the wedding stuff happened.

> I guess that's a challenge—get ready for the best
> margaritas you've ever had. Do you need me to get
> more fizzy water, too?

Maddie suppressed her grin at her phone as Alexa walked back outside.

"But speaking of guacamole, let me see if Theo can pick up some more snacks. You'd better prepare yourself for some shop talk; Theo's pretty consumed right now by this campaign he's working on. I'm going to try to get him to relax, though; I told him to bring a book. It'll probably be something about history or basketball."

Maddie lay back in her lounge chair and smiled as the sun hit her face. She was outside in the sun with a good book and her best friend, the guy she was secretly sleeping with was on his way over with snacks and margarita fixings, and she was at least eighty percent sure this meant she was going to have sex later tonight.

She looked down at her bikini.

Maybe ninety percent.

Theo walked up Alexa's front steps carrying a grocery bag and wondering how the hell he'd gotten himself into this situation. He was about to go into the house of his close friend and coworker, to hang out and drink tequila with her and her best friend, who, coincidentally, he'd been secretly sleeping with on a regular basis for the past month.

Today had the potential to be either a train wreck or enormously awkward, but he didn't bother lying to himself: he'd take any excuse at this point to be around Maddie. The past month had been way too much fun. Sometimes he wished he wasn't always so tense, so earnest, never spontaneous or relaxed or just fun. But for some reason, he could be all those things with Maddie.

He was pretty sure this whole thing was going to blow up in his face at some point, but he had chosen not to worry about that. Between dealing with fifteen elected official–size egos, and their accompanying staffers, along with doing the rest of his job, he didn't have time to worry about how much Alexa was going to flip out when she eventually found out he and Maddie were sleeping together.

He pulled out his phone to text Alexa, since he didn't think her doorbell would reach to her backyard.

I'm outside, open up

A minute later, the front door opened to Maddie in a bikini.

Holy fucking shit.

"Come on in. Alexa's out back." She waved him into the house, but he didn't move. He definitely hadn't imagined he'd be this lucky today.

"How the hell is it possible to look that good in any article of clothing? And why the fuck do you look that sexy when I'm going to have to sit there with you and Alexa, and I can't jump on you and peel that bikini off your incredible body?"

He looked over her shoulder to make sure the coast was clear and then stepped into the house and wrapped his arms around her. He pulled her flush against his body and brought his lips down on hers. She laughed against his mouth as he kissed her, and she kissed him back just as hard.

"Who's playing with fire now?" she asked when they finally broke apart.

He picked up the grocery bags again.

"What the hell was I supposed to do with you answering the door looking like that? I'm going to get back at you for this later."

She grinned sideways at him as he preceded her into the kitchen and started unloading the bags.

"If I remember correctly, your method of 'getting back at me' is a very pleasurable one, so I'm not going to make any arguments."

He shook his head as he plunked the bottle of tequila on the counter.

"You win this round, Forest. I know I'm going to win one eventually."

He opened the sliding glass door to the backyard and yelled to Alexa.

"I have snacks and the makings of margaritas. Come help."

He took a bag of limes out of the grocery bag and handed them to Maddie.

"Here, make yourself useful. Slice all of these in half."

Maddie looked from the bag of limes, to the bottle of tequila, and then back to Theo. She didn't move.

"Why, exactly, am I slicing limes in half?"

Theo opened one of Alexa's cabinets and took down the bag of sugar.

"So I can juice them. For lime juice? For margaritas? You two did order margaritas, didn't you?"

Alexa walked into the kitchen.

"Oh, is Maddie being introduced to the way Theo makes drinks?"

While he'd made plenty of cocktails for Maddie by now, he realized most of those had been easy ones. Well, maybe she'd learn something.

Theo measured out sugar and water into a saucepan and turned it on.

"Hi, Alexa, how are you? Great to see you. Yes, I am making the drinks you ordered me to come over to your house to make, while you're standing there about to make fun of me for how I'm making your drinks, that is correct."

Both women ignored him.

"How . . . exactly . . . does Theo make drinks?" Maddie asked.

"Very, very slowly. Look, you ask the man for chips and salsa, he goes into the kitchen and fries tortillas to make the chips, and roasts tomatoes to make the salsa, okay?"

That made him turn around.

"That only happened one time! I bought you salsa this time!"

Alexa kept talking like he hadn't even said anything.

"So, I'm just saying, if you expected his margaritas to start with anything so pedestrian as margarita mix, or even bottled lime juice, you were barking up the wrong cocktail tree here."

Theo shook his head and swirled the saucepan full of sugar and water.

"Margarita mix. Like I would ever."

Maddie opened up one of the bags of chips he'd brought and poured them into a bowl.

"Why didn't you warn me?" she asked Alexa. "I thought he was going to come over, plug in a blender, zuzz us up some margaritas, and we'd be happy. Now he's in the kitchen . . . cooking sugar?" She walked over to Theo at the stove and peered over his shoulder. "What the hell are you doing?"

He swirled the pan again as Alexa popped open the jar of salsa with a big grin on her face.

"Making simple syrup, of course," he said. "You can't just pour sugar into lime juice. It won't dissolve. Simple syrup is the basis for many great cocktails, you know."

Maddie looked over at Alexa, who was now doubled over with laughter. Theo was having a hard time keeping a straight face himself, even though most of what Alexa had said about him was the absolute truth. He was pretty sure Maddie was questioning what she'd gotten herself into.

"How have you worked with this man for so many years without killing him?" Maddie asked Alexa.

Alexa handed her a knife.

"I've learned it's just easier to go along with it when he does stuff like this. Plus, unfortunately, it almost always turns out great. Here, you cut the limes. I'll squeeze them."

Thirty minutes later, the three of them were outside in the backyard with margaritas, chips and guacamole, and an ice bucket full of cold grapefruit sparkling water. Theo watched Maddie as she took a sip of her drink. Her smile made him feel victorious.

"Worth the wait, wasn't it?"

She ignored him and turned to Alexa, which only made his grin get bigger. He dug into the bowl of guacamole with his chip and took his biography of Ida B. Wells out of his bag.

Alexa looked over at him and laughed.

"I knew you'd be reading a book like that. Didn't I say that, Maddie?" She lifted up her magazine to show it to him. "This, Theodore, this is how you take an actual break from work." She dropped the magazine onto her lap. "How'd the call go yesterday? We didn't get to talk about it afterward."

He leaned back in his chair and shook his head.

"I'm fighting so hard to have the kickoff rally in Berkeley, and every conference call is two steps forward and one step back. This time, I had answers to all of their arguments and talked about the many parents we know who will be able to speak at the rally, and how we'll get such favorable press here, and I think I won Sybil over, but then all the Central Valley people brought up protestors."

Maddie looked over at him.

"Aren't *you* worried about protestors?"

He shrugged.

"Like there won't be protestors anywhere in this state, but who cares? So what, a handful of people will have some ugly signs and bad chants. We'll turn up the sound system and deal with it. Saying, 'But protestors!' is just their excuse to get the rally out of Berkeley and into their boss's city. It's so frustrating, and I really hope it doesn't work."

Alexa turned to Maddie.

"This is the initiative I told you about that Theo was working on for universal pre-K in California."

Maddie raised an eyebrow at him, with an expression on her face like this was all brand new to her and she hadn't listened to him rant about this campaign for fifteen minutes the other night.

"I know that would have helped my mom a lot when I was a kid. Do you think it has a shot at winning?" she asked him.

She hadn't asked him that question the other night.

He thought about whether to give the politic answer or the real one, and shrugged.

"Anything has a shot. Wild things happen on Election Days, for good and bad. But, do I think it'll win? No. That doesn't mean it's not worth fighting for, though. The better job we do this year, the more people will be inspired by it, and the more likely it'll be that we'll win the next time. The great and terrible thing about politics is you have to play the short and the long game all at once."

Maddie held up her glass.

"Okay, now that you're done boring us, can I get a refill?"

He tried not to show his irritation at her brush-off and reached for her glass.

"Lex, you want another, too? There's more inside."

Alexa nodded.

"I do, but do you know the other thing I want?"

He looked at her sideways.

"What?"

"Pizza. Chips and salsa and guacamole aren't a meal. I'm hungry."

Maddie drained the dregs of her margarita glass.

"Okay, but I'm very confused," Maddie said. "I really expected you to say tacos just now."

So had Theo, actually.

"Obviously, I want tacos, but the good taco places don't deliver, and none of us can drive after Theo's margaritas, so I forced myself to crave something more easily deliverable. Plus, then there will be pizza here waiting for Drew when he gets home from work, so I'll be the best fiancée any man has ever had, and you know I really like to be the best at things."

Theo and Maddie looked at each other and shrugged.

"Get roasted garlic on the pizza, please."

Maddie made a fake gagging noise.

"Roasted garlic on a pizza sounds disgusting. Do we have to?"

They'd had this argument so far every time they'd ordered pizza together, which was . . . four or five times now. Now he usually let her have her way.

When he came out of the kitchen bearing the pitcher of margaritas, Alexa had her phone out.

"Is it too much to get two large pizzas for four people?" She set her phone down and shook her head. "What am I thinking? Of course it's too much. I have to fit myself into a wedding dress at some point here. I should be on a green juice and quinoa diet." She picked up her margarita glass Theo had just filled up. "And I should definitely not be drinking this!" Despite her declaration, she took a long sip.

"Oh no." Maddie sat up and turned to Alexa. "You've been talking to your mom again, haven't you?"

Alexa sighed and nodded.

"Stop that!" Maddie said. Alexa put her glass down. "No, not stop drinking the margarita! Stop talking to your mom about what you need to do or look like to get into a wedding dress, I mean."

Theo picked up Alexa's margarita glass and handed it to her.

"I didn't drive to the store and buy all of those limes just so you could reject my margaritas because of some as yet unpurchased dress. Plus, if you've been talking to your mom this much, you need more tequila."

Alexa took a big gulp.

"That's better," Maddie said. "I'm making it my mission to find you a fantastic wedding dress, and I will never tell you to put down your margarita. Now, please order two pizzas, and let Theo get his roasted garlic on half of one so he doesn't whine for the rest of the day—we can't handle that, on top of everything else. And plus, we're going all out today, so everyone might as well get whatever they want."

Whatever? Theo mouthed to Maddie from behind Alexa.

Maddie winked at him when Alexa was distracted by her phone.

Drew got home moments after the pizzas arrived.

"Is that a pitcher of margaritas I see?" he asked as he opened the sliding glass door to the backyard. "Oh, hey, Maddie. And hi, Theo. Holy shit, there's pizza, too? You're the best fiancée a man has ever had!" He walked over to Alexa and bent down to kiss her.

"We tried not to get her too drunk, Drew, but she started babbling about wedding planning and Theo had to make extra margaritas to calm her down," Maddie said.

"Good call. Thank goodness she has you guys." Drew picked up Alexa's margarita and took a sip and opened his eyes wide. "Wow, okay, those would relax anyone. And I guess the pizza was because none of the good taco places deliver?"

Theo looked at Maddie and they both laughed out loud.

"Drew, it kills me to say this, but sometimes you know Alexa even better than I do," Maddie said.

Drew sat down at the foot of Alexa's lounge chair and leaned over to kiss her again.

"I think that's the biggest compliment you've given me so far, Maddie."

The four of them finished the pitcher of margaritas and made a big dent in the pizzas, as Drew told them about a surgery he'd done that day, which segued into him talking about his greatest hits of kid accidents.

"My favorites were the two cousins who convinced each other to jump off their grandparents' roof. One broke an arm, the other broke two ribs, but they were both triumphant after their surgeries and kept talking about how fun it all was. Their parents may never let those two kids be together and unchaperoned until they turn thirty."

After a while, Theo saw Maddie looking pointedly at him and stood up.

"Okay, guys, I have to take off. Alexa, thanks for forcing me to relax in the sun today. I needed this."

Alexa stood up and gave him a hug.

"Thanks for obeying my summons and coming over to make us margaritas. This was exactly the Saturday I needed."

He turned to leave, then glanced over at Maddie.

"Do you need a ride home? No judgment, Maddie, but I don't think you're in any state to drive yourself."

She glared at him and stood up.

"Whenever anyone starts a sentence with 'No judgment, but,' you know judgment is coming. It's just like 'No offense, but' is always offensive, and 'Not to be racist, but' is always racist. Plus, you're probably the most judgmental person I know. And I wasn't going to drive myself home, but just for that, sure, you can go out of your way and drive me home. You deserve it."

He rolled his eyes and slung his bag over his shoulder. Maddie used to say stuff like that to him all the time. So why did it sting so much when she said it now?

Theo waited as Maddie threw her dress on over her bikini and tossed her magazines in her bag.

"Bye, man. See you later," he said to Drew.

"Basketball Monday night?" Drew asked.

Theo nodded.

"I'll be there."

As soon as they got into his car, he turned to Maddie.

"I'm the most judgmental person you know? Am I done boring you yet?" He'd planned on letting the boring her thing go, but after her crack at the end, he was really annoyed.

"I was being too nice to you!" Maddie said. "I was trying to course correct. We can't have Alexa suspecting we don't hate each other anymore. That's a slippery slope to her realizing that I took a really long time to come back outside when I went to open the door for you!"

Theo tried to figure out the best way to express himself but decided to just let it out.

"Okay. I get it. But also, it doesn't make me feel great. You think maybe next time you can dial it back a little?"

Maddie opened her mouth, closed it again, and sighed.

"Will do."

He put his hand on her warm, brown, mostly bare thigh and smiled at her.

"Just don't say 'course correct' around Alexa. She'll know you've been talking to me too much."

She laughed.

"Oh shit, you're right. God, I can't say 'slippery slope' like that, either. I can't believe you're affecting my speech patterns like this. What a nightmare."

He moved his hand up underneath her dress.

"Do you know what my nightmare was today? Sitting there all day with you, watching the way you sat and turned and arched your back and walked around and wanting so badly to put my mouth on your breasts and squeeze those hard nipples and I wasn't even able to touch you." He slid a finger under her bikini bottoms and smiled at her gasp.

He started to slide his hand back out so he could start the car, but she reached down and held it in place.

"It was pretty hot though," she said. "Watching you watch me like that."

He kissed her on the lips, so hard she was breathless when he finally pulled away.

"You'll see how hot I thought it was when we get back to my place."

He put the key in the ignition but stopped again.

"Hey, the Fourth of July is in a few weeks, do you have plans?" he asked.

She sighed.

"My cousin invited me to her party, but . . ."

He nodded.

"Want to bail on the parties we both got invited to and eat take-out barbecue on my couch?"

She grinned.

"That's the best idea you've ever had."

Chapter Ten

THEO WALKED HOME FROM WORK LATE FRIDAY NIGHT. HE'D REALLY meant to get home earlier, but he'd managed to fuck up his own day. He was still furious when he left the office, but his walk home helped him decompress a little. He couldn't wait to get home, sit on the couch in his boxers, order a pizza, and watch whatever the hell sporting event was on. Golf, baseball, bowling; he didn't care, just something that would involve people playing a game on his television where he could make up a rooting interest for one side and yell at the TV.

He walked up his front steps and reached in his pocket for his keys. Not in that pocket. Not in the other pocket, either. Okay.

He reached into the big pocket at the back of his messenger bag, but all he found were a handful of receipts and three punch cards from coffee shops. This was not the night for this.

He sat on his front steps, flipped open his messenger bag, and dug around inside. And then he froze.

He'd pulled his keys out of his pocket to lock his office door before he'd left. And then he'd stopped by his assistant's desk to drop a file on his chair so it would be ready for him on Monday morning. He'd left his keys sitting right on top of the file.

He dropped his head in his hands. No part of him felt like walking the mile plus back to City Hall and then having to deal with the security guard who hated him and would almost certainly pretend he didn't know who he was.

He picked up his phone, made a face, and called Ben.

You've reached Ben Stephens. I can't come to the phone right now, but leave a message, and—

Voice mail? He went straight to his brother's voice mail? The one time he needed his brother, the only person with a spare key to his apartment, and he got kicked to voice mail? He texted Ben instead.

Where are you? I'm locked out, I need my key.

Just thinking about how he'd have to sit here and wait to hear back from Ben made him tired. The true exhaustion came when he thought about how, when he got in touch with Ben, he'd either have to plead with him to come to the East Bay to bring the key— if Ben even knew where the key was—or would have to pay God knows how much to get a ride into the city to meet him.

Theo thought longingly of his couch.

Any other night, he'd call Alexa, who'd pick him up, take him to City Hall, and smile her way past the security guard to get his keys, but she was out of town. Some romantic getaway with her fiancé. How inconvenient for her friends.

Maybe he could break into his apartment. Wasn't that what a

ground-floor apartment was good for? If he went around the side, he was pretty sure his bedroom window was open a crack. He could get that open and then . . . Yeah, sure, Theo, that was a great idea. He could see the headlines now, when his neighbors called the police on the black man trying to break into an apartment in Berkeley. How likely were the police to believe that he lived there? Or that he worked for the mayor? Would his brother come faster when he needed him to bail him out of jail?

He shivered. Sitting on concrete steps in a cotton button-down shirt and no jacket wasn't all that comfortable. It had been so warm when he'd left home this morning he thought he wouldn't need a jacket. Of course, that was before the sun went down.

He was going to have to walk the mile back to work, deal with the annoying questioning by the security guard who hated him, get his keys, and then walk home.

"Come on, Theo, this was no big deal."

He stood up, and then immediately sat back down. It had been an awful day at the end of a stressful week, and this one last fuckup overwhelmed him. The last thing he wanted was to have to talk to one more person who treated him like shit.

He picked up his phone again and scrolled to Maddie's number. He paused before he clicked on it; should he really call Maddie here? Their thing so far had been lots of fun, but they weren't in the habit of doing each other favors, and this would be a huge favor. Plus, she'd never invited him over to her place; they'd only ever been at his place together, and he had a feeling that wasn't just a coincidence.

Hell with it.

"Hello?"

He didn't blame her for sounding confused. He'd be confused, too, if she had called him. A Friday-night text, now that made sense, but not a phone call. But he needed to plead his case.

"Hey. Are you home? Are you busy tonight? Can I come over?"

Okay, he sounded a little too desperate there.

"Um . . ."

He really should have set this up better.

"I'm sorry, let me back up. I've had the worst day, I'm locked out, my keys are at work, the only other person who has the key to my place is my ridiculous brother, Alexa could get me into City Hall but she's somewhere with Drew. Can I come to your place and sleep there tonight and buy you pizza or expensive wine or whatever the hell you want and figure out the solution to this tomorrow?"

There was a long pause. She was going to say no, he just knew it. And now he'd have to walk back to City Hall and throw himself on the mercy of the security guard with her "no" ringing in his ears

"Okay, sure. Do you know where I live?"

Oh thank God.

"You're my savior. Text me your address. I'll stop and get the pizza on the way."

He hung up and sighed from relief. He should be at her house in thirty minutes. He couldn't wait.

Shit shit shit shit shit. Okay, she had, what, thirty minutes before he'd get here?

Maddie turned in a circle and looked at her disaster of a home. This was why she had a whole separate space for her business, so no one would ever see what a mess she was.

She filled her arms with the clothes on her floor and pushed them into her already overstuffed closet. Cleaning like this unfortunately destroyed her system—the clothes in *this* corner needed to be folded and put in drawers, the clothes in *that* corner needed to be hung up, and the clothes on her bed had been worn but were still mostly clean. But she didn't have time now to try to keep that straight. The dirty clothes all went into her hamper behind her bedroom door, and any other crap on the floor she kicked under her guest room bed.

She really should have said no to Theo. But he'd sounded so exhausted, and she'd had those nights. She couldn't help but sympathize with him.

Plus, she already knew why he'd had such a bad day. Some asshole reporter had been mocking the universal pre-K campaign for weeks, and today had come out with a terrible article about how much money it would cost California and how worthless pre-K was anyway. That had apparently been the last straw for Theo, because he'd refuted the article with a point-by-point rant on Twitter that used a lot of all-caps words like "ACTUALLY" and "FURTHERMORE." He deleted it five minutes later, but the damage was done: the reporter kept tweeting screenshots of it with "Looks like I hit a nerve!" and the Friday-afternoon-slow-news-day local press had a field day talking about how the mayor's normally unflappable communications director had flipped his lid. Knowing Theo, he was mortified.

The bed! She dumped the books and clothes that were on top of her bed into her top dresser drawer and pulled all the bedclothes off her bed. She grabbed clean sheets out of the linen closet and remade her bed the fastest she'd ever made a bed. She ran into the bathroom, grabbed the many pairs of underwear and bras that she'd hung to dry weeks ago, and threw them, still on their hangers, into her bedroom closet to join everything else. After five minutes of straightening up, she sprayed some bleach in the toilet and the sink, and then lit a candle so her whole place wouldn't smell like cleaning products.   .

The only room in her home that was marginally clean was her kitchen. Thank God for that dishwashing bet. But she devoted two minutes to sweeping her kitchen floor, then whirled through her living room and tossed everything on a surface into one of her many empty boxes from online orders, and then pushed it and the rest of the boxes into her guest room and shut the door.

Shit, she had like two minutes before he arrived.

She washed her hands and ran back into her room to change into . . . something. She really should have figured out what the hell she was wearing to this impromptu sleepover before she'd thrown all her clothes in her closet, shouldn't she? She heard her phone buzz on the other side of the room as she pulled on leggings and the first tank top she could find.

I'm outside

She sprayed on perfume and dabbed a touch of blush on her cheeks, just enough to make her look like she always looked this refreshed when she was at home wearing leggings and a tank top.

Be right there

At least her hair looked presentable.

She glanced around her house before she went to the door. It actually looked pretty good. Maybe she should keep it like this all the time.

She laughed at herself as she opened the door.

"Hey." Theo looked as exhausted as he'd sounded on the phone. He was wearing that blue pin-striped shirt she liked, but with no jacket. No wonder he'd stopped on the way for the pizza; he needed it to warm him up.

"Hey, you look freezing."

She opened the door all the way to let him in. He dropped a kiss on her cheek as he walked past her.

"Thanks, I am freezing." He held up the pizza, and she beckoned for him to follow her through the living room into the kitchen. "It was so warm yesterday that I didn't wear a jacket today, and then I stayed at work for twelve hours, and when I left, the fog had descended on Berkeley and I froze the whole walk home."

She took down two plates from the cabinet.

"Only to not have your keys when you got home."

He set the pizza down on the counter.

"Only to not have my keys when I got home. Thank God you were at home tonight."

She reached for a wineglass and poured him a glass of the red wine she'd been drinking.

"Here. Drink this. It'll warm you up. Good timing on the pizza. I was just about to order some. Go sit down on the couch— you look like you're about to collapse. I'll get everything else."

She put slices of the pepperoni and black olive pizza on their plates and grabbed a stack of napkins, a jar of red pepper flakes, and the bottle of wine before she joined him on the couch.

"You got my favorite kind of pizza," she said.

He smiled at her. No, she refused to let that smile make her the slightest bit gooey inside. That's not what this was about.

"It was the least I could do." He picked up the bottle of wine and poured more into her glass. "Not only are you letting me crash here, but you're sharing your wine with me. Getting your favorite pizza toppings seemed necessary."

She shook some red pepper flakes on top of her slice.

"Even though you thought this would have been vastly improved by the addition of roasted garlic?"

He took the jar of red pepper flakes from her and sprinkled them on his own slice.

"It *would* have been vastly improved by the addition of roasted garlic, but that's not the point."

She shook her head but didn't argue. She was starting to like roasted garlic on everything now—not that she'd ever tell Theo that.

But when he reached for his pizza, she pushed his plate to the other side of the coffee table.

"Why is that shirt still on? You can't eat pizza wearing that. You'll get grease all over it!"

He blushed and dropped his hands to his knees.

"Oh. I've never been here before; I didn't want to act like I could just walk into your house and start throwing my clothes off."

Maddie started to roll her eyes, and then she realized he was serious. That was unexpectedly charming.

"Theo. I've walked into your house and thrown my clothes off numerous times. It's your turn to return the favor."

He grinned and unbuttoned his shirt.

"Well, if you put it that way."

She waited until he'd taken off the shirt and carefully draped it over the back of the couch.

"Plus, I love that shirt. It would be a travesty for it to get ruined by my favorite pizza toppings."

He looked down at his pale blue T-shirt and then back up at her with an injured look on his face.

"What, you don't like my T-shirt? You don't care if I get pepperoni grease all over it? Its feelings are hurt."

She pushed his plate closer to him and he picked up his pizza.

"It's going to have to get over those hurt feelings. Or it can choose to make you drape a bunch of napkins over it before you eat. The shirt can call me a snob all it wants, but it's from Target, and your other shirt is Paul Smith. I know which one is easier to buy again."

He put his arm around her and leaned back against the couch, pulling her with him.

"I got it on sale. A city salary doesn't usually extend to Paul Smith. I was going to ask how you knew where my shirts come from, but then I realized it's your job to know. Though I'm impressed that you know men's brands, too."

She relaxed against his chest. Even though she'd been freaked out when he'd called, it was sort of nice to have him here on her couch, for once. Just as long as he didn't open any drawers. God only knew what would fly out at him.

"Only some of them, but I'm learning more. I have some clients who have more of a masculine style of dressing, so I've been trying to learn a lot more about menswear over the past few years. I've found them some great stuff."

He reached for the glass of wine she'd poured him and took a big swallow.

"That's awesome. Do you ever think you'll start to work with men, too? I bet lots of men around here could use you; you know what terrible dressers they are."

Maddie never would have guessed a year ago that the Theo

who thought she couldn't rub two brain cells together would be sitting here on her couch giving her compliments. Or that she'd be sitting next to him, in the circle of his arm, pouring him more wine. Maddie of a year ago—hell, Maddie of a few months ago— would die laughing if someone told her this.

Alexa of present day would simply die if someone told her this. Maddie wished she could tell Alexa just to see the look on her face.

She wasn't going to. But still.

"Oh, plenty of men around here need to hire me—that part is true. But I'm still trying to really establish myself. I don't want to dilute my brand too much in the beginning. Plus, I don't like to do something unless I can really throw myself into it; I would need to know a lot more about menswear to start that. And also, I really like working with women . . . I'm not sure the same would be true for men."

He laughed and pushed the hair away from her face.

"You're probably right about that."

He inhaled a second piece of pizza and flopped back against the couch.

"You want another slice?" she asked.

He shook his head.

"In a minute, but please, don't get up and get it for me. I barged in on you here tonight. I refuse to let you keep being so nice to me."

She shrugged.

"I heard you had a bad day, so I thought you deserved a little something, but don't worry, I won't let it happen again."

He narrowed his eyes at her.

"What do you mean, you heard I had a bad day? Outside of what I told you, you mean?" She looked down at her pizza. Shit, he wasn't supposed to know she already knew about that. "Oh

Lord, you heard about the Twitter thing? You don't even pay attention to local politics. If you heard about it, the entire world must have!" He dropped his head into his hands.

She patted him on the head.

"No, really, that's not it. I saw it accidentally, just because I follow Alexa on Twitter, and I had some downtime this afternoon and was clicking around, and . . ."

That was a lie. That wasn't how she knew. She'd started following a bunch of local news reporters on Twitter in the past month, just so she would know what he meant when he talked about work.

"I'm so mad at myself. I never do shit like that, but this guy has had it in for me for a long time, and I finally snapped. The mayor just laughed it off, but I still don't know if he was serious about that. What a nightmare. No wonder I was so distracted that I left my keys at work."

Maddie ran her fingernails over his short hair, again and again. He closed his eyes.

"That feels nice. You shouldn't reward me for being a jackass."

She pushed his head into her lap.

"You weren't a jackass, you were just pushed to the brink, that's all. I've been there. I don't blame you."

The weird thing was that if this had happened just a few months ago, she would have laughed at smug, mansplaining, know-it-all Theo being publicly humiliated. Now she just felt bad for him.

He swung his legs up onto the other end of the couch.

"That makes one of us, at least. I never should have let that guy bait me in the first place, but I'm just so fucking sick of guys like that thinking I don't know what I'm talking about." He sighed. "The problem is, people like me can't get away with blowing their fuse at work. Ever. One false move and it could all come tumbling down. I know I have to work twice as hard and be twice as good, but sometimes that just really gets to me."

She could relate.

"I get it. Sometimes it really gets to me, too. But don't you think you have enough credit with your boss by this point that he won't fire you for popping off at a reporter one time?"

He shrugged.

"I mean, I hope so. But I'm always paranoid about stuff like this." He sat up. "My brother thinks I'm neurotic about everything because . . ." He shook his head. "Well, for a lot of reasons we don't need to get into. But I've been like this for a long time now. I always feel like I can't take a step out of line."

She and Theo were very different people, but she really got how he felt.

"Yeah. Other people get the benefit of the doubt when something goes wrong or when they have an off day, but we never do."

He looked up at her and nodded.

"Yeah, exactly. Sometimes we just have to explode, you know?"

That part, she was good at.

"Oh, I know." They grinned at each other. "That's one of the reasons I got into this kind of work: we have to prove ourselves over and over and over again, and maybe you think it's stupid, but the clothes you're wearing while you prove yourself matter. I know you're going to say they shouldn't matter, it should all be about abilities and qualifications, et cetera, but that's not how it is, especially for women of color, and we have to work with the world we live in."

He shook his head.

"I don't think it's stupid, and I wasn't going to say that. I totally agree with you. You see what I wear to work every day. I know this stuff matters." He looked down. "You know, Maddie, I've been meaning to . . . I don't think your work is silly or frivolous or any of those things. That first time we met . . ." He let out a breath. "I mean, speaking of a time I was a jackass. Before that I didn't know stylists even existed, so I didn't understand what you meant. I know I asked you about it in the worst way possible. But I don't want you to think that I ever thought—or think now—that the work you do is somehow less than."

Oh. Wow. That was something she'd never expected to hear from Theo Stephens.

She squeezed his hand.

"Thanks for saying that. I really appreciate it."

He squeezed back.

"Sorry it took me so long to say it, and that I had to have a very public humiliation that reminded me how insufferable I can be first. I guess that's why I waited years to say it; I was so pissed at how true what you said about me was."

She opened her mouth to deny that. The weird thing was, she didn't think it was true anymore. Though . . . it had felt pretty true at the time. She bit her lip, and he laughed at her.

"See? You were about to try to make me feel better, but you couldn't lie to me."

She shook her head.

"Look, I'm not going to say you didn't deserve what I said, but if you'd ever been as bad as I thought you were, Alexa would have murdered you. But no matter what, you definitely aren't the person I thought you were."

He kissed her cheek.

"Thanks for that. I appreciate it." He reached for his wineglass.

"Speaking of your work, what's going on with that TV show? Last time you said you were playing phone tag with the station manager?"

She smiled. She'd been waiting to tell him.

"I have a real interview in a few weeks. I'm talking with people from the station, and he said they're going to bring in someone from the shelter they're working with so they can see how I work with her."

He pulled her into a hug.

"That's great! You'll be fantastic! Let me know if you need help preparing or anything like that."

She laughed.

"I think you've done a lot of the prep with me already—all this reality TV we watch together helps show me how it's done." She paused. "Except for *The Great British Baking Show*. Unfortunately, American networks don't like their hosts to be that nice."

She'd been thinking a lot about that, actually. Even the nice makeover shows wanted their hosts to have an edge at the beginning, to help set up the heartwarming thing at the end. Luckily, she was great at being bitchily funny when she needed to be.

"I'll watch whatever you want." He pulled her into a kiss before he stood up. "I'm getting more pizza. You want another slice?"

When he came back from the kitchen, he poured them both more wine before he sat down.

"I can't believe I was so stupid as to leave my only spare key with Ben, of all people. I bet you anything he has no idea where my key even is. I'm getting two extra keys made and leaving one with you and one with Alexa." He glanced at her and paused for a second. "I mean, if that's okay with you. You probably don't need me barging in on you the next time I lose my temper and then leave my keys at work."

She took her glass of wine out of his hand.

"No problem. I'm probably a safer person to have your key than either your brother or Alexa. She's always off doing wedding stuff these days. That's where they are tonight, by the way—they're up in Wine Country looking at some venue."

He settled back onto the couch with his pizza.

"Oh, that's right. I'm sure she told me that, but I was distracted by everything else that happened today."

They curled up on the couch as they finished the pizza; first sitting up straight on the couch, and eventually both lying on the couch, some reality TV show in the background. Theo's arm was around her, and her head was tucked into the hollow of his chest. She did really like that blue T-shirt he was wearing. It was so soft against her back that she moved a little just to feel it slide against her bare skin. She took a deep breath and closed her eyes; this was the first time all week she'd really been able to relax, and it felt so good.

She popped her eyes back open. This was altogether too comfortable. What the hell was even going on? Why was she all cozy on her couch snuggled into Theo, for the love of God? Had they really just had a conversation about him giving her a key to his apartment? She knew this thing wasn't going to last for all that much longer—there was no way it could. Why were they both acting so out of character tonight? This thing was about sex, remember?

She turned to Theo to get the whole sex part of this evening going, and found him sound asleep, his arm still around her, the look on his face so peaceful that she didn't want to disturb him.

No, come on, Maddie. What had she just been thinking? Who cared if she disturbed him!

She reached out and shook him, not so gently.

Finally, he half opened his eyes and smiled at her. His lashes were far too long to be on a man; it was just unfair. She would pay for lashes that good. She *had* paid for lashes that good.

"I'm sorry, I didn't mean to fall asleep," he said.

She stood up.

"Come on, bedtime." She reached out her hand to him. He grabbed it and pulled himself off the couch.

She led him into her mostly tidy bedroom and disappeared into the bathroom to splash water on her face and attempt to pull herself out of this weird, schmoopy mood. When she got out of the bathroom, he was already in her bed, looking right at home.

"Hey," he said as she approached the bed. "Thanks. For letting me come over, tonight, I mean. Even aside from a place to stay, I needed a friendly face. Thanks for being that."

Damn it, why did he have to say something so nice? She didn't want to actually like him!

She slid into the bed next to him, and he pulled her close. She didn't even try to resist; it was all too comfortable. Every time she changed her sheets and had a just-made bed, she was so cozy that she thought she should turn into one of those people who made their bed every morning. Maybe this time she'd really do it.

"You're welcome. Thanks for the pizza."

He kissed her gently, and they lay like that for a while, kissing slowly, nothing moving except for their lips, tucked into her best sheets and under a big pile of fluffy blankets. She knew at some point one of them would move faster, and she knew when that happened it would be good; it always was. But for now, the slow, sleepy kissing was so soothing she could let it go on forever. She closed her eyes and let herself float along with the stroke of his lips and the touch of his tongue.

Theo woke up in Maddie's bed, his arms still around her. She was still sound asleep, so he snuck out of bed and into the bathroom. She'd left a new toothbrush next to the sink for him, thank goodness, so he brushed his teeth before getting back in bed.

She stirred and nuzzled her head against him as he put his arms back around her. Maddie was always so much softer and less prickly when she was half-asleep. It wasn't that he didn't like sparring with her—he enjoyed it far more than he tried to let her know—but he also really liked when she unexpectedly dropped a kiss on his cheek, or let her head rest on his shoulder, or rubbed her face against his chest.

This thing with Maddie was so weird. He still wasn't sure if he'd been right to come over last night. She was still so hot and cold with him, but he couldn't deny it to himself any longer that he had it bad for Maddie. He knew it would pass; this was just one of those early relationship–type crushes that would never progress to something bigger, but it had only made it worse that she'd been so great the night before.

He brushed the soft hairs that had escaped from her loose bun back and kissed her gently on her temple.

"Good morning," she mumbled, her face still pressed against his chest.

He kissed her again.

"Good morning. Did I fall asleep on you last night?"

She tilted her head back to look up at him and smiled.

"You fell asleep on me twice last night, as a matter of fact. First on the couch, then here in the bed. But you were pretty exhausted last night."

He shook his head at himself.

"God, what an asshole I am. First I barge into your house, take advantage of your hospitality, and then I fall asleep in the middle of kissing you. I'm surprised you put up with me."

Maddie nodded. Of course she did.

"I'm surprised I put up with you, too. You also drank a bunch of my wine before conking out on my best furniture. And it was really good wine."

He pushed her onto her back.

"It *was* really good wine, thank you for that. Apparently, I have a lot to make up for this morning." He knelt between her legs and smiled down at her.

Once her trembling subsided and she could breathe again, he lifted his mouth and moved back up and kissed her.

"Thanks for taking care of me last night," he said. "Not just giving me a place to crash, but . . . the rest, too."

She kissed him back.

"Thanks for taking care of me this morning," she said.

He grinned and rolled out of the bed.

"It was the least I could do. Now I'm going to see what kind of ancient mechanism you have to make coffee, and I'm going to make the best coffee you've ever had with it. You just wait."

He wandered naked into her kitchen. First, to see if she even had coffee. She must, right? He spied a familiar brown Peet's Coffee bag and sighed with relief. He looked on the counter: okay, she had an enormous Mr. Coffee coffee maker. Not the best option, but he'd use that if there was nothing else. He opened a few cabinets to see what else she had.

"I thought you were making coffee. How are you making all this noise in here?" Maddie walked in wearing a silky patterned robe, with, he was pretty sure, nothing underneath. He very much wanted to take that robe off her and . . . No, he needed to stay focused. He could take that robe off her after the coffee.

"Don't you have an electric kettle?" he asked her.

He bent down to double-check her cabinets.

"No, what would I do with one of those?" she asked. "What do you even want with one of those? I have a coffee maker right there."

He stood up and turned back to Maddie. She quickly looked away. She'd been looking at his ass again. He hid his grin.

"Okay, fine. I'll make coffee your way. But . . . do you have measuring spoons? Or a measuring cup?"

Maddie rolled her eyes.

"I just use a normal spoon and the measuring lines on the side of the coffee maker. You're so weird."

He smiled at her.

"Humor me?"

She shook her head at him and shrugged, but he was pretty sure he saw a hint of a smile on her face.

"Fine, do what you want, as long as I get coffee at the end of this."

She dug a set of measuring spoons out of a drawer and took down the measuring cup from the cabinet.

He kissed her cheek and measured four tablespoons of coffee and thirty-two ounces of water into the coffee maker.

"See? I'm adaptable," he said before shutting the lid.

She was just about to retort something when her doorbell rang.

"Who is ringing my doorbell at nine a.m. on Saturday morning?" She walked out of the kitchen and through the living room toward the front door.

"It's me! I hear you in there! Open up!" Alexa's voice came through the front door.

What the hell was Alexa doing here? Just as Theo was about to wave at Maddie to pretend she wasn't there and that Alexa didn't hear anything, or failing that, to give him time to hide in the bedroom, Maddie opened the door.

Maddie opened the door.

To Alexa.

With him buck naked.

In her kitchen.

He had just enough time to leap into the corner of the kitchen that wasn't visible from her living room. And there he stood, staring at Maddie's spice rack and the many boxes of Girl Scout Cookies in the far corner of her kitchen. Naked.

"Lex? Is everything okay?" Maddie said.

Couldn't she have asked that with the door still closed?

"I'm okay, I think, but I might have lost my mind, I'm not sure." "Alexa sounded like she was at least on her fourth cup of coffee. I called and you didn't answer, and I figured you were asleep and I know I woke you up and I'm sorry but I had to talk about this right now! The most amazing and also terrifying thing just happened!"

He heard the door open all the way and Alexa walk in. Great, now he was really trapped.

"I stopped to buy you coffee since I figured you wouldn't have made it yet and because I knew I wouldn't be able to let you stop to make some."

Great. Maddie had coffee. Alexa had coffee. All he had was a coffee maker full of meticulously measured coffee and water on the other side of the room. A coffee maker he hadn't even had time to turn on before Alexa barged in.

"Thanks for the coffee, but you'd better spill this news immediately," Maddie said. There was a short pause. "Wait. Something happened that made you show up at my house on a Saturday morning. You're already engaged. Are you pregnant?"

Alexa laughed.

"No, God, no. At this point that would definitely be more terrifying than amazing. No, it's . . . Okay, so you know how I really wanted to get married at the Berkeley Rose Garden, but they were booked for weddings every weekend day straight for the next year? And every time they open a new Saturday I try to call to get the date but someone always gets it ahead of me?"

He heard Maddie sip her coffee. He looked at the coffee maker on the other side of the kitchen with longing.

"Yeah, of course I know. We had a plan that Olivia and I would call for you for the next date, remember?"

"Yes, right, I forgot, it's been a wild morning. Well, okay, I know someone who works for the Parks Department—I did them a big favor a few years ago around that Harvest Festival thing—and she kept saying I was at the top of the waiting list, but I didn't really believe anything would come of that. Well, this morning I checked my work voice mail, and she called late last night to tell me an October date just opened up and I should call her today on her cell if I want it, because otherwise someone else would grab it."

October? *This* October?

"October of this year?" Maddie repeated his thoughts.

"I know, I know, it's really soon. But . . . Mads, was somebody over here? Your place is so neat! I mean, for you."

Huh, this was neat? He'd been thinking that Maddie's place was kind of cluttered.

"I just cleared out some stuff, that's all. For, um, a charity drive." Had she cleaned up for him? "Can we get back to your news? October?"

Theo looked down at Maddie's spice rack. Why the hell was turmeric next to *herbes de Provence*?

"Right, sorry. Okay, so I listened to the message in the car when Drew and I were driving back from Napa—we had to come back early this morning because he's on call today—and we had been trying to talk ourselves into having the wedding at the perfectly nice but totally generic site we saw yesterday. And when we heard October, we both just looked at each other and grinned. So I called her back right away and said yes."

"You just grinned and said yes? To getting married in less than four months? Just like that?"

"Just like that!" Alexa said. "Drew was so excited and said all this sweet stuff about how he couldn't wait to marry me and he was so glad it was going to be in just a few months, and it got me excited, too, but what the hell was I thinking? Does he have any idea how much we have to do in the next four months? I don't have a dress! Maddie, what the hell am I going to do? See why I said this was terrifying?"

Less than four months.

Maddie had said, back in May when she set down that list of rules, that this thing would only last until the wedding.

He'd agreed to that then, partly because she was naked and so was he and he would have agreed to anything she said, but also because the wedding felt so far into the future. At least a year away. Maybe more.

Now it was October. That felt way too soon.

Granted, he'd always sort of assumed they wouldn't actually last until the wedding. Their relationship felt too tenuous for that. He'd never quite believed Maddie could keep the secret from Alexa anyway, and he'd figured that she'd end it as soon as that happened.

But it was one thing to assume it would all blow up at some point, and a very different thing to know for sure they were going to be done by October.

"Don't panic," Maddie said. "Please, this is you and me we're talking about. Four months is nothing. We can put together a wedding in that time, easy. No one needs huge amounts of time to plan a wedding; that's just what the wedding industrial complex wants you to think. Here: go home right now and make a list of all the things you have to get done for this wedding, and then send it out to me, Olivia, Drew, Carlos, and Theo. Theo will be very useful here."

That was probably the nicest thing Maddie had ever said about him.

"I will figure out your dress. I was born to do this," Maddie said. "We can get this done."

Theo tried to think of what task Alexa and Maddie would come up with for him to sort out. Probably the DJ. Or the bartender.

Probably the DJ and the bartender.

And definitely something that involved spreadsheets.

"Oh God, my MOM," Alexa said. "She's going to flip OUT. I haven't told her about this yet. I have to work up to it."

"Did you talk to Olivia?"

He heard Alexa stand up.

"Yeah, and of course right before I called her I had a moment of panic that she had a trial or something scheduled for that week and so I'd have to cancel after all, but no, the date is clear."

"Okay." The door opened. Could it be? Was she actually leaving? "We can do this! I'm going to go home and make a list of everything we have to do and try to chill out for a second. Thanks, Mads. You always know what to say. I'm sure I'll email you a spreadsheet in a few hours."

"I look forward to it," Maddie said.

He held his breath and waited for the door to close.

"Wait!" Oh God. Why was Alexa doing this to him? He was freezing in here! "What's going on with the show? Did they schedule your big interview yet? Do you know if it's going to be on camera, or . . . ?"

"We can talk about that later. Go home and make your list!" Maddie said.

The door closed, but Theo didn't move. Alexa might come back. Or she might still be there, or . . .

"You ever coming out of there?" Maddie stood at the door of the kitchen with a grin on her face.

"Oh thank God. I love Alexa like a sister but I thought she was never going to leave."

Maddie laughed.

"I kept thinking about you hiding in here naked and almost lost it more than once as she talked and talked. Do you know how much of a struggle it was to keep a straight face? Especially when I saw your work bag in the corner of the living room and just kept praying she wouldn't notice it. Every time I thought we were almost done and I could get her out of here, no, she had something more to say. And then I would think of you naked in here and almost laugh again."

This made him laugh, and soon both of them had dissolved into giggles.

"I was dying! In addition to trying to silently react to the news that the wedding is in less than four months, and not freeze to death in your incredibly cold kitchen, I kept thinking about the look on her face if she knew I was hiding naked in here while she was pouring out this story to you." Theo wrapped his arms around Maddie and shivered. "And I had to listen to you two drink coffee and not have any of my own."

Maddie handed him her cup.

"Here, I took pity on you and saved most of mine for you. I felt like the worst friend in the world; here Alexa was dealing with something super stressful and I was trying to help but I was so distracted envisioning you naked in here."

He leered at her.

"I'm glad thinking about me naked distracts you."

She swatted his butt, and he grinned. Damn it, why did he have to have so much fun with her?

She led him into the living room and tossed him the blanket that was draped over the couch.

"Okay, fine. Here, I'll take you out for some of your stupid fancy coffee. Will that make you feel better?"

Oh thank God. This lukewarm coffee wasn't going to do it for him. He wrapped the blanket around himself and smiled.

"Blue Bottle? Please? I know it's not your favorite but it's only a few blocks away."

She frowned at him.

"Don't give me those puppy-dog eyes. It doesn't work on me."

She picked up Alexa's cup and turned to take it into the kitchen. "But fine, Blue Bottle. Get dressed, naked boy."

Theo walked down the hallway to Maddie's bedroom, trailing the blanket behind him like a cape. He heard her call out to him from the kitchen.

"Did you alphabetize my spice rack?"

He shrugged.

"I had to do something to keep myself busy in there!" he yelled back.

Chapter Eleven

AGAINST HIS BETTER JUDGMENT, THEO WAS IN THE BACK SEAT OF AL-
exa's car two weeks later, along with Maddie and Olivia, on their
way to go wedding dress shopping. Olivia had flown into town for
the weekend to help Alexa find a dress, and Alexa had invited
Theo to come along, too. She'd made it clear he didn't have to go,
but he felt like he had to support her. And when would he ever get
this opportunity again?

Plus, he hadn't seen Maddie for well over a week, not since their
relaxed—and very hot—Fourth of July at his apartment. They'd
texted funny—or sexy—notes to each other almost every day for
the past week, but the night he'd texted her to see if he could come
over, she had been out on a doomed wedding dress shopping trip
with Alexa and had an early-morning client the next day. A few
days later, she'd texted him, but he'd been at an event with his boss
and ended up getting home past midnight.

Now she was on the other side of the back seat, and it took all his willpower not to reach over to touch her.

"There's a plan B, right?" Alexa asked the car at large. "In case the people at this boutique are assholes, too, and all these dresses also look terrible on me and I can't find a wedding dress anywhere in the nine Bay Area counties? Maddie, do you have some sort of white fabric in your studio that you can, like, drape around me for me to walk down the aisle so I don't have to do it naked?"

When he said he'd come shopping, he hadn't accounted for Alexa's wedding dress–related breakdown.

"I told you, don't worry. This place is great—you'll see," Maddie said.

"Don't worry? Don't worry?!? It's already July! My wedding is in October! I don't have a dress, and from what people tell me, it's virtually impossible for me to GET a dress when you look like me and have this little amount of time to go before a wedding. How can I not worry???"

He'd never seen Alexa this panicky. She'd told him the first two trips had been disastrous, but he didn't realize she'd be this stressed about it. Maddie should have warned him that today was going to be like this. He still would have come; he just might be more prepared for it.

"Lexie, come on, this will be fun!" Olivia said. "I can't wait to see my little sister in a wedding dress."

Alexa turned to look at Maddie.

"That's what I thought the first time! 'This will be fun!' I thought. 'I can't wait to see myself in a wedding dress!' I thought. That was before the women in the bridal shop all made me feel like I was too fat to ever find a man to even look at me, much less to marry me. And between their attitude and Mom asking me if I was sure about having the wedding date so soon because it didn't give me much time to lose weight before the wedding, I almost lost it."

Olivia winced. Theo had always thought Alexa and Olivia got along well with their mom, but then he'd also heard that weddings make everyone go over the edge.

"Lex, I could have told you not to bring Mom. You knew she would do that!"

Alexa glared at all three of them in the rearview mirror. Why him? He hadn't even said anything!

"I got lost in the moment, okay? I got all excited about having a wedding date and trying on dresses and wanting my mom to see me in dresses and I kind of forgot what she would be like. Don't worry, it won't happen again; as you know, today is a secret from anyone except the four of us and Drew. If I ever find a dress, she can come back then to see it, but that's not looking likely."

Olivia and Maddie exchanged worried glances.

"Lexie, I'm sure we'll find you a great dress," Olivia said. "That was just one place!"

Alexa changed lanes to head toward the Bay Bridge.

"Maybe that was just one place, but every dress I tried on at that place looked terrible on me. I'm not even exaggerating, am I, Maddie? Tell them!"

Maddie sighed and shook her head.

"Unfortunately, no, she isn't. But that's all my fault. I shouldn't have taken her to that store. They were awful there. I don't do bridal often enough to know how they are with non-standard-size brides. But trust me, none of my clients will go there ever again."

Olivia patted her sister on the shoulder.

"Okay, that sucks, but that was just the one shop. What happened at the other shop?"

Alexa slowed as they approached the tollgates for the Bay Bridge.

"They weren't as terrible about what I looked like there, but they flipped OUT about the wedding date. Apparently, unless it's at *least* nine months before your wedding, you shouldn't even think about getting a wedding dress."

"Wait, really, they need nine months of lead time just to make a dress?" Theo asked. "Are you kidding me? What the hell are they doing to it?"

Alexa pointed at him.

"Thank you! And I have no idea what they're doing to it. It's all a mystery! They give you some bullshit about craftsmanship and blah blah blah. Come on. My great-aunt was a seamstress. Making a dress doesn't take that long! But apparently if you're getting married with less time than that, you should just find scraps of fabric on the floor of a thrift store and piece them together, because that's all you deserve."

Maddie looked at Theo and opened her eyes wide.

"Okay, now you're exaggerating a little," she said.

"A LITTLE, maybe, but not that much. They had literally three dresses they thought it might be possible to get made before the wedding, and they were all very, very ugly."

Maddie poked the back of Alexa's seat.

"Two of the dresses were very, very ugly, I'll give you that, but I liked that last one! I'm not saying you had to like it—it's your wedding—but still."

"It was very, very ugly on me. I don't care what it looked like on the hanger." Alexa glanced back at Theo. "Are you ready to watch me put on a bunch more dresses that look fine or even good on the hanger but very, very ugly on me? Well, you're in luck. Looks like that's what's going to happen for hours this afternoon!"

He hoped Maddie and Olivia knew how to talk Alexa down. He knew exactly how to do it in a work context, just as Alexa knew how to talk him down. But when it came to wedding dresses? His role today was going to be to stay silent and let the women talk.

"That is not what's going to happen today," Maddie said. "There will be plenty of things for you to try on, and at least half of them won't be ugly, I promise. And like I told you, I've heard good stuff from a lot of people about this place and their options for brides of all sizes. And I called ahead to make sure they're aware of your wedding date. It'll be better here. Trust me."

He never should have doubted. Maddie was so good at this.

Alexa shrugged and was quiet for a moment.

"You guys, is my mom right?"

"NO!" all three of them shouted. Olivia was the loudest.

"Not about the losing weight thing, that's not what I mean. But were we rash to jump on this wedding date? I was so excited about it, but everything that's happened since we decided on it has been . . . deflating. The Rose Garden is perfect, and I'm not at all worried about marrying Drew, but . . . everyone seems so upset about the time line, between the dress people and the catering people and even the damn makeup artists. Am I going to be able to get this done?"

Now this Theo knew how to deal with.

"*We* are going to be able to get this done, Lex," he said. "You're not doing this alone, you know that. You have the three of us, and Drew and Carlos, and your parents, and a ton of other friends who will be ready and willing to pitch in and do whatever you need us to do to make sure you and Drew have a great wedding. Don't let the assholes get to you! Do you really think Maddie will let anything get in between you and a perfect wedding dress? Absolutely not. The wedding will be awesome, don't worry."

Maddie turned to him and mouthed "Thank you!" They smiled at each other.

"Theo is exactly right about all of that," Maddie said. He wished he'd recorded that statement. "You've got this. We've got this. I know you have problems delegating sometimes, but when you've got only a few months to plan a wedding, you need to delegate the hell out of your list. And like I said, the dress is my responsibility, and we're going to get this done."

"Okay," Alexa said, "but just in case, between me and Olivia we have three bottles of champagne with us, if I need to drown my sorrows and prepare to buy a white nightgown from Target. Theo, you're driving home, FYI."

"On it," he said.

Alexa changed lanes.

"I'm tired of talking about dresses and my wedding. Good God, I'm turning into one of those brides. Let's talk about all of you. Maddie has a very exciting job interview coming up soon. Tell them all about it, Maddie!"

Theo turned to Maddie and put his hands under his chin expectantly.

"A job interview? Tell us all about it, Maddie," he said.

She rolled her eyes at him but smiled as she did it.

"A local TV station is hiring for a new show; a kind of *What Not to Wear* with a twist—it's all about helping women get back on their feet. I'm interviewing for the stylist job on the show, though they call it the 'host.'"

Olivia applauded and peppered Maddie with questions the rest of their way into San Francisco. Theo smiled as he watched Maddie answer them. She really knew what she was doing.

As they walked from the car to the bridal salon, he held Maddie back a few steps.

"You seem on top of things, but let me know if you want help to prep for the interview."

She smiled at him.

"I've watched a lot of reality TV; I know the drill. I know what they're looking for. But we could definitely watch a little more of that, for, you know, practice."

He grinned.

"Done."

When they walked in, a woman by the door jumped to greet them.

"Welcome! Do you have an appointment?"

Alexa nodded. She still looked nervous.

"Yes, for two p.m. Alexa Monroe?"

The woman smiled.

"Alexa, great. I'm Jill; nice to meet you. I talked to your friend Maddie the other day." She looked between the two other women. "Is one of you Maddie?"

"That's me," Maddie said.

"Great. Thanks for calling ahead with all of that information. Let me take you all over here and we can get started." She turned to Theo and raised her eyebrows. "And is this the groom?"

The four of them laughed. Alexa's laughter was just on the edge of hysteria.

"No, he's my bridesman," Alexa said. "I don't think he's ever been to a bridal salon before, so this will be a brand-new experience for Theo in so many ways."

Jill escorted all four of them to a bunch of white couches. Theo ended up sitting in between Maddie and Olivia. Just as they sat down, Maddie scooted over so she was closer to him. He rested his arm along the back of the low couch and brushed her shoulder with his hand.

Olivia immediately pulled out a bottle of champagne and opened it, and they forced Alexa to toast before they did anything else.

"Okay, so I know you have a short time frame you're working with, which does make things more complicated, but we definitely have plenty of dresses that will work for you, don't worry about that. Almost all our dresses can be done in time for your wedding, though they will incur rush fees."

Alexa shrugged.

"I know this is how they get you, but honestly, at this point, I don't even care about extra fees if I can find a dress that I like and fits my body."

Olivia put her arm around her sister.

"I don't care, either, and that's a lot more relevant, because I'm paying for this dress."

Alexa gasped and spun to face Olivia.

"Livie, you don't have to do that. I budgeted for this, and I know you . . ."

Olivia shook her head and put her finger up in front of Alexa's mouth.

"I know I don't have to. I'm doing it anyway. No arguments."

Alexa and Olivia hugged, and everyone toasted again. No wonder they needed three bottles of champagne; it seemed like they'd
get through all of it pretty quickly, whether they found a dress
or not.

As Jill and Alexa talked about wedding dresses, using lots of
words like "glamorous" and "chiffon" and "sparkle," Theo took
the opportunity to whisper in Maddie's ear.

"I missed you this week."

She kept looking straight at Alexa and Jill, but her smile turned
from sappy to dirty.

"I missed you, too."

He ran his hand up and down her back, and her smile grew
wider.

"Careful!" she said under her breath. He dropped his hand but
didn't move it too far.

"Okay!" Jill clapped her hands. "I think I have all the information I need. Alexa, come with me. Let's get you in some dresses."

Alexa turned to glance back at them as she walked down the
hallway with Jill. She looked like a little kid being dragged off to
get shots.

"You'll be great!" Maddie shouted after her.

As soon as she disappeared, Olivia turned to Maddie.

"How bad was it really?"

Maddie sighed.

"Awful. The time we went with your mom was the worst; the
second place wouldn't have been as bad if she hadn't already been
crushed from the first time. I'm so worried about today, you guys.
I promised her she'd find a dress here, but . . ." She sighed. "I really
hope I was telling the truth."

Maddie looked so worried. Theo was on the far side of Olivia; she wouldn't be able see him touch Maddie. Theo moved his hand up to the small of Maddie's back, and she leaned against it.

"You heard good things about this place though, right?" Olivia asked.

Maddie nodded.

"I did, and I'm pretty confident she'll at least find some dresses that fit her here, but what if she just decides to buy the first dress that fits, to get it over with? I want her to love her wedding dress, and I know she does, too, and it would kill me for her to get something she only sort of likes just because she's so demoralized from the whole process."

Theo traced circles around Maddie's back, and she leaned in closer to him.

"Okay." Olivia poured more champagne in their glasses. "We'll just make sure that doesn't happen. Everyone here is very good at reading Alexa. We can't let her pretend to us."

Maddie lifted her glass.

"I'll toast to that."

Maddie saw Theo pull his phone out of his pocket. Really? Now? She always made fun of him about how addicted he was to his phone, but he couldn't take a break for an afternoon while they did this for Alexa? She moved away from him—how had she let him sit this close to her with Olivia right there, anyway?

A few seconds later, she heard her phone ding in her purse. Shit, she'd meant to turn off her phone for the day so she wouldn't get interrupted. She reached for it and saw the message on her screen.

Sitting this close to you is driving me crazy

She glanced over at Theo. He was looking off into the corner of the room, as a smug smile hovered around his lips.

She moved closer to him, so they were sitting hip to hip.

Is that better?

She looked at Olivia to make sure she wasn't paying attention, but Olivia was buried in her own phone.

Better and worse, all at the same time. Do you have just an
endless amount of those thin dresses where when I touch
you through them, it feels like you're wearing almost
nothing?

She grinned.

I have a few such dresses, I'll admit. Why, don't you like
them?

His text came back within seconds.

Let's put it this way: I'm about a minute away from dragging
you into an empty dressing room. We wouldn't even have
to take the dress off

Holy shit, how did Theo manage to do this to her? The worst part was that she was about a minute away from letting him drag her wherever he wanted.

"How much time does it take to put a dress on, anyway?" Theo asked. "What's taking them so long?"

Maddie grinned.

"Most dresses take a few seconds to put on . . . and take off," Maddie said. "A wedding dress? Those take a long time. Those things weren't built for quick changes. Or for getting into and out of by yourself. They're a throwback to the days of rich women having someone help them get dressed. That's why you're here, don't you know? That's our job on Alexa's wedding day."

Theo looked stricken, and they laughed at him again.

"Don't worry," Olivia said. "We'll let you do a snack run while we get Alexa into the dress. It'll be useful to have an errand boy that day. In my experience as a bridesmaid, there are never enough snacks before the wedding. And they basically starve you for hours after the wedding. No wonder bridesmaids always get drunk and hit on groomsmen—there's always lots of champagne and not enough food!"

"Olivia. Do you really think there won't be enough snacks for the wedding party at *my* wedding?" Alexa said as she walked down the hallway. "I'm honestly insulted that you don't know I've already drafted the list of our wedding-day snacks."

Maddie sighed in relief as soon as she saw Alexa. She had a smile on her face! She had a wedding dress on *and* a smile on her face! She was cracking jokes! Oh thank God.

"What do you guys think?" Alexa stopped in front of the three of them, and then turned to look at herself in the big mirror. "I don't hate it. I mean, I don't love it, either, but not hating the dress on my body is already, like, a thousand times better than how I felt at the last two appointments."

Maddie didn't hate it, either. It wasn't Alexa's dress, she could tell immediately—it had a lace skirt, and Alexa wasn't a lace kind of person, and it had spaghetti straps, and Maddie had never seen Alexa in spaghetti straps—but it still looked good on her. And most important, she was smiling.

"It's a good first dress, but let's see some more," Olivia said.

"Okay, Jill," Alexa said. "This dress is a no, but we all like it anyway. On to the next one!"

Jill and Alexa walked back down the hallway. Maddie, Theo, and Olivia all grinned at one another.

"I'm so relieved," Maddie said, as soon as Alexa was no longer in earshot. "She found a dress where she looked in the mirror and smiled instead of bursting into tears. The bad kind of tears."

They'd both cried that time. That whole trip had been awful. Maddie had felt like a failure as both a friend and a stylist.

"Wow," Theo said. He put his hand on the small of her back. "Alexa almost never cries. She must be so stressed about this." He patted her back. "You must be, too."

She leaned back against his hand.

"A lot better now."

She really shouldn't be this close to Theo. Could Alexa have noticed anything when she came into the room?

No, there was no way. Alexa was way too occupied by her wedding and everything going on at work for something as unlikely as her two friends—who she knew hated each other—having secret sex with each other on a weekly . . . or sometimes even more frequent . . . basis.

After another long wait—and some more surreptitious texting—Maddie heard Alexa's laugh. Okay, that was a good sign. A few seconds later she appeared in a dress with a simple satin tank on top and layers and layers and layers of tulle on the bottom.

"This dress is an enormous amount of fun," Alexa said, as she stopped in front of the mirror. "It's absolutely the wedding dress I desperately wanted to be mine someday when I was fifteen." She twirled in front of the mirror and grinned at them. "It is not the dress I desperately want to be mine at age thirty-four, but I'm still glad I got to try it on."

Olivia also had a big grin on her face.

"Are you sure you don't want that dress? Because you look so pretty in it! I remember you drawing pictures when you were little of dresses a lot like that." Olivia stood up and walked around her. "It just looks so great on you."

Oh no. Olivia wasn't going to do that thing where she tried to convince Alexa to get a dress because she loved it, was she? Hadn't they talked about this?

Alexa laughed.

"I should have known you would love this dress; you always liked dressing me up as if I was one of your little dolls. But no, as much as I love tulle to the depths of my being, I don't think a wedding dress with this much tulle is me, and I want to feel like me on my wedding day."

Olivia dropped her hand from Alexa's shoulder and sat down.

"You should absolutely feel like you on your wedding day. But . . . can't we find you some tulle for the rehearsal dinner or something?"

Maddie sighed in relief. Thank goodness, Olivia didn't look like she was going to be difficult.

"Good idea," Maddie said. "I think we can manage that."

Alexa held up a finger to Maddie.

"Let's not get ahead of ourselves here. We still haven't managed to find me a wedding dress yet!" She took one last look at herself in the mirror. "All I can say is, thank God we didn't bring my mom today. She would have insisted on this dress. She also wants me to look like the pretty princess I used to draw when I was a little girl. I'll have that fight with her once the dress is ordered."

She turned and floated back down the hallway with Jill.

Theo turned to Maddie once she was gone.

"I already know you're going to get mad at me for asking this question, but I've got to know the answer."

Oh no. What was he going to ask her?

"Well, I'm already mad, but what's your question?"

He gestured around the room.

"Just how many dresses is she going to try on today? Is it going to be the whole store? I just need to know so I can mentally prepare for this."

She tried to summon up a scowl, but she was pretty sure it was mostly just a smile.

"Anywhere between three dresses and the whole store, so buckle in, bridesman."

Theo sighed and leaned back all the way against the couch, bringing Maddie with him.

"Great, okay, that's awesome; I really wanted there to be a lot more dresses, so that was exactly what I was hoping you'd say. Just one more thing: what the hell is tulle?"

Maddie and Olivia burst out laughing. Maddie struggled to sit up. The long, low couch was far too comfortable, especially with Theo right there.

"That ballerina skirt type stuff," she said.

Theo just looked at her.

"Right, I guess that has no meaning for you. The stuff that made the underskirt of her dress stick out?"

His eyebrows squeezed together.

"That sort of scratchy stuff?"

Maddie nodded.

Theo shook his head.

"I need some sort of reward for undergoing fashion school."

She rolled her eyes at him and reached for her phone.

Reward? What kind of reward do you think you're going to get for this?

He grinned down at his phone.

Maybe you can let yourself into my place later on tonight with nothing on but that trench coat of yours and we'll see what happens from there

She crossed her legs. How did he always do this to her?

Mmm, keep talking

She opened a second bottle of champagne to keep herself occupied as she saw his thumbs flying over his keyboard.

I don't care how long we're out looking for wedding dresses, or what other kind of wedding nonsense Alexa has you doing later on tonight, we are going to be naked in bed together before midnight, damn it. It's been way too long

She poured champagne into all of their glasses before she texted him back.

Mmm, naked, yes, but does it have to be in bed?

She felt Theo's eyes on her and shivered.

"Oooh, I like this one!" Olivia said. Maddie's head shot up.

This dress had a very vintage vibe to it: short lacy sleeves over a simple silk chiffon sheath with a sweetheart neckline. Maddie liked it immediately, but she couldn't tell if Alexa liked it.

"What do you guys think?" she asked. Maddie and Olivia both jumped up.

"What do *you* think?" Olivia asked.

Alexa turned around to see herself in the mirror.

"I like it. I didn't think I would like lace, and I didn't think I would like this shape of a skirt, but Jill convinced me to try it on, and I like it a lot more than I thought I would. I think I could see myself getting married in it? It would fit the venue really well. But I just don't know."

Maddie and Olivia looked at each other and shook their heads.

"I like it a lot," Maddie said. "But there are plenty of other dresses here to try on. You don't have to convince yourself to get the first one that seems like it might be right to you."

Alexa turned back around and looked from Olivia to Maddie.

"Okay. That sounds right." She raised her voice. "Theo, any thoughts?"

The three of them turned to stare at Theo, still sitting on the couch.

"I think you look beautiful in that dress, but I also think you shouldn't get it if you're not positive."

Maddie nodded at him and he winked at her.

"Excellent thoughts, Theo," Olivia said. She put her hands on her sister's shoulders and spun her around in the direction of the dressing room.

"Okay, we're all agreed," Maddie said. "On to the next one."

When she disappeared down the hallway, Maddie turned to Olivia.

"What if this keeps happening? What if she keeps finding dresses that look good on her and one of us likes, but *she* doesn't like them? I don't want her to get that second dress because you liked it, or the third one because I did. I want her to get one she falls in love with."

She felt herself tearing up, which seemed silly. It was just a wedding dress.

But it was Alexa's wedding dress.

Theo put his hand on her shoulder. If he made fun of her for crying over a dress, she might have to kill him.

"Hey." His voice was more tender than she'd ever heard it. "She'll find a great dress. You won't let her down."

She wiped her eyes and smiled at him.

"Thanks. I just want everything to be great for her, you know?"

The other two nodded. They did know.

She was glad to be here with both Olivia and Theo, two people who she knew loved Alexa as much as she did, and only wanted the best for her. In her years of scorning Theo, she'd somehow managed to ignore what a genuinely good friend he was to Alexa.

Maddie took a deep breath.

"Okay. Let's all just look at the tiaras and try to relax a little."

Theo swiveled his head around to look at her.

"That's how you relax?"

She grinned and looked into his eyes.

"Well, that's one way."

He opened his mouth to respond, just as Olivia said, "Here she comes! Lexie!"

Olivia jumped out of her seat. When Maddie saw Alexa emerge from the hallway, she stood up, too.

Alexa glowed like she was lit from within. This dress was pure white, with a sweetheart neckline that gave Alexa plenty of cleavage, but not grandma-can't-come-to-the-wedding amounts of cleavage. The full skirt had pleats and folds that swayed as she walked toward them. As she moved, the dress floated around her, which made her look like she was dancing with every step. She stopped in front of them, a huge smile on her face, and spun in a circle. The folds of the skirt rose and fell and swirled around her as if they were set to music.

They all grinned at one another without saying anything.

"Why wasn't this the first dress she tried on?" Olivia finally asked.

Jill grinned.

"We only have one sample in the store, and someone else grabbed it for their client. But I knew she needed to try this one on, so I pulled rank and took it back."

Alexa turned around to look at herself in the mirror, with Maddie, Olivia, and Theo all behind her. Maddie didn't even realize she had tears streaming down her face until Theo reached up to wipe them away.

"It's perfect," Alexa said to them. "It's me. It's mine."

Olivia laughed.

"She used to say 'it's mine' just like that when she was a little girl, anytime she really wanted something. But this time, she's right. It's hers."

Twenty minutes later, the four of them left the salon. After four steps down the street, Alexa stopped them.

"I'm not even going to apologize for doing this. GROUP HUG."

Before she'd even gotten the words out, the other three enveloped her, and one another, in a huge hug.

"I'm so happy. I love you guys so much," Alexa said. "I'm so glad all three of you were here with me today. Thank you so much."

"Damn it, Alexa, now I'm crying again!" Maddie said.

"I'm crying, too!" Alexa said from inside the curve of Maddie's arm. "I expected you to cry—you always cry at *Say Yes to the Dress*—but why am I crying about a dress?"

"We're all crying about a dress!" Maddie said.

They all laughed as they let one another go. All four of them wiped their faces, even Theo.

Olivia pulled Alexa into a solitary hug.

"I'm so happy for you, Lexie. It's everything I wanted for you."

They continued their walk to the car, with Olivia and Alexa up in front of Maddie and Theo.

Theo slid something small and cold into her hand.

"For the next emergency," he said. She opened her hand and found a shiny new key in there. She was so emotional right now, she pushed back her reservations about having a key to his place, and just slid it into her purse.

"Let yourself in as soon as you can get to my house later. I can't wait to get you naked," he said. "Do you know how much what you said turned me on?"

She raised an eyebrow at him.

"Which thing I said? The thing about being naked not in your bed? Or the thing about how you'd get a reward?"

He patted her on the butt.

"Oh, those things were good, too. But I meant the best thing of all. 'Theo is exactly right.' I'm going to make you repeat that a few times later."

She narrowed her eyes at him. She wanted to yell, but Alexa was just up ahead.

"Oh, I'd like to see you try to make me do that."

He smiled.

"Trust me. You're really going to like the way I make you do it."

Her whole body tingled at the growl in his voice. She looked at him, but the way he was looking at her made her blush and turn away.

She knew one thing. She couldn't fucking wait to be alone inside Theo's apartment with him.

Chapter Twelve

ALMOST TWO WEEKS LATER, THEO WAS IN THE MIDDLE OF HAVING THE same conversation about the rally with the governor's press secretary he'd had twice before. They'd tentatively agreed to have the rally in Berkeley, but the rest of the group was getting to her.

"Sybil, I completely understand your worries about protestors," he said. That was a lie; he knew the worries about protestors were all bullshit, but he needed Sybil on his side. "And while, yes, the risk of protestors is marginally higher here in Berkeley, I think the reward is much higher here, too. We have a community here who is really passionate about universal pre-K, and who I know will be fantastic in front of the cameras. I've already vetted a handful of parents who will be strong advocates for us and can talk about how universal pre-K has helped their lives and the lives of their children. Now, I'm not saying that there aren't families like this all over California. I know there are. But I am saying the rally will be a great success in Berkeley."

There was a long silence on the phone, and he took a bite of the chocolate chip cookie on his desk while he waited. Finally, Sybil sighed.

"I know we keep having this conversation, but you and I both understand how high stakes this whole campaign is. Okay, I'm trusting you here. Start getting those parents media trained."

He threw his arms up in victory but tried to keep his voice even.

"Will do. Talk to you soon. And let the campaign know that I'll handle everything with the city of Berkeley."

He turned to his computer to email the mayor.

He'd just typed Rally is a go for Berkeley! when he heard his door click shut. He glanced up, expecting it to be either Alexa, with some advice for him on the question he'd emailed her earlier, or Peter, his assistant. It was neither of them.

"Maddie? What are you doing here?"

She didn't answer him but dropped her bag by the door and turned to look at the knob.

"Does this door lock?"

He saved his document and stood up.

"It does, but I never lock it from the inside. Why do you ask?"

She turned around and smiled at him. That wasn't a smile he'd seen before. She looked wild and sexy, but something seemed off about her.

"Because I want to do this." She came around his desk, wrapped her arms around his neck, and pulled his face down to hers. This was like their first kiss, but better; it had all of the passion and urgency of that first time in his living room, but they knew each other now, knew exactly how the other person liked to be kissed. She knew that if she bit his lip, just like . . . oh God, just like that . . . he would go wild. He knew that if he tangled his fingers in her hair and tugged a little, she would make a moan, just like that.

He lost himself in the kiss. He stopped thinking about where he was, and what he should be doing, and everything he was stressed about, and concentrated on this moment, this woman, their lips and tongues and bodies coming together. He could have kissed her for hours. But after not long enough, she pulled back. He started to step backward, but she put her hand on his arm and motioned for him to stay right where he was, and he obeyed her.

She smiled at him, that same wild smile from when she'd walked into his office. It unsettled him. She unbuttoned the top three buttons of the white shirtdress she was wearing, until it fell open to her pale pink bra. As hot as that kiss was, this was taking it too far. And she should know that. What was going on?

"What the hell are you doing?" At any other time, in any other situation, in any other place, he'd be delighted for her to barge in and interrupt what he was doing and start taking her clothes off, but not right now, on a Thursday afternoon, in his office in City Hall.

"What does it look like I'm doing?" she asked, unbuttoning two more buttons, until her dress was open to her waist.

He'd been standing frozen at his desk, staring at her. He'd be dead if he wasn't excited by this, but he needed to end this. Now.

"Maddie." He started buttoning her dress back up. "Stop this. What's gotten into you? I'm at work; we can't do this now."

She pushed his hands away and pulled her belt off.

"I know you're at work—that's the fucking point." She pushed him backward, until his butt hit the back of his desk. "Don't you want to fuck me on top of your desk? You told me you did; you said it would be so hot. Well, now's your opportunity."

He had told her that, but he hadn't been seriously suggesting that she come to his office in the middle of the day and start taking her clothes off.

She reached for his belt and unbuckled it before he could stop her. But as she reached for his fly, he took ahold of her wrists.

"We can't do this right now. I'm at work. Anyone could walk in at any time. Including my boss, the mayor, who would rightly fire me on the spot. And including your best friend, the one who you're desperately keeping it a secret from that you're sleeping with me, remember?"

She pulled her wrists away and stepped back.

"She's at a meeting in San Francisco. Along with your boss, by the way." She turned away from him and buttoned up her dress with her back to him. "I texted her earlier to see if she was around, and she said she was just walking into the meeting, so I knew it would be a while. But never mind, you're obviously too scared to take a little risk, even though it would be the hottest thing you've ever done in your conservative, boring, pathetic life, so I'm just going to go now."

Ouch. He'd always known this thing would blow up when it ended; he just hadn't quite expected it to happen so soon. Or like this.

"Fine. If you're so self-absorbed that all you care about is yourself and what you want right now, and you can't think about how your little stunt could affect me, then I guess you're the person I used to always think you were. Enjoy the rest of your day. Lots of other people work in this building—why don't you try one of them for your striptease routine, since it doesn't seem to matter who you fuck right now."

He started to turn back to his computer, but he couldn't help but see the tears in her eyes. He'd said that to hurt her, but now that he had, he felt awful.

He walked back over to Maddie and looked at her. Something weird was definitely going on. Maddie could be a real bitch sometimes, but usually not like this.

He stepped around Maddie and stopped her from opening the door.

"Maddie." He put his hand on her shoulder, and she shook it off. "Hey. What's going on? Is something wrong?"

She threw her head back and crossed her arms.

"No, nothing's wrong. Why would you think something's wrong just because I want to do something fun for once, something adventurous, something spontaneous, something different from normal? Why does something have to be wrong? What if I just wanted a break from regular life, and wanted to live a little? Oh, right, I forgot; your version of living a little is to get Chinese food instead of pizza on a Friday night to go with your home improvement television shows geared toward middle-aged women. Why would I think I could rely on you to be there for me when I needed you?"

She reached for the door again, but again he blocked her.

"Hey. Can we just press the reset button for a second?"

The rage left her eyes, and her whole body deflated.

"Yeah." She bent down to pick up her bag. "Sorry. I won't bother you anymore."

He looked harder at her. Oh shit, he knew what this was about. He felt like the biggest jackass in the world now.

"Your interview. It was today, wasn't it? What happened?" He didn't wait for an answer but wrapped his arms around her. He wasn't sure if she would pull away again, but instead she nestled herself deep into his chest. They stood like that for a while, with him afraid to move, or say anything. When he stroked her hair, she started to sob.

She cried in his arms for a long time. He didn't ask any questions; he barely moved. He just stroked her hair and rubbed her back. Finally, she took a deep breath and pulled away.

"Do you want to talk about it?" he asked.

She shook her head, then nodded. He wasn't sure which one she actually meant, and he was still kind of mad at her for her insults earlier, but he knew he couldn't let her go home alone.

"Okay." He looked around his office and shook his head. "Not here. I have a call later, but I can do it from home." He threw his computer and phone in his bag and pulled his jacket on.

"Here." He took a few tissues from the box on his desk and dabbed at the damp makeup stains on her face. She forced a smile and took the tissues from him.

"How terrible do I look?" she asked.

He touched her cheek.

"You could never look terrible." He handed her another tissue. "But . . . you do look like you've had an awful day."

She wiped her face and dropped the tissue in the trash can. When she looked back up at him, she laughed.

"Your poor shirt. I think I ruined it. I'm sorry."

He looked down at his shirt, which was now mottled by a variety of damp makeup stains. He zipped up his jacket and shook his head.

"No problem. Luckily, it was cold this morning and I wore a jacket that will cover this all up on my way home. And I'm very good at laundry; I bet I can get these stains out."

He started to open his office door, but this time she stopped him.

"Should we not leave your office together? I mean, with the closed door and all, I don't want people to think . . . I don't want to embarrass you or get you in trouble."

He touched her cheek, just for a second.

"Thanks for that." He cleared his throat. "Did you drive here? Do you want to meet me outside?"

She adjusted her bag on her shoulder.

"Yeah, my car's just around the corner. Meet me there in a few minutes?"

He opened the door and went back to his desk.

"See you then." He tried to say it offhand, for the benefit of the people who might be walking by, so it wouldn't seem like this was a big deal or like they'd had some big emotional moment. Then he forced himself to look back down at the papers on his desk and not watch her walk away.

As Maddie walked through the hallway to the stairwell, she prayed the whole time she wouldn't run into anyone who knew her. Plenty of Alexa's coworkers other than Theo had met her, and the last thing she wanted was for one of them to stop her and force her into a conversation with them, when she felt wrung out and humiliated, after the day she'd just had and then what had gone on in Theo's office.

She couldn't tell what part of today was worse: how terrible she'd felt after her interview; Theo rejecting her and trying to button her clothes back up when she'd been convinced he would be thrilled by her little striptease; or her lengthy sobbing fit against Theo's warm chest and beautiful shirt.

And on top of all that, now she felt like an asshole for not thinking of how her little stunt could affect Theo. She really hoped no one had noticed her walk into his office; the last thing she wanted was for him to get in trouble because of her.

When she made it to her car, she put her head in her hands. What an awful day. After the disastrous interview, she'd texted Alexa and asked if she was busy—she'd known Alexa would be able to talk her through this and make her feel better. But Alexa had said she was just about to go into a meeting in SF with her boss, and was it important? Maddie had lied and said it could wait.

Then she'd had the—she now recognized—unhinged thought that what would really make her feel better was some really hot animal sex with Theo on top of his desk. His desk, at City Hall. In the middle of the day, when everyone was at work. What the hell had she been thinking?

She sat up and put her key in the ignition. Why was she sitting here waiting for Theo to come to her car, anyway? She already felt terrible about what she'd done. Seeing him again would just make it worse. She should just drive away, text him she was sorry, and then ignore him for the rest of her life.

She jumped at the knock on her passenger-side window. Theo. Great timing.

"Oh good, you're still here," he said as he got into the car. "I was worried you'd just drive away and leave me here."

She started the car and pulled out of her parking space. This guy was getting to know her far too well.

"I don't know why you'd think I'd do that," she said. He just looked at her and didn't respond.

"Um, do you want to go to my place, or yours?" he asked when they got to the end of the block.

"Yours," she said. Her place was unnaturally clean lately, because he'd come over a few times now, so it wasn't that she needed to clean up for him. It was that she was pretty sure she wanted to abort this whole "telling Theo everything that went wrong today" mission, and just flee back to her own space. He'd managed to get into the car before she'd driven away, but that didn't mean she had to sit around and confess every one of her flaws to Theo of all people. That sounded like a nightmare she'd had before. Maybe she could walk into his place with him and then suddenly remember a client meeting she had later on today and could run out the door without having to talk about any of this.

"I'm ordering pizza," he said, looking up from his phone. "The usual toppings?"

Her stomach rumbled. She hadn't eaten since the coffee and half a muffin she'd forced down early this morning. Maybe she would stay just until the pizza came.

"Yeah," she said. "The usual toppings sound great."

They walked into his apartment, and instead of immediately asking her questions or pulling her into another hug that she didn't think she could handle right now, he dropped his bag and jacket in his living room and kept walking down his long hallway to the kitchen. She followed him, expecting him to pull out his bar cart and make her a fancy drink, like he'd done that first night.

Instead, he walked to a closet in the corner of his kitchen that she'd never noticed, and opened it. Inside, there were many racks full of wine.

"Where did all of that wine come from?" she asked.

He laughed as he scanned the rows of bottles.

"Lots of places. Some were gifts; most were from tipsy purchases on trips up to Napa with my brother." He bent down and pulled a bottle of wine off the second to the bottom shelf. "Here, I think this one works for now." He pulled a corkscrew out of a drawer and opened the bottle with a few quick turns.

He turned and walked back out of the kitchen with the open bottle of wine in one hand, and grabbed two glasses out of a cabinet on his way. Again, she followed him, back to the living room, where he set the bottle on the coffee table and poured wine into both glasses. He sat down on the couch and gestured for her to sit next to him. She sat and felt some of the tension drain from her shoulders.

Theo picked up a glass and handed it to her.

"You don't have to talk to me. If you don't want to, I mean. If you just want to sit here and drink wine and maybe eat some pizza and not talk, we can sit here and drink wine and eat some pizza and not talk. Or I can show you the spreadsheet I made for Alexa's wedding invitations and you can tell me how beautiful it is." He picked up his own glass and took a sip. "But if you do want to talk, at any point tonight—at any point ever—I'm here to listen. I just want you to know that."

She set down her glass on top of a magazine on the coffee table.

"Why are you being so nice to me? I don't deserve any of this. I was the world's biggest bitch today. What you said about me was right: it was completely self-absorbed to go to your office like that. I wasn't thinking of you at all—I was just upset and trying to make myself feel better, and I wanted some attention. That was really shitty of me." She stood up. "I should go. I shouldn't sit here drinking your wine and letting you be nice to me when I don't deserve it."

He glared at her.

"Maddie. Sit down. Please."

She didn't want to sit down. She didn't want him to see her cry, yet again, or have to talk about the interview and why it had made her feel like the biggest asshole in the world.

"Theo, I think I really should just go."

He shook his head.

"Maddie, I'm serious. Stay so we can talk about this. We don't have to talk about why you were upset today, but . . ." He took a deep breath. "We both said some shitty things to each other in my office—I'm really sorry about what I said, by the way—and if we want to keep doing"—he waved his hands in the air—"this, I don't think we can do so if you leave now and we both just feel bad and unsettled and uncomfortable with each other." He shook his head. "Maybe that's what you want; maybe you're ready to be done with this, which . . . if that's the case, just tell me now."

She sat down.

"No, Theo, that's not . . ." She sighed. "That's not what I want. I'm just so humiliated about the whole day today, about what I did, and how I acted, and what you think of me now, and I'm scared to look you in the eye."

He put his arm around her and pulled her into his chest.

"So don't, just yet. Just sit here and drink wine with me."

She was less than half a glass in before she started talking.

"The problem is, I was exactly what they wanted me to be. They brought in clients for me to work with, and I made fun of the clothes they were wearing, and I told them how they needed to reinvent themselves, and I told them all of the stuff that was wrong with them, and I was funny and everyone loved it and I made these women feel terrible, and that's not the kind of person I want to be."

He rubbed the side of her neck with his thumb, and she leaned into the pressure.

"The way I grew up . . ." She stopped herself and looked at him. Did she want to trust Theo with all of this? Oh hell with it, she'd already sobbed her eyes out to him in his office; she might as well. "It was just me and my mom, and she worked hard to get me everything I needed, but we were often right on the edge. Which meant a lot of things, but one of them was Mom always sacrificed her needs for mine. That took me an embarrassingly long time to realize; I used to make fun of her clothes for years when I was a bitchy preteen. And suddenly one day she was preparing for an interview and I asked her what she was going to wear and she said some old out-of-date outfit of hers, and I remembered the new clothes she'd bought me just a few days before, and I realized I couldn't remember the last time she'd bought herself anything new."

She still felt the shame that had washed over her that day.

"My mom used to do the same thing," Theo said. "I don't think I realized until I left for college."

Maddie closed her eyes. A few tears still seeped through.

"I'm glad . . . I'm glad I wasn't the only one." He wiped her tears with a tissue and she smiled. "Anyway, after that, I made it my mission to ensure my mom was well dressed. I even found a sewing machine secondhand and taught myself how to do alterations for her. But it was when I tried to figure out what 'well dressed' meant for her, a woman going to job interviews for all these corporate jobs while she was going through school, I discovered how complicated all this stuff is. There are so many unwritten rules, and if you don't follow them, you're 'not a culture fit.' And of course, it's even harder if you're a woman of color, or you're plus size, or you speak accented English. There's no one to teach this stuff to women who don't already know it."

She glanced up at Theo. How was he taking all this? But he was looking at her with his open, interested expression that she knew by now he couldn't fake.

"Right, white men can show up to important meetings in ripped jeans and hoodies, and people still take them seriously," he said. "I have to wear a suit just for people to even consider taking me seriously."

She nodded.

"Exactly. I think that's one reason I got so excited about doing this show. It would be my opportunity to help women who really need me. But as things started getting more serious, I guess I forgot about all that, and thought about it in terms of what would make good TV, and not what would be something I could be proud of. And today, the old mean girl Maddie came back. I'm just so ashamed of myself and what my mother would think of me." She shook her head. "I'm ashamed of what *I* think of me. I'm ashamed of what you must think of me; you do volunteer work all the time. I'm sure you're so great at it."

He opened his mouth and then closed it. Oh God, what did he want to say? Probably something about how she *should* be ashamed of herself.

"What? Just say it."

He dropped his arm from around her and looked away.

"I do things I'm ashamed of all the time. I don't do this any-more, but I always used to be that guy who would look down on other people for not dressing exactly right, or not knowing the rules for any professional interaction, or for stepping out of line even for a second. I've stopped—for the most part—being an ass-hole to other people about that kind of stuff, but I still get mad at myself when I fuck up anything, as you saw a few weeks ago." He shook his head. "My brother—who has had far more therapy than is good for him—says I blame myself for our dad leaving when we were kids, and that's why I'm such a perfectionist, and it's not healthy to expect everyone else to be one, too. I say I had to grow up really quickly, and I didn't want to make life even harder for my mom, so I learned how to put my head down and get things done, look right, dress right, act right."

Theo was looking straight down at the coffee table. This was clearly hard for him to talk about.

"Which one is it?" she asked him.

He sighed and looked up at her.

"Probably some of both. Ben somehow learned the opposite from what I did, and I'm always in a panic when he tells me about one of his half-cocked plots and I think he's headed for disaster, and yet he's ended up okay so far." He shook his head. "He thinks I'm a walking spreadsheet without a spontaneous bone in my body; I think he's a flighty bro who never plans past the next day. Put the two of us together, and we might make one normal person."

She poured more wine into both of their glasses. He took a sip and laughed.

"When I'm feeling uncharitable, I think Ben's had all that therapy because he loves to find ways to talk about himself, but in reality, he's probably just better at being a person than I am."

She nudged him with her shoulder.

"I think you're pretty great at being a person. Sometimes."

He laughed.

"Sometimes indeed. I don't think that time is right now, though—we were talking about you, and I made it all about me."

She laughed.

"That's okay. It helped. Speaking of a few weeks ago, I'm glad we've managed to have our respective breakdowns at different times so we could calm each other down."

He put his arm around her.

"I promise one thing: I absolutely won't tell you to calm down. I've learned not to do *that* the hard way." She laughed and leaned her head against his chest. "But really, do you just want me to listen, or do you want advice? I can do either one, but I don't want to be that pretentious asshole we both know I can be, who'll butt in with advice when it's not necessary or wanted."

Apparently, tonight they were both admitting their flaws to each other. She smiled at him.

"Thanks for asking that. Advice is okay, I think. Just, be gentle?"

The doorbell rang, and he stood up.

"I promise."

When he came back with the pizza, she looked up at him.

"Okay." She took a deep breath. "Do you have advice for me now?"

He nodded, but he looked worried.

"Don't worry," she said. "I'm not going to yell at you and try to storm out again, I promise. You're stuck with me for the rest of the night, no matter what you say."

He laughed, just as she'd meant him to.

"Okay. First, what are the next steps in the interview process?"

She'd almost forgotten to ask that but had done it right at the end, when all she wanted to do was flee from the building.

"This time it was just a panel from the station who watched us; if I get through to the next one, it'll be filmed."

He nodded.

"Great. Then, if you get through to the next round, do everything differently. Help these women in a way that will make you feel proud of yourself, show the people at the studio how fantastic you are at making your clients feel good about themselves, show everyone involved that you don't have to be mean and mocking in order to make a great show. Be the black female Tim Gunn!"

Maddie laughed at Theo's last line and then sighed.

"That all sounds great, but what if they hate that? What if they want the funny, bitchy mean girl Maddie they saw today, and not . . ."

He ran his fingers through her hair.

"Not the warm, kind, encouraging Maddie I saw at the bridal store? That seems like the real Maddie."

She shrugged.

"Both are the real Maddie, but it's a lot easier to show the other Maddie to the world. The snarky Maddie has a lot more armor." Easier to show the other Maddie to everyone, and a hell of a lot less scary. Very few people saw the emotional, soft-bellied Maddie she'd shown at the bridal salon . . . and to Theo today. "Plus, most people only like one side of me, not both."

He pulled her against him.

"I like both sides of you. I bet other people will as well. Think about it?"

Theo had surprised her a lot this summer, but never as much as he had this afternoon, with the amount of respect he'd shown her and her job, even after her meltdown.

Now that she thought about it, she wasn't sure if she believed it. What did he really think about her—the kind, thoughtful things he was saying now, or the stuff he'd said in his office about how self-absorbed she was? Could she really trust him with her real self? She had no idea, but she did know talking to him like this was

starting to make her feel way too vulnerable. She needed to change
the subject.

"Okay. I'll think about it." She reached for the remote control.
"Can we watch some British people bake now?"

He took the remote control from her and put it back down on
the coffee table.

"I have a better idea." He stood and pulled her up with one
hand. What was he up to? He had a sly look on his face.

"Come here." He put his hands on her hips, and steered her to
the corner of the room. With one hand, he swept the orderly piles
of books, papers, and plants off his desk, and then he picked her up
and set her on top of it.

"Theo!" She looked at the disorder on the floor and grinned
widely. "I didn't know you had it in you."

He pushed her skirt up around her hips and moved himself in
between her legs. This was better than an emotional conversation
any day.

"Look, you wanted sex on my desk, I'm going to give you sex
on my desk. Sure, we're swapping one desk for another, and this
one isn't quite as risky, but . . ."

She leaned forward and pulled his belt off and dropped it on
the floor.

"No, it's even better. There was way more stuff on this desk
than your one at work. Do you know how hot it was to see you
sweep everything off this onto the floor?" She pulled open his
pants. "So, so fucking hot."

He hooked his thumbs around her underwear and pulled it off
her. See, she'd been right. Sex was just what she needed to get over
today.

"Do you know what's going to be even hotter than that?" he asked her.

She shook her head, her fist wrapped around his cock.

"No, tell me."

He pushed her legs open wider and slid his fingers inside her.

"It's going to be so hot when I fuck you right now. With all your clothes on, and your nipples hard, and your pussy so wet for me." He pulled a condom out of his desk drawer and rolled it on. "How much do you want this right now, Maddie?"

She looked him in the eyes. He was intent on her, with that serious look on his face she'd seen there before, often when he was deep into work. She loved it when he directed that look to her.

"I want it so much. I want you so much," she said.

He brushed her hair off her face and stroked her cheek with his thumb. The look in his eyes was so tender, so open, it made tears spring to her eyes. She pulled him toward her and kissed him. All of her emotions from the past few hours came out in that kiss: her anxiety, her relief, her gratitude, her joy. He kissed her back with the same power and warmth she gave to him. She was almost relieved when the kiss ended.

He finally drove into her, and she gasped. She wrapped her legs around his to hold on to him, and she felt his strong arms around her, holding her up, as they moved back and forth against each other. At first they went slowly, as they both stared at each other, neither of them smiling. He leaned forward and kissed her again, this time harder, and suddenly they moved together faster and faster. He held her tightly with one arm and reached in between the two of them so he could rub his thumb against the exact place he knew would put her over the edge.

She bit his shoulder as she came, and then he pounded his

release into her. She rested her head against his chest as she tried to catch her breath, and for some stupid reason fought back tears.

"Well." He kissed her hair. "That was even better than I fantasized it would be."

She kissed his collarbone. It had been the best sex they'd ever had; they both knew that. She couldn't say that, though. She'd said too much today already. Instead, she sat up and grinned at him.

"If I had known this was what happened when I called you conservative, I would have done that weeks ago."

He laughed and tossed her onto the couch.

Chapter Thirteen

THEO WALKED INTO A NEW BAR IN OAKLAND AND SCANNED THE crowded room. Ah, there was his brother, perched at the bar, already in deep conversation with the bartender. He slid onto the empty stool next to Ben.

"Hey," Ben said. "Another Manhattan for my brother here, please, Dahlia."

The bartender winked at Ben.

"Coming right up."

Theo shook his head as she walked over to grab bourbon off the shelf.

"Why do bartenders love you so much? I don't understand it."

Ben grinned.

"I tip well, I ask good questions, and I sympathize with them when other people are being assholes. It gets me great service and interesting conversation." Ben nodded in the direction of the bartender. "I think you'll like this drink; they've got some great bourbons here."

The bartender set Theo's drink in front of him and smiled at both of them before going to the other side of the bar.

Theo lifted his drink and took a sip.

"You're right: this is great." He looked around at the rest of the bar. "You live in San Francisco. I can't believe you've been to a new bar in Oakland before I have."

Ben plucked the cherry out of Theo's drink and ate it.

"Well, *I* can't believe I got my brother to come out for a drink. I haven't seen you since, like, mid-June, and it's almost August!"

Ben had tried to get him to come out a few times in the past month, but one night he'd been working late, and the other two nights he'd been with Maddie.

"Work has been crazy," he said. "I'm working with this ballot initiative campaign, and everything is about to heat up in September for it, so we're doing a ton of planning for—"

"Yeah, yeah, the rally, I know, you told me about it," Ben said. "But you and I both know you're not at work every damn time I text you at night. What's going on with that girl?"

Theo shrugged.

"Who, Maddie? It's no big deal. We're just having sex sometimes, that's all. I've been too busy this summer with work for anything else."

Theo knew that was a lie, but he definitely wasn't ready to tell his brother the truth. Things between him and Maddie had been a lot more than just sex for a while now. After he'd confessed his faults to her, and she'd cried on his chest, it had felt like their relationship had become different. Deeper. More real.

At least, it had felt like that to him. He didn't really know how she felt. Sometimes, when they laughed together, or when they curled up on the couch in easy silence for hours, or when she gave him advice and listened to his, he thought she must feel the same way he did.

But when she snapped back at him like she had in his office, or like now, when he hadn't heard from her for a few days, he had no idea what she thought or felt. Maybe she was looking forward to the wedding so this whole thing could be over. He was starting to dread it.

Ben shrugged.

"Must be nice. I never manage to find women who just want me for sex. Either they want too much of me, or they don't want me at all." He reached into his pocket. "Actually, speaking of—do you want this?"

He handed Theo an envelope. Theo opened it to find a gift certificate to one of the hot restaurants in San Francisco, for an amount that made Theo's eyes get big.

"Of course I want this, but why don't you want it?"

Ben sighed.

"I got it from work as a reward for a project I just finished, and they even made a reservation for me, since that place is impossible to get reservations for." He made a face. "The problem is that I had a thing with one of the waitresses there, and . . . it didn't end so well. And I obviously can't tell my boss to take it back and get me into a different restaurant. But someone should get something out of this."

Theo slid the gift certificate into his messenger bag.

"That is such a Ben problem, and I'll happily benefit from it. When's the reservation for?"

He hoped Maddie would be able to go. If she couldn't . . . well, he'd worry about that later.

"In a few weeks, I think? I don't know. I wrote down the date on the envelope."

When Ben went to the bathroom, Theo texted Maddie.

My brother got a gift card and reservation at Fields & Bone but he can't use it so he gave it to me. Want to go?

What if she said no? Or worse, didn't even respond?

He'd at least know how she felt.

Maybe he didn't want to know how she felt after all.

Seriously? Yes! That place is impossible to get into and it's supposed to be really good. Why can't your brother go?

Theo grinned.

Oh, wait until you hear this reason

He waved at Ben's bartender buddy so he could order them more drinks.

Maddie's phone rang as she was washing dishes. She didn't even have to look to know who it was.

"Hey, Mom," she said. "You're on speaker. I'm washing dishes."

"Hey, girl," her mom said. "I haven't heard from you for days. How are things? I was about to call the highway patrol!"

Maddie made herself laugh. Usually, when Maddie hadn't

talked to her mom for a few days, it was just because life got in the way for one or both of them. But this time Maddie had been actively avoiding talking to her mom, which she'd felt guilty about. She'd texted her the day after the interview to tell her it had gone okay but not great, and she knew her mom would want details. And the details would disappoint her.

She'd tried to stop thinking about the interview, ever since the day it happened. That afternoon and evening with Theo had been a little too soul baring for her taste, so she'd avoided him for a while afterward, too. But when he texted about his brother's woman issues and how they were getting a free fancy meal out of the deal, everything seemed light and jokey again between the two of them. Thank goodness, especially since Alexa had taken her whole "delegate things to your wedding party!" to heart, and had assigned her and Theo to go together to check out some DJ.

"I texted you, didn't I?" Maddie said to her mom as she rinsed out her coffee cup from that morning. "Things are okay, just busy. How are you? Anything fun going on at work? How are Kathryn and Michelle? Did you guys end up going out to dinner this weekend?"

Sometimes changing the subject away from herself worked to get her mom to move from the topic Maddie didn't want to talk about.

"We did. It was fun. So, tell me about the interview at the station. What happened?"

And sometimes it didn't.

Maddie turned off the water and dried her hands. She couldn't avoid this conversation forever.

"I think they really liked me. But . . ." she sighed. "You know that part in makeover shows where they tell the person being made over everything wrong with them? I was really good at that. Too good. I didn't like myself. I felt pretty bad afterward."

Her mom sighed, too.

"So you were too much of a bitch, huh? I was afraid of that."

Maddie laughed out loud.

"Thanks for putting it so bluntly, Mom!" Theo had been a lot more tactful, but she supposed he'd said more or less the same thing. "But yeah, that was exactly the problem. And I made the woman I was working with feel terrible, which I think probably makes for good TV. From the way the people with the station acted, I think they think so, too, but it wouldn't make me sleep well at night." She moved out of the kitchen and sat down on her couch. "I was afraid to tell you about this. I didn't want you to . . ."

Her mom laughed.

"What, think less of you? Madeleine, please, I know you far too well for that. After all those times you asked me if I was really leaving the house like that?"

Maddie put her head in her hands.

"Oh God, I've always been this much of a bitch."

Her mom's voice softened.

"No, that's not what I meant. You can take things too far sometimes, it's true. But you've also always had a good heart, and you manage to correct yourself. The older you get, the faster you get at doing it."

Maddie put her legs up on the couch and hugged her knees into her chest.

"I'm going to try—they called me the other day and said they want me to come back in for an official filmed mock episode. That'll be in a few weeks."

The filmed audition was going to be the same day as her dinner with Theo, and she kept going back and forth about whether or not to cancel dinner. On the one hand, she might just want to go home and crawl into a hole and not have to deal with Theo or anyone else after the audition. On the other hand, their texts about dinner had made things feel normal between the two of them again, and she didn't want to ruin that.

"Are you nervous about the audition?" her mom asked.

Maddie stared into the kitchen at the glass of wine she'd left in there. Maybe this time she could actually move it with her mind. She closed her eyes and thought hard.

Nope.

"Oh, I'm definitely nervous, but I'm trying not to think too much about it for now. I need to forget about the cameras and try to remember who I am and why I wanted to do this in the first place. We'll see if I manage to do that." She sighed. "Who knows, maybe they only like Maddie the bitch. Most people do."

Her mom clicked her tongue.

"You're lovable any way you want to be. Anyone would be lucky to have you, and if they don't realize that, you don't want them anyway."

Maddie wiped her eyes with the bottom of her shirt.

"I'm lucky to have you, you know."

Her mom cleared her throat.

"Likewise. Now. How are the plans for Alexa's wedding going? Have you found bridesmaids dresses? Is she ready to kill her mom yet?"

Maddie laughed.

"We did find bridesmaids dresses; Alexa and I found them just this weekend, actually. It helps that it's just me and Olivia wearing

them and we look good in the same colors. I know we're all relieved that part is done. And no, Alexa doesn't want to kill her
mom yet but . . . we'll see how the next two months go."

"That sounds great," her mom said. "I'm excited the wedding
is so soon. I can't wait to meet Theo, and see Olivia again and
Alexa in her wedding dress. However, I hope you're not too busy
with this whole job interview and bridesmaid thing to help your
mother find a dress for this wedding. I have no idea what *I'm* going
to wear!"

Maddie laughed.

"Don't worry, Mom. I'm on it."

Chapter Fourteen

MADDIE PULLED A TISSUE OUT OF HER BLAZER POCKET AND WIPED
her eyes after releasing Dominique from a hug.

"You look fantastic," she said.

Dominique stared at herself in the mirror.

"I love it, I really do. I thought I was going to come here and
you were going to put me in a bunch of, like, pale pink cardigans,
or whatever, but this just looks like the business lady version
of me."

Maddie forced herself not to cry again.

"That's just what I wanted you to look like," she said.

"CUT!"

Maddie and Dominique both turned around to the camera-
man. Weird as it was, Maddie had forgotten they were being
filmed. She'd talked to Dominique like she was back in her own
studio with any client. No. Like she was with a friend.

"Thank you both." Allen, the producer, came on set and nodded at them. "Dominique, Talia here will show you back to your dressing room. Maddie, you can follow me."

Maddie said good-bye to Dominique and pressed her card into her hand before following Allen down the hall. She hadn't intended to cry today, but she was glad she'd put on waterproof mascara, just in case. She was surprised at how emotional the audition had made her feel; Dominique's story and worries and needs had affected Maddie more than she'd expected them to.

She turned to smile at the producer walking her down the hall. She couldn't tell from his demeanor if he'd liked her audition or not, or if he liked how different she'd been from the last time. She just wanted to whisper, "Blink twice if you thought it was good!" at him, but somehow she didn't think that was a wise idea.

He led her back to her dressing room and shook her hand.

"Maddie, it's been a pleasure. Not sure exactly when we'll be making decisions, but you should hear from us within a few weeks."

She tried to make her smile as confident as she could.

"Thanks so much, Allen. I look forward to hearing from you."

She waited until she got into her car before calling Theo. He picked up right away.

"Maddie. How'd it go?"

She loved that he knew exactly why she was calling.

"I feel a lot better about this than I did the last one, that's for sure. No matter what happens, I'm proud of what I did in there."

She heard the sound of his office door closing and thanked him mentally for that.

"Oh, Maddie, I'm so glad," he said. "I can't wait to hear the details and celebrate tonight."

She was glad she hadn't canceled dinner with him tonight. It would be good to relax and tell him all about it.

"Let's not get too far ahead of ourselves," she said. "I have no idea if I got the job, but at least I know I gave it my best shot."

"That's definitely something to celebrate. Remember, the reservation is at seven thirty. Since you're already in the city, are you going to meet me there?"

That would make the most sense, but no one had ever accused her of being a person who made sense.

"No, I want to go home and change first. My 'going out to a fun new restaurant' outfits and my 'interview for a dream job' outfits are in two very different categories. But I'll meet you at your house after I change and we can go together?"

"See you then."

Maddie turned her car on, waited for her Bluetooth to connect, and then called her mom.

"Hey, Mom! I think it went well!"

She talked to her mom, and then Alexa, the whole way back across the Bay Bridge.

Theo had planned to wear the same thing to work as he did out to dinner, but Maddie and her whole outfit categories thing had shamed him into coming home in time to change before dinner. If he was evaluating her categories correctly, she'd be most likely to wear a dress or a jumpsuit tonight. He'd seen her admire his favorite blazer in the past—the tweed one with the elbow patches—so he switched to dark jeans, took off his tie, and slipped the blazer on, just in time for her to ring his doorbell.

He padded down the hallway and opened the door.

"You know, you have a key now. You can just let yourself in."

She shrugged as she walked in. Yep, a flowy pink dress with a jean jacket.

"I don't want to assume that just because I have a key I can use it whenever I want."

He leaned down and kissed her.

"You can definitely use it if we already had plans for you to come over, which we did in this instance. Or obviously in any emergency."

She rolled her eyes.

"Okay, sure, I anticipate a lot of 'I need to get into Theo's apartment or else the dinosaur on the loose might capture me' emergencies. Thanks for letting me know."

He smacked her butt lightly and she grinned.

"I see we've been watching *Jurassic Park* again."

She laughed as he slipped his shoes on.

"You caught me. It was on TV the other night, and I couldn't not watch when I flipped channels."

He grabbed his keys and they walked out to his car.

"This place had better be good; it takes a lot to get me to drive across the bridge on a weeknight."

She put her seat belt on and turned the radio from NPR to music.

"If it's terrible, we'll both blame Ben."

He nodded.

"Excellent call. Okay, so tell me everything about the audition. I'm so glad you're happy about how this one went."

She turned to him with a smile. When she smiled like that, she was so stunning he could hardly believe it.

"I really am. I'm not going to lie: it was scary to put myself out there like that—it was a lot easier the first time, when I managed to not think of them as real people. This time, I got so emotional. I even started crying at the end, which I felt weird about, but then, so did the woman I was working with. But when I saw the look on her face, and the way she thanked me afterward, I felt like what I said to her made a difference." She laughed. "Is this how you and Alexa feel all the time? Now I get why you both love your jobs."

He put his hand on hers.

"Not all the time, but those magic times when it does happen . . . it's an incredible feeling. I know exactly what you mean."

She squeezed his hand.

"I know you do. Thanks for helping me get there."

He hadn't been prepared for her to thank him. Or for how incredible that would make *him* feel.

"No thanks needed. This was all you."

She leaned over and kissed him on the cheek.

"Well, you helped me figure out how to be the best of me—let's put it that way."

Maddie did that for him, too, and had since the very beginning, when she'd told him what a pompous jerk he could be.

Granted, it had taken him a while to admit that, but still.

"I'm glad I could help," he said.

As they walked into the restaurant, he wondered if Maddie realized this was the first time they'd been out like this. Up to this point, their entire relationship—or whatever someone might call it—had occurred in private. They'd hung out and talked and had sex and watched TV and eaten lots of food and had more sex, but all that had happened either at his place or hers. But he'd missed the feeling of walking into a restaurant, or a party, or just down the street, with the woman he was with by his side.

He looked down at the menu once they were at their table.

"Okay, I've been dying to go to this place, and I'm very thankful my little brother got us in here, but this is the issue I always have with restaurants like this: why do the menus all have to be so minimalist? Like 'squid, lemon, herbs, beans'—that's a list of ingredients, not a dish! How is it cooked? Deep fried? Roasted? Stewed together? No one knows!"

Maddie looked at the menu and laughed.

"Okay, but I don't need to know much more than 'burrata, bread, tomatoes' to know that I want that. It's like a deconstructed pizza!"

They ordered the squid, and the burrata, and a bunch of other things. Once they were halfway into a bottle of champagne, they found humor in everything around them. Or maybe he just got that way around Maddie these days.

"Don't forget, Alexa assigned us the job to figure out the signature cocktail for the wedding," Maddie said. "Who did you hire to be the bartender again?"

Theo laughed.

"One of the many bartenders my brother knows. I'll ask her what she thinks, and hopefully we'll get some taste tests out of this."

They were halfway through their appetizers when Maddie looked across the room, jumped, and turned her whole body around to face the back of the restaurant.

"It's Alexa!" Why she whispered in that loud hiss to him, he had no idea; the place was so noisy no one could hear anyone past their own table. "She's over at the bar! What should we do? If I get up and go to the bathroom, it might draw her attention to me. But

what if she's waiting for a table? How can we get out of here without her seeing us?"

Theo turned from Maddie to look over at the bar at the entrance of the restaurant. What was Alexa doing here? She hadn't
said anything about going to San Francisco tonight. Well, maybe
Drew had surprised her.

Wait. He saw a black woman at the bar, wearing a red floral
dress like one Alexa would wear, but . . .

"That's not Alexa," he said to Maddie. "Not all short black
women look alike, Madeleine."

She glared at him and shook her head.

"I know that, asshole, but I also know how to recognize my best
friend of more than twenty years."

He kept eating the burrata and grilled bread appetizer.

"If you say so, but also, I promise you, Alexa does not have a
tattoo on her forearm, and that woman does." He narrowed his
eyes. "Well, that's either a tattoo or a big scar—I can't quite tell
from here, but either way, unless Alexa has some great makeup
that she's been using every day on her arm, that's not her."

Maddie turned back around and peered at the bar from behind
the champagne bottle.

"Oh." She sat up straight and took a gulp of champagne.
"You're right. That isn't Alexa."

He took another bite of the gooey cheese. It had suddenly stopped
tasting as good.

She scooped up the rest of the burrata and put it on her plate.

"You have to admit, she looks a lot like Alexa. Same height,
same hair, same skin color, and she has a dress just that color. Can
you blame me for freaking out?"

He dropped his fork.

"Yeah, actually, I can. You were about three seconds from hiding under the table for the rest of dinner. What would you have done if that had actually been Alexa? Run to the bathroom and just stayed there all night? Would it be so bad if Alexa saw us here together?"

Come to think of it, why had one of her conditions from the beginning been that they never go out anywhere? Was this not about Alexa, but about something else altogether? Was she embarrassed to be with him?

She put down the piece of cheese-covered bread she'd been about to put in her mouth.

"Yes, of course it would be so bad if Alexa saw us here together. Come on now, we talked about this months ago. You know Alexa almost as well as I do; you know how she'd react. Maybe you want to deal with her acting like we're meant for each other and then the fallout when we tell her that isn't the case, but I sure as hell don't."

Right. *When we tell her that isn't the case.* He guessed that answered the question of how Maddie felt about him. And about them.

How the hell had he gotten this involved with and—fine, he'd admit it to himself at least—attached to Maddie?

"Like you said, you know her better than I do," he said when he finally looked up at her. "It just sort of makes me feel like I'm your dirty little secret, that's all."

He regretted that as soon as he'd said it. He didn't need her pity compliments. And he definitely didn't want her to know he'd gotten way too serious about all this.

He made himself laugh like he meant it and reached for his glass of champagne.

"On the other hand . . . being someone's dirty little secret is kind of fun."

Maddie didn't trust that smile. She could tell he was pissed; he was looking everywhere in the restaurant instead of at her.

"Grilled squid with citrus and flageolet beans," a waiter said, as he laid a plate down in the middle of the table. Theo mouthed "GRILLED" at her, and she looked down at her lap so she wouldn't laugh.

When the waiter walked away, Theo shook his head.

"I don't understand why they couldn't tell us from the beginning that this squid was grilled."

He was smiling, but she didn't think he'd recovered that quickly from the hurt she'd seen in his eyes. But just like he always did, he'd jumped to the worst possible reason for her reaction to Not Alexa. That didn't really put her in the mood to reassure him.

She wasn't lying to him, but she wasn't quite telling the truth, either, about why she didn't want to tell Alexa, or anyone else, about them. But she didn't know if she could explain it in words Theo would understand. Or if she even wanted to.

If she told Alexa, or her mom, or anyone else—it would change everything. This whole thing with him this summer had been so perfect. Even keeping the secret had turned out to be surprisingly fun. It felt like their own private thing, where they didn't have to take each other as dates to things, or introduce each other to family and friends, or go out to dinner and drinks and parties and all that nonsense. It was just the two of them, without all the pretense that had gone into every other relationship she'd ever had. Just Maddie and Theo, being comfortable together. Sitting on the couch, making each other laugh, eating food they regretted later, talking about things that mattered to them. If she told people, it would ruin all of that. It would turn what they had, what they'd been doing, into something else, something she didn't want. It would ruin everything.

She took a bite of the squid.

"No matter what the menu said about the squid, this is fantastic, and you know it."

He picked up his fork.

"I haven't even tried it yet. Give a man a second to take a bite!"

He made a face at her as he put the piece of squid in his mouth, and she relaxed a little. Maybe everything would be okay, and they'd go back to normal.

"Fine, now you're right. This is amazing."

She speared the tentacles with her fork and dangled them in the air. They both giggled like they were five years old.

The waitress came by and brought two more of their complicated-sounding but delicious-looking dishes to their table. They spent the rest of dinner speculating on which one of the waitresses was Ben's ex, and loudly giggling whenever one of the prime suspects approached their table.

On the drive back across the bridge, Theo started talking about his big rally the following week and stopped himself.

"Sorry, I've been boring your ears off about this for months. I'll stop now. I bet you're glad that after next week you'll never have to listen to me talking about this rally again."

He'd never bored her when he talked about the rally. She didn't know if he'd changed from the pedantic mansplainer she always thought he was, or if he was never that person in the first place. He just seemed passionate, or caring, or worried, or frustrated, or excited, sometimes at the same time.

"It's okay, you can keep talking about it. I don't mind. You've certainly listened to me talk for hours." She pulled out her phone and checked her calendar. "Wait, speaking of—it's next Thursday, right? What time?"

He glanced over at her with a questioning look on his face.

"Two in the afternoon. Why?"

Oh good, she didn't have any clients scheduled yet that afternoon.

"Like you said, you've been talking about this rally all summer; now I feel like I'll be missing something if I don't come. Alexa's always trying to get me to come to more events you guys do anyway, and I haven't been to anything since Black History Month. And I'm a great woo girl. I cheer very loudly."

The lights were bright on the bridge, bright enough for her to see the genuine smile on his face.

"You? A woo girl? I can't picture that."

She put a look of mock outrage on her face.

"Hey, I can woo with the best of them!"

He laughed.

"Yeah," he said. "Come to the rally. Cheer us on and be a woo girl. I can't wait to see this."

She put her hand on top of his and squeezed.

Chapter Fifteen

BY SEVEN A.M. ON THE DAY OF THE RALLY, THEO WAS IN THE OFFICE, dressed in his favorite gray suit and pin-striped shirt, and with an enormous cup of coffee. The governor, five mayors, and seven state representatives would be there today, all with their accompanying staffs and newspapers from their various cities and constituencies. All he wanted for the day was good press for the campaign and good press for his boss. Maybe not in that order.

He was really glad Maddie was coming today, even though she'd be there to see what a stress case he was on days like this. He'd worked so hard on this, and she'd listened to him talk about it for months; it would be great to have her there to see it all happen.

He'd just gotten off the phone with Sybil for the second time that morning when Alexa stopped by his office.

"How's it going? Are you sure you don't need me to come to the rally? I'm on my way to the bakery around the corner. Do you need anything? Other than more coffee, obviously."

He picked up his cup to see how much was there. Yes, he absolutely needed more coffee.

"You're an angel, thank you. One of their chocolate chip cookies—you know I love those. And no, you don't have to come. I think it's all under control, but thank you for the offer. I'm sure I'll send you many frantic texts later this afternoon."

She grinned.

"I'll be happy to answer them, just like you always answer mine. I can't wait to hear how it all goes."

Alexa would hold down the fort in the office, while Theo, the mayor, and a handful of other staffers would be at the rally. Theo wondered if Maddie knew Alexa wouldn't be at the rally when she'd said she'd come. He had no idea. He wished he did.

Maddie kept saying Alexa would flip out and get too excited and want them to live happily ever after, and be super upset when they ended things, but Alexa had dealt with it fine when he and Maddie had quietly hated each other for years; she'd deal with it fine when they stopped sleeping together after the wedding and—most likely—went back to avoiding each other.

He stared at his email box without seeing it. Maddie had somehow become one of the people he went to first about things he was struggling with, or happy about, or just needed to vent about. He didn't want that to end.

And she'd certainly reached out to him for advice a lot recently, and had seemed to value what he said. She'd seemed to value *him*. Were they really going to go back to being two people who occasionally saw each other at Alexa's parties and nothing else?

Apparently, that's what she wanted.

His phone rang again and he snapped back to reality. Why was he thinking about Maddie right now? His kickoff was in four hours and counting.

Two hours later, he was at the school, helping the campaign staff set up. It was too early for any of the elected officials or other speakers to arrive, and none of the press would likely be here for at least another hour at the earliest, so he was trying to use up his nervous energy. Thank God for the interns—they'd managed to deal with the overly complicated mechanisms to hang up the banners with ease, so he and the other more senior staff were left to do the important tasks of setting folding chairs in a row and testing the microphones.

Finally, people started arriving: his assistant delivered the mayor, reporters trickled in and set up all their equipment, and all the parents who were speaking arrived within minutes of one another, thankfully. As he was checking in with one of the fathers who had seemed the most nervous about today, he saw a familiar movement out of the corner of his eye and turned.

Maddie was here early. Yep, there was that hair toss of hers again. For so long he'd thought that hair toss was so affected, until he realized how much she hated her hair in her face. She pushed her hair back even when it was just the two of them on his couch watching TV, whenever a breeze from the window drifted through the room. Why she almost never just put it up in a ponytail he had no idea.

He wanted to go over to Maddie right away, but he saw the reporter from the *L.A. Times* arrive. She was one of the best political reporters out there, so it was both great and terrifying that she was at the rally today. Great because it seemed like the *L.A. Times* was really paying attention to this, and terrifying because he knew that meant everything had to run like clockwork.

"Hi, Theo," she said. "Looking like you'll get a good turnout today. I heard that there might be some protests during the event; how worried are you about that?"

Good thing he'd already been on guard before he even said hi.

"Hi, Mallory, glad to see you here. We welcome lively political debate, and we're glad that there's going to be a great turnout of Californians to find out more about the issue of universal pre-K. As with any major political issue, we imagine there will be protestors, but this is Berkeley: we have a long, proud history of protest here. We just hope that the press will be sure to cover the issues as well as the protest."

She smirked at him.

"We'll be sure to do that—thanks for the advice."

He smirked back.

"Always a pleasure. Hope to talk to you again soon."

Finally, he went over to Maddie.

"Hey," he said. He didn't know if he was allowed to give her a hug with all these people around, so he just smiled at her. "Thanks for coming."

"Hey, yourself," she said. "Who were you just talking to? She looks scary."

He laughed.

"Oh, she's scary, all right. She's a reporter for the *L.A. Times*, and she's very good at what she does, which means now I have to warn everyone that she's here."

Maddie looked around at the people starting to fill up the seats, the reporters and photographers all setting up, and the colorfully decorated stage, with the campaign signs at just the perfect level for the cameras to get them.

"It looks like you're on track to be great already. But you're busy. I don't want to keep you. Is Alexa here yet?"

So she didn't know Alexa wasn't coming.

"No, she's staying back at City Hall to keep track of everything else."

He couldn't tell whether the look on her face was surprise, or relief, or something else.

"Oh. Okay. Well, I'll be right here. Let me know if you need an extra hand for anything."

He touched her arm.

"Thanks. I will. Have you—"

"Theo?" He turned, to find one of the campaign interns at his elbow. "The mayor sent me to find you. He says he can't find his talking points?"

Theo shook his head.

"I was waiting for this. I brought extra copies. I'll be right there." He turned back to Maddie. "I have to run, and I'll probably be running around all through this, but thanks again for coming."

Maddie clasped his hand for a second.

"Of course. See you later."

The next thirty minutes were frantic, as that time before an event like this always was. He ran back and forth from the mayor to the press to the families to the mayor to the governor to the campaign staff, and finally back to the mayor right before it was go time.

"I'll be in the back, watching and taking some pictures for social media. Mimi from the campaign is in charge of getting everyone on and off the stage at the right times, but if anything goes wrong, I'll be right there."

His boss waved him off.

"You have that anxious look on your face, Theo!" He turned to the governor, being briefed by Sybil. "Does *your* staff always have that anxious look on their faces when they're talking to *you* before you go on stage?" He and the governor both laughed like he'd said something hilarious. Theo and Sybil just sighed.

Theo walked back out to the schoolyard and took a deep breath. Everything was tentatively looking good. There were so many people, they'd had to run more folding chairs over from City Hall, which was great, and there was lots of press to witness that, which was even better. He looked for Maddie in the crowd and found her: a few rows from the back, on a seat along the center aisle. She waved and smiled at him, and he smiled back.

The local high school jazz band kicked into gear, and the crowd cheered for them, and then again for the politicians who all came out to the music. Some of them—oh God, including his boss—were dancing. He made a note to tell his boss, yet again, to never dance in public.

The speeches started: his boss went first, which was one of the benefits of this being on his home turf, and he introduced one of the parent speakers. It was the one Theo had been the most nervous about, but she drew a huge round of applause. Theo let out a deep breath for what felt like the first time in weeks.

Just as one of the state representatives started to speak, he heard the protests start. Everything had been going too well.

At first, it was just indeterminate yelling, but eventually he could make out some "Not MY tax dollars" and "Don't pollute our schools!" chants. So uncreative. The protestors from the left could always at least rhyme.

He could tell Mimi had done what they'd talked about in

advance, and cranked up the sound on the microphones, because everyone on their side suddenly got a lot louder and almost drowned out the protestors.

The protestors kept chanting, but the police kept them a few yards back from the last row of seats. Thank goodness most of the reporters were still looking at the stage and taking notes. Granted, a bunch of the photographers had turned around and were shooting pictures of the protestors, but he'd expected that.

Theo heard a commotion behind him, a shout, cheering, and more shouting. He turned around to see a cop on the ground, and protestors, now with masks on, running toward the seats as they waved their big wooden sticks that had moments ago held protest signs.

One of the masked protestors was running toward him, maybe to attack the politicians, maybe to attack the crowd—he didn't know which one. If he charged at the crowd, Maddie was right there in the middle. And Theo couldn't get to her in time. He spun back around.

"Maddie!" Theo yelled. "Watch out!"

She jumped up, turned around, and tripped the guy running toward her. She grinned at him, and he grinned back. Until he saw the look of panic wash over her face. She pointed and started to run toward him.

"Theo! Oh no, Theo!"

And then everything went black.

Maddie screamed. She raced toward Theo, lying still on the ground, and in the process knocked over the protestor in her way, who was just getting back to his feet. She'd tried to warn Theo, but she'd clearly done it in the stupidest way possible. He'd said, "Watch out," to her—why didn't she just repeat him, or point, or do anything but say, "Oh no!" What was that supposed to communicate to him? Definitely not that someone was about to hit him over the head with a two-by-four.

She got to him just as the medic did.

"Theo? Theo, are you okay?" She knew she wasn't supposed to shake him, but she now understood why people always did that when someone was unconscious. Anything to try to make them wake up, sit up, smile, tell you everything was going to be okay. Instead of shaking him, she reached for his hand and squeezed. He didn't squeeze back.

She was worried that the medic would make her let go of his hand, but he just reached for Theo's other hand to take his pulse.

A photographer came over and tried to take a photo of Theo, lying there on the ground, and she jumped to her feet to block him.

"I swear to fucking God, if you try to take a picture of him like this, I will destroy every camera you've ever owned."

The man tried to stare her down. Oh please, she was the mother-fucking queen of the stare down. She pushed his camera out of the way again, as he tried to move it around her to get a picture of Theo.

"Have some fucking decency," she hissed. Two police officers walked over to them, and the photographer turned away. Maddie knelt back down next to Theo and watched the medic working over him.

"Is he going to be okay?" she asked. She tried to keep silent, but she couldn't help it. She needed to know.

The guy didn't answer at first and kept working on Theo, but he finally looked up and nodded, though he wasn't smiling.

"Vital signs are okay, but I can't tell you anything for sure. Stay with him. Someone will be back."

Like she would do anything other than stay with him. She stared at him after the medic left, as she held tightly to his hand, like doing that would make some of the strength seep out of her body and into his. She watched his chest go up and down and was a little reassured by his regular breathing. But his eyes were still closed and his hands were still slack inside of hers.

Please be okay, please be okay, please be okay, please be okay. She chanted it over and over in her mind, like a mantra or a prayer.

After what felt like forever, the medic was back, and this time he had two other people and a stretcher with him.

"Ma'am, we're going to need you to let go of his hands. I'm sorry." She forced herself to let go of him and stood up.

"Where are you taking him? He's Theo Stephens; he works for the Berkeley mayor. I need to come with you."

They all shook their heads in unison as they put the stretcher down where she'd been kneeling.

"You can't come in the ambulance, but you can meet us at the hospital."

Maddie finally looked up from Theo, for the first time since she'd come running over to him. It felt like hours had passed, but it had probably only been five or so minutes. The protestors were all in handcuffs, way back against the fence, and there was only one other person being worked over by the medics. She looked up toward the stage and got a shock: the politicians were still talking. And people were just sitting there, listening to them, like nothing was wrong, like Theo wasn't lying here on the ground. What were they doing?

Maddie wanted to run up the aisle, yell at them, shake the

mayor, Theo's boss, for the love of God, who was just sitting there looking unconcerned. But then she looked back down at Theo, as they strapped him in before wheeling him toward the ambulance. This is what he'd want, damn him. He'd want the stupid show to go on. He'd been working toward this for months, and he cared about these people, this issue. He wouldn't want to derail the whole day because some racist asshole hit him on the head.

She went back to her seat to grab her purse so she could follow the ambulance to the hospital. She picked it up and turned to go, but a blond woman holding a clipboard grabbed her arm on her way out.

"Is he okay?" the woman whispered. "My boss said to keep going, so we did, but it was killing me to see him over there."

Maddie looked back up at the stage and saw the mayor's eyes on her. Okay, maybe he wasn't so unconcerned.

"His vital signs are okay, they said. I'm following them to the hospital now. Can you tell the mayor that for me?"

The blond woman nodded.

"I will. I'm Sybil. I work for the governor. Here, this is my number." She tore a scrap of paper from her clipboard and scribbled a number on it. "Can you just text me and let me know what's going on?"

Maddie tucked the piece of paper into her wallet.

"Okay. I have to run."

As soon as she got outside the school grounds, she did literally that, and ran to her car. The hospital was close by, a straight shot down Ashby, thank God. But of course there was traffic, and horribly long red lights, and a nightmarish parking garage, so it wasn't until almost twenty minutes later that she ran into the ER.

"I'm here for Theo Stephens. He should have gotten here maybe about ten or fifteen minutes ago? I'm his . . . wife."

Was she going to have to prove that statement? Apparently not; the woman at the front desk just checked Maddie's ID and gave her Theo's room number. She hid her left hand, just in case.

She forced herself to not run through the halls of the emergency room, so it felt like forever until she got into his room. There were two doctors standing there blocking him, so she couldn't see his face.

"Theo?" She looked at the doctors. "Is he okay? Is he awake?"

"Maddie?" His voice was weak, but it was his. He looked up at her and reached out his hand. She almost pushed one of the doctors out of the way so she could grab it.

"Theo. Oh, Theo, you're awake." His eyes were open, but he looked bleary and out of it. She looked back up at the doctors. "I'm sorry for rushing in here—" She wasn't sorry at all, but she assumed she had to say that. "Is he going to be okay? Did they tell you what happened?"

The doctor who she'd almost knocked over patted her on the shoulder.

"Mr. Stephens, do you feel okay to receive visitors? And can I—"

Theo stopped her with a wave of his other hand.

"I want her in here. And you can tell her everything."

The doctor turned back to Maddie.

"He should be okay, but we need to check him out for a bit more time. He has a concussion, but we're still figuring out what the effects from it might be. I'm Dr. Stewart. The medics told us what happened, but if you were there, we'd love to hear it from you, too."

The doctor's voice was gentle and soothing, and she looked at Maddie and at Theo like she really cared. She made Maddie feel better immediately.

"I was there. I can tell you."

Maddie told the doctors the story of the rally and then the protest turned riot, and just as she got to the end, she gasped.

"Alexa! Oh God, I have to tell her what happened. What am I saying? She probably already knows what happened. She's probably freaking out." She pulled her phone out of her pocket and looked back up at the doctors. They looked confused. "Sorry. Theo works for the mayor—no, right, I already told you that—but Alexa is my best friend, she also works for the mayor, they're all going to be so worried, I just want to make sure everyone knows where he is."

Dr. Stewart nodded.

"Sounds good. Oh, and I'm sure he'll get this instruction multiple times, but the concussion means he should avoid screens for a while."

Maddie looked down at the phone in her hand, and then up at the TV in the corner of the room.

The doctor smiled.

"Exactly those kinds of screens. They'll just make everything worse. We're going to let him rest and go check on some other patients, but someone will come back in a little while to give him a few more tests."

Maddie nodded.

"Okay, thank you. I'll be here."

She started to step outside the room to call Alexa so she wouldn't wake Theo up. But Theo had gone back to sleep still holding her hand tight, and she couldn't let go. She pulled her phone out of her pocket to see missed calls from a bunch of numbers she didn't recognize, along with two from Alexa. She clicked to call her back.

"Peter told me you were at the rally. Are you with Theo? How is he?" Alexa had a note of panic in her voice that Maddie hadn't heard in a long time.

"I'm with him in the ER. He woke up sometime between getting in the ambulance and me getting here. The doctors didn't say much to me, but they said someone will be back to give him more tests soon."

Alexa let out a sigh.

"He woke up. Okay, that's a good sign. Oh thank God. When I called you and called him and didn't hear anything . . . I was panicking a little." Maddie should have thought to call Alexa earlier, at least just to let her know she was heading to the hospital. But she'd been so panicked herself, she couldn't even think that far. "I'm chained to my desk because my phone is ringing off the hook. Text Drew anything the doctors say; he'll be able to tell us what they really mean."

Maddie looked down at Theo, but he was still sound asleep with a faint smile on his face.

"I will. Do you have Theo's brother's number? Someone needs to tell him what happened before he sees it on the news. He can call their mom. She's . . ." Maddie stopped herself before she told Alexa that Theo's mom was on vacation. Alexa might wonder why the hell she knew that.

Luckily, Alexa seemed distracted by everything going on and hadn't seemed to hear that part. She wasn't kidding about her phone ringing off the hook; Maddie could hear it in the background as they talked.

"Yeah, I'll text it to you so you can let him know. You know more than anyone else right now."

Maddie suddenly realized that Alexa—and Ben, if Theo hadn't told him what was going on between the two of them—would probably wonder why the hell she of all people was the one there at the hospital with Theo, the one talking to the doctors, the one who knew more than anyone else right now.

"Um, okay, sure, I can get in touch with him. I'm just here because I went to the rally today because you guys kept talking about it, and then when he got hit I thought someone should be here with him, and everyone else there who knew him was working, so . . ."

"Sure, right, of course. I'm glad you're there. I have to go, but please text any updates."

I'm glad I'm here, too, she thought, but didn't say.

As soon as Alexa sent her Ben's number, Maddie clicked on it to let him know what was going on, but she got stuck right after, "Hi Ben, it's Maddie." It turned out that texting the brother of the dude you'd been sleeping with for months to tell him in the least alarming way possible that his brother had been hit over the head and was in the hospital was difficult. Theo and Alexa were the ones good with diplomacy; Maddie was decidedly not.

"Damn it, where's Theo when I need him?" she said out loud.

"Right here," he said. She almost jumped and turned from her phone back to the bed. "What do you need me for?"

She put her phone down and touched his face, making sure to stay away from the bandage on his head.

"Hey. How are you feeling?"

He tried to sit up and gave up quickly.

"My head hurts. What do you need me for? And . . . what happened? What are we doing here?"

He'd forgotten. She'd just told the story of what had happened to him and the doctors a little while ago before Theo had fallen asleep, and he'd already forgotten. The doctors had said that might happen, but it still freaked her out.

She picked up the water jug next to the bed and offered him the straw. He drank gratefully before he pushed the straw away. He was still holding on to her hand.

"We were at the rally. There was a protest. Someone hit you."

"The protest. Right." He shook his head. "Damn it, this is all my fault. Everyone kept saying something like this would happen, but I refused to listen. Disaster." He sighed. "How'd the rest of the rally go?"

Maddie almost laughed. What a Theo question to ask.

"I don't know—I've been with you the whole time—but I know they kept going. I need to text your brother to tell him what happened. I was just trying to do that without freaking him out."

Theo looked down at her phone.

"Don't worry about it. My brother's an asshole sometimes but he's great in a crisis. Where's my phone? Do you have it? And my glasses?"

Maddie looked around the room and found a plastic bag in the corner with what looked like his clothes in it. She let go of Theo's hand to pick it up.

"Here's all your stuff, but you shouldn't have your phone. The doctor said no screens or reading for now." She dug through the bag and handed him his glasses. Then she gasped. "Oh no. Your clothes! They're all cut up! They must have cut your clothes off you in the ambulance. I loved that shirt."

Theo looked as horrified as she felt. She reached for his hand again.

"I loved that shirt, too," he said. "It's my favorite shirt. That's why I wore it today." They both went silent, mourning Theo's perfect navy and white pin-striped button-down shirt.

Maddie forced herself back to the matter at hand.

"I need to text your brother before he finds out from someone else."

Hi Ben, it's Maddie, Alexa and Theo's friend, we met last year at Theo's birthday party. Theo got hit over the head during a protest today, I'm with him in the ER right now. He's awake—

She looked over at Theo and saw he'd fallen back to sleep.

—on and off but they're still giving him tests. Text me if you have questions, I'll be here

There, that seemed as unalarming as she could make it. She pressed send.

Thirty seconds later her phone buzzed.

Yeah someone told me they heard a news report and they thought it was about Theo, so I was texting him but he wasn't responding. Glad you're with him. I'm in SF, going to go home to get my car and meet you there, keep me posted about where to go and what's going on. You'll stay with him?

She texted back.

I'll text when we know anything. Can you stop at his house first to pick up a pair of sweatpants and a t-shirt so he has

something to go home in? You have his key, right? I'll be
with him, don't worry.

He sent the blowing kisses emoji in return. She had to laugh,
even though he hadn't answered any of her questions.

After a while longer of sitting next to a sleeping Theo while
texting one handed, she reached into her purse to get her portable
charger. Thank God she'd had it in this purse; her battery was
draining quickly.

"Maddie."

She looked up at him, but his eyes were barely open.

"I'm here."

He smiled and opened his eyes wider.

"Just checking to make sure. Glad I didn't dream you."

She smiled and patted his hand.

"Why don't you ever put your hair up?" he asked.

Now she wondered how bad his concussion really was.

"Why don't I what?"

He lifted his hand to his face and made a gesture like he was
pushing his hair back. She laughed at how familiar it was.

"You do that all the time, so I know you don't like your hair in
your face, but why don't you just put it up in a ponytail?"

She started to push her hair back again and then stopped herself, suddenly self-conscious.

"Oh. It gives me headaches. Ponytails, I mean. Sometimes I do,
like if I'm at home, but I do it really loosely. Otherwise my head
will hurt for hours. Why are you thinking about that now?"

He reached for her hair, and she leaned in closer to him so he
could push it off her shoulder for her.

"I think I was thinking about it earlier. I don't know why." He brushed his fingers against her cheek. "Glad you're here."

She ran her hand up and down his arm.

"I'm glad I'm here, too."

He smiled and closed his eyes again.

About an hour later, Alexa appeared at the door of his room. Maddie dropped Theo's hand and stood up. Had Alexa noticed her holding his hand? No, she must not have; she was staring up at the machine with Theo's blood pressure and heart rate on it.

"Drew told me to take a picture of this and text it to him." She held up her phone and snapped the photo before she looked at Maddie. "How is he?"

Maddie stretched. Her body was stiff from being in the same position in that chair for so long. And her hand felt cold and empty. It felt weird to not be touching him, after holding his hand for so many hours.

"I can't tell. He wakes up every so often and says a little something, then falls back asleep. He asked me what we were doing here; he didn't remember what had happened. He's thrown up a few times. But the doctors—and the Internet—say all of that is normal." Maddie had spent the last hour looking up a lot of information about concussions on her phone. "We're still waiting on the CT scan. How's everything at the office?"

Alexa pulled up a chair on the other side of Theo's bed and sat down.

"Still wild. I can only stay here for a second, but I just had to see him. The mayor was on all the local news—and some local news shows elsewhere in the state—talking about what happened, but Theo will be very proud: in all of the interviews, the mayor managed to turn the subject back to statewide pre-K and how important it is."

"I am very proud." Theo opened his eyes halfway and smiled at Alexa. She reached out and grabbed his hand, which gave Maddie a pang.

"Hey, there you are," Alexa said. "We're barely managing without you in the office, you know. But everyone is trying to pull themselves together until you get back. Leave it to you to play the hero."

Theo laughed, a stronger laugh than he'd managed so far.

"Me, play the hero? It's my fault this whole thing happened in the first place. Plus, I couldn't have been less of a hero; I was just standing there and got knocked to the ground."

Alexa looked at him, then at Maddie, with her eyebrows raised.

"That's not the story I heard. Peter said you yelled for Maddie to watch out because one of the protestors was near her, and when you started to run toward her, his friend knocked you out."

Now Theo and Alexa were both staring at her.

"Oh." Was Alexa going to make some big deal out of this? "Yeah, that is what happened. It was"—she closed her eyes for a second—"a pretty scary few minutes there. I shouted your name and tried to warn you, but . . . it was too late." She refused to cry. "Anyway, no, you weren't just standing there."

Theo reached for her hand. She wanted to grab on to his, but Alexa was right there. She turned to pick her phone up from the table and pretended she hadn't seen. After a second, he dropped his hand.

Theo sighed.

"I'm never going to get Mallory from the *L.A. Times* to take me seriously again now that she's seen me being loaded into an ambulance. Her article about the rally probably rightly blamed me for this whole thing."

Alexa pulled her phone out.

"One, you're not to blame for this whole thing. Two, let's check to see if Mallory's piece is up."

Theo reached for her phone.

"Let me read it."

Maddie snatched the phone out of his hands.

"Did you not hear what Dr. Stewart said to you? No phones! No reading! No screens at all! You have a traumatic brain injury."

Theo rolled his eyes again, but his yawn kind of destroyed the effect.

"That's just a fancy word for a concussion. People get concussions all the time. It's no big deal. I feel fine."

Maddie handed Alexa's phone back to her.

"Don't let him have it. He says he feels fine, but just wait: he'll fall back asleep within seconds after you leave the room."

A nurse appeared at the door.

"It's time to take you down for your CT scan, Mr. Stephens!" Why did nurses always sound so cheerful?

Alexa stood up.

"It seems like Maddie has this in hand, and I should get back to the office. Theo, feel better and do what Maddie and the doctors say. Maddie, text me any updates, please, especially anything from the doctors that we can get Drew to translate. If you're still here in an hour when he gets off, he'll come by."

Maddie met Alexa at the door.

"He keeps trying to make light of this, but I'm worried. We'll know more after the CT scan, but he was out of it for a while."

Alexa nodded.

"I could tell you were worried. I am, too."

Alexa wrapped her arms around Maddie and held her tight. Alexa's big, warm, loving hug felt so good.

"Thanks for taking care of him," she whispered in Maddie's ear.

God, why did that make her want to cry? She was glad Alexa couldn't see her face.

"You weren't there, and I knew you'd want someone you trusted watching over him, so . . ."

Alexa pulled back and smiled at her.

"He's lucky to have you here," she said. "How are you doing? Are you okay?"

Maddie pulled away.

"I'm fine. He's sleeping a lot so I have plenty of time to answer emails."

Alexa patted her on the shoulder and waved at Theo. His eyes were already drooping again.

When Alexa was safely down the hall, Maddie returned to her chair next to Theo's bed and dragged it closer to him. He reached for her hand just as she reached for his.

Chapter Sixteen

THEO WOKE UP WHEN HE HEARD HIS BROTHER'S VOICE. WHAT WAS Ben doing at his place?

He opened his eyes. Oh, right, he was in the hospital. The rally. Sybil had been right, and he'd been wrong. He looked to his left and sighed in relief—Maddie was still there next to him. She squeezed his hand, and he squeezed back. He looked over at Ben.

"It's not as bad as it looks," Theo said.

"Isn't that my line?" Ben leaned over him. He must look pretty bad for that worried look to be on his brother's face. "Sorry it took me so long to get here. There was a ton of traffic."

"You didn't tell Mom, did you?" Theo asked. "She'll freak out."

Ben shook his head.

"Oh no, of course I didn't tell Mom. I figured the best way for her to learn that her oldest and most beloved son had been hit over the head and rushed to the emergency room was to get a text interrupting her vacation from any of her fifteen best friends, all of whom watch the local news religiously. Your brain must really have been damaged; of course I told Mom! She would whoop me so hard if I just, what, decided to pretend that if I didn't tell her she wouldn't find out? I tried that a lot as a kid; it didn't work any of those times. Occasionally, I learn from my mistakes."

His little brother sometimes made good points.

"You're right. Please tell me she's not getting on a plane back here right now."

Ben shook his head.

"I talked her out of that, and hopefully it'll last. But you can imagine what she said when I told her that you'd been attacked and were in the emergency room."

Nope, Ben was back to his brother Ben again.

"You told her I'd been attacked? Benjamin, really? Did you also tell her I have a traumatic brain injury, like Maddie keeps calling it?"

Ben grinned.

"Don't 'Benjamin' me. I didn't actually say that, but I did tell her you were in the ER. I also said Alexa and her doctor fiancé were here with you—I know that wasn't true, but it made her feel better, okay? She wants to talk to you, but we can do that later. Be convincingly well when you talk to her, please, otherwise she'll be on your doorstep by nine a.m. tomorrow."

"You do have a traumatic brain injury, you know," Maddie said. "You keep saying it like it's a big joke, but this isn't a joke. I don't care how much better you're feeling right now." She looked up at Ben. "They took him down to get a CT scan a while ago, but we haven't heard anything yet."

Theo looked over at his brother and sighed.

"I know this isn't a joke. I'm just ready to go home. I hate this

IV, I hate this hospital gown, I want to go home to my bed and my clothes and without so many things attached to me, and I want to be able to at least help deal with this public relations disaster I created."

Why had he ignored everyone who was so worried about protestors fucking up the rally? Now they would be the whole story, instead of the families he'd worked so hard for.

Maddie shook her head.

"I've been googling, and what if there's bleeding in your brain that they haven't caught? Depending on the results of the CT scan, they might need to admit you so you can stay overnight for monitoring. The first twenty-four hours are crucial—everyone says that."

"Who is everyone?" Drew asked as he walked in. Theo was both embarrassed and touched that Drew had come by. Of course Alexa had told him to, but still.

"Hey!" Maddie dropped his hand again and stood up. "'Everyone' is the whole Internet and all the doctors."

Drew put his arm around Maddie. Theo wished he was the one doing that.

"First, that's true. Second, never google when someone is in the hospital; it just makes you terrified. Have the doctors come back yet since the last time you texted?" He turned to Ben. "You're Theo's brother, right? I think we met a while ago?"

Ben nodded.

"That's me. Good to see you again. And if my mother asks, you've been here watching over him since the ambulance brought him in."

Drew nodded.

"Good to know. Is she on her way here?"

"No!" Ben and Theo both said. "And we hope it stays that

way," Theo said. "She's on vacation, and it would kill me to ruin her trip like this."

Ben slapped him on the shoulder a little too hard.

"And she will kill *me* if anything happens to you, so please listen to what Maddie said and take this head thing seriously, okay?"

Theo sighed. He knew head injuries were bad, he had not at all enjoyed the experience of waking up in an ambulance and not knowing how or why he'd gotten there, and he was ready to do whatever the doctors said he had to. He just wanted to get the hell out of the hospital first.

"I am taking it seriously," he said to the room at large. He looked at Drew. "But really—do you think they're going to let me go home tonight? No offense, but hospitals are nightmares."

Drew laughed.

"None taken. I haven't done adult medicine in a while, but from what I remember, we usually wouldn't keep concussions in overnight unless there was some evidence of something wrong, something more than just a sore spot and a headache."

Maddie looked like she wanted to argue with Drew, and Theo couldn't figure out why. Couldn't she see how much happier he'd be at home, in his own clothes, without any needles in his arm?

Maybe she was tired of being here. He had no idea how long they'd been at the hospital, but he was pretty sure Maddie had been with him the whole time. She must be exhausted.

Drew and Ben were in the corner talking about baseball, but he lowered his voice anyway.

"Now that Ben's here, you can go if you want."

Oh no, now she looked pissed.

"Do you want me to go? I don't have to stay if you don't want me here."

He shook his head. Shit, why did he keep doing that? Shaking his head hurt like hell.

"Of course I don't want you to go. But it's getting late, and you've been in that chair for I don't know how many hours. I know I'm grumpy and tired, so I'm assuming you're getting grumpy and tired and probably hungry. Ben can take over."

She glared at him.

"I'm not going anywhere. I promised Alexa I'd stay, and I'm staying until you're out of here." She frowned as she looked at him. "You look tired. Are there too many people in this room right now?"

Now she was looking at Ben and Drew like she was going to throw them out.

"No, they're fine. It's good to have some entertainment while I'm in this stupid bed. And I'm sure Alexa will flip if Drew leaves before he gets a chance to talk to the doctors."

Maddie nodded and sat back down next to him. She didn't reach for his hand again.

Ben turned on the TV, then quickly turned it back off after Maddie yelled at him that his brother had just gotten a traumatic brain injury and no screens were allowed. Oh good, she could be mad at Ben instead of him.

Finally, the doctor came back in.

"Okay, Mr. Stephens, how are you feeling?" She looked around the room. "You have a lot of visitors, I see." She smiled at Maddie. "You, I've already met."

Ben reached out his hand.

"Hi, I'm Ben Stephens. Thanks for taking care of my big brother."

Dr. Stewart shook his hand and turned to Drew.

"I'm Drew Nichols, a friend of Theo's. I'm a doctor over at Children's."

Ben jumped in.

"Our mom is out of town, and she demanded that Drew be her eyes and ears—forget her own son."

Theo sighed.

"And yes, Doctor, feel free to speak frankly with all of them in here. Anything to get me home faster."

The doctor laughed and turned to Drew.

Did the doctor have the test results or not? Were they going to keep Theo tonight or send him home? Just give them the news and stop the suspense.

"So, Doctor, do you have an update for us?" Maddie finally asked.

The doctor stopped chatting with Drew about people they both knew and turned back to Theo.

"Your test results were clear. We're sending you home tonight. I bet you're thrilled about that."

Theo sat up and smiled. Was she the only one who noticed how much he winced whenever he moved? Why were they letting him go home like this?

"I'm very thrilled, Dr. Stewart. Thanks so much for everything."

"Are you sure about this, Dr. Stewart?" Maddie couldn't help herself. "Shouldn't he stay overnight for monitoring? What if there's bleeding in his brain that didn't show up on your tests? Or what if he forgets things again, like he did when he first woke up? Shouldn't he stay here, in case any of those things happen?"

The doctor smiled at her. Maddie could see condescension in that smile.

"I see someone has been looking on the Internet for worst-case scenarios. Don't worry, we have a list of things to watch out for, but he can easily be monitored by friends and family at home. He might forget things and feel kind of foggy for the next few days, but that's normal." She looked around the room. "I can tell he'll be in good hands, and he'll be able to rest and recuperate a lot better at home than in the hospital."

She took out her phone to text Alexa.

> The doctor says Theo gets to go home tonight but I really think they should keep him to monitor him but no one seems to be paying attention to me. She's talking to Drew now

Alexa was clearly waiting for news, because her little bubble popped up immediately.

> I wish he was staying overnight too! Glad Drew's there hopefully he'll either get the doctor to change her mind or tell us why this makes even the slightest amount of sense

Theo leaned over and peeked at her phone.

"Oh great, you're getting Alexa on your 'Keep Theo in the hospital' side, I see."

Maddie tucked her phone in her pocket.

"I'm just keeping her posted, since her fiancé doesn't seem to be doing that!"

Dr. Stewart finished talking to Drew and shook hands with everyone before she left the room.

"If I don't see any of you again before he's out of here, it was a pleasure. Don't worry, the nurses will give you a whole list to consult in the next few days." She patted Maddie on the shoulder after she shook Theo's hand. "He'll be okay."

Maddie showed all of her teeth when she smiled back at her.

"He'd better be."

Drew picked up his bag shortly after the doctor left.

"I'm pretty sure that all you need is a lot of very boring rest—Maddie's right that you won't get to use screens for a while, so say good-bye to your phone and computer, too."

Theo dropped his head into his hands.

"For how long?"

Poor Theo. He was on his phone more than she was on hers.

"A week at a minimum, more than likely more," Drew said. He turned to Ben. "I'll send you a text you can send to your mom, if that will make her feel better."

Ben nodded.

"I'm sure it will, thanks."

Drew waved at the door.

"Okay, text me if you need anything. I'm sure you'll hear from Alexa very soon."

After Drew left, the nurse came back in with Theo's discharge papers and a stack of other paperwork.

"Do you have someone to stay with you overnight tonight?" she asked Theo as she was disconnecting the IV cord.

"Yes," both Maddie and Ben said.

Maddie looked at Ben, and he looked back at her, then down at Theo. Part of Maddie wanted to just let his brother deal with him overnight. Theo had told her to go home. Maybe he was tired of her. Maybe he wanted his brother to take care of him instead of her.

Too bad if he did; she was going to do it no matter what. Had his brother sat there all day looking up danger signs for head injuries, or listening to what every doctor said? Had his brother already read through the list that the nurse had handed her about what to do over the next few days and when to take him back to the hospital?

"I'll be the one taking care of him overnight," Maddie said to the nurse. Neither Theo nor Ben argued.

The nurse nodded at Maddie.

"Okay, you have the list of danger signs there, and the numbers to call if there are any problems. Do you have any questions?"

Boy, they really didn't give you a lot of time to look over the list and think of questions, did they? They were just ready to turn over his bed and get them out of there. They had apparently never met her before.

"Yes, quite a few, actually. First of all, this line says vomiting is common, but then this line says to be concerned if there's too much vomiting. Those two things seem to contradict each other. Can you clarify?"

Chapter Seventeen

THEO AND BEN EXCHANGED GLANCES THROUGHOUT MADDIE'S LITANY of questions for the nurse. Theo was very glad Ben had obeyed his "Don't argue with her" look after the nurse had asked who was staying with him tonight.

Theo had no idea why Maddie was so intent on taking care of him overnight. She was such a hard person to figure out: on the one hand, she'd been there with him basically since he'd been injured, had answered him every time he'd woken up confused in this bed, and was now grilling the nurse on proper postconcussion procedures. On the other, she'd dropped his hand like it had burned her as soon as Alexa had walked into the room, and had made a point to say she was only at the hospital to do Alexa a favor. If this had happened after the wedding, would Maddie have even been here at all? He had no idea.

All he knew was that he'd felt so relieved every time he'd woken up and had seen her right there by his side. Especially since he had a rock in the pit of his stomach because of the rally. He couldn't believe he'd made every wrong decision about something he'd worked so hard to make perfect.

"Okay, Mr. Stephens," the nurse finally said. "Let's get you out of that bed and you can get some clothes on."

Theo sat up, slowly this time. Okay, good, it didn't hurt as much as it had the last few times he'd tried it.

"Speaking of clothes, what am I going to wear out of here?" He looked at Maddie. "Or . . . did they really cut my clothes off me?" Everything that had happened so far today felt like it was one big dream.

Maddie took a deep breath.

"It happened. Don't remind me." She shook her head. "But you have other stuff to change into. I got Ben to stop by your house and pick up sweats and a T-shirt." She narrowed her eyes at Ben. "You did do that, didn't you?"

Apparently, in the last few hours in the ER together, Maddie had started talking to Ben like he was *her* little brother.

Ben reached into his messenger bag and pulled out Theo's gray sweats and an old Harvard tee.

"You think I'd forget to do that and risk your wrath?" Ben tossed the clothes on the bed next to Theo.

Theo swung his legs over the side of the bed and stood up. Okay, yes, that took a little more effort than usual, and he had to hold on to the side of the bed at first, but he was okay. He looked at Maddie, who was staring intently at him, and smiled.

"I can stand up all by myself, really I can."

She glared at him again and turned to leave the room.

"Ben, hold on to him while he changes, please. Though maybe if he falls down and hits his head again, the hospital will take this more seriously. I'm going to call Alexa to tell her we're about to leave."

As soon as Maddie was safely out of the room, Ben leaned over to him.

"Don't tell Maddie, but I totally forgot to go to your house and get the clothes. I was all the way in the parking garage before I remembered. I had to turn around and race over there and come back, because I knew she'd kill me if I didn't come in with them."

Theo sat back down on the bed.

"Good call. Now please don't tell her I sat down to put my pants on, but I really didn't want to risk actually falling down again and having the hospital make me stay overnight."

By the time Maddie came back in the room, Theo was dressed and ready to go. A nurse came in with a wheelchair right behind Maddie.

"We know you can walk; this is just until you get into the car," the nurse said.

Ben looked at Maddie.

"I'll walk him to the door if you want to go out and get your car?"

Maddie looked at them both for a moment, clearly trying to decide if they could handle the wheelchair without her. Finally, she reached for her purse and the plastic bag with all of Theo's possessions.

"Sounds good. I'll meet you outside in a few minutes."

Theo hadn't really realized how long he'd been in the emergency room until they got outside. The last he remembered of the day, it had been the middle of the afternoon, and now it was pitch-black outside.

"What time is it?" he asked Ben as they stood there waiting for Maddie.

Ben pulled his phone out of his pocket.

"Just after nine." He clapped his hand on Theo's shoulder. "It's been a long day. Don't do this shit to me again, you hear me? I almost had a heart attack when I got Maddie's text."

Theo punched him lightly.

"I'll be fine, no heart attacks necessary."

Ben nodded toward Maddie's car as she pulled up in front of them.

"I'm glad you have her to take care of you. I'm really glad you're okay."

Maddie jumped out of the car before Theo had a chance to respond. Ben opened the passenger-side door, and Theo got out of the wheelchair and walked the few steps to get into Maddie's car.

"See you soon, man." Theo put his hand on his brother's shoulder before getting into the car. "I'll be fine, don't worry about me. Don't you remember Mom always used to say how hardheaded I was?"

Ben pulled his phone out of his pocket and shut the door.

"Shit. Mom." Ben let out a long sigh. "I need to send her, like, a twelve-paragraph text just so she won't get on the next plane."

Theo was still laughing as Maddie got in the car. He was suddenly delighted to be alive, to be outside the hospital and in a car with the windows down on this warm September night, to be in this car right now with Maddie.

"Careful," she said as she put her key in the ignition. "You shouldn't move your head too much. If you have to laugh, do it gently."

He turned toward her and grinned.

"Who ever heard of laughing gently? That's not much of a laugh at all."

Maddie wasn't smiling back at him. She obviously wasn't as happy with the world tonight as he was. He patted her on the arm.

"Relax, Maddie! I'll be fine, don't worry. Isn't it a glorious night? I can't wait to get home and open the windows and smell the flowers from the garden next door." And to be with her.

She shook her head.

"Now I'm even more worried about your poor brain. I can't believe you're waxing poetic about smelling flowers."

He leaned his head back against the seat and smiled at her as she drove him home.

Maddie parked right outside Theo's apartment. Thank God the space in front was open. She jumped out of the car and went around to help Theo out. He'd been so wobbly in the hospital, she'd worried every time he'd gotten up to go to the bathroom that he would fall down. Once he was standing up, he put his arm around her waist, and they walked slowly up the path to his building.

Maddie pulled her key to his place out of her bag.

"Your keys are in the hospital bag with your phone and your ruined clothes. Let me get you inside and comfortable, and I can run back to the car and get everything."

As soon as they got inside, Theo steered her into his living room and pulled them both down on his couch. He kicked off his shoes, plopped his feet onto his coffee table, and sighed. When Maddie tried to get up, he held on to her.

"I just want to run outside and get your hospital bag out of the car," she said.

He squeezed her hand.

"Don't leave me yet, okay?"

She put her arm around him.

"Okay."

He dropped his head onto her shoulder.

"I can't believe I fucked up the rally. Did Alexa say anything else about the press? I'm sure they barely mentioned universal pre-K at all, and the whole story was the protests."

She reached down to stroke his head, then remembered she shouldn't, so she dropped her hand to his shoulder.

"Don't worry about that right now. There's nothing you can do about it. Just let yourself rest."

They sat like that for a while, until his regular breathing made her think he'd fallen asleep. So she almost jumped when he said her name.

"Maddie?"

She turned toward him, and he kissed her on the cheek.

"I'm here."

He kissed her on the lips softly.

"Thank you for being here. Thank you for everything you did for me today."

Something inside of her melted.

"You're welcome. I'm here as long as you need me." She rubbed her thumb over the back of his hand. "You'll probably get sick of me before these next forty-eight hours are up. They told me to watch you, so get ready for me to be following you around this apartment, staring at you the entire time."

He stroked her hair.

"I look forward to it. Now: can we please order some pizza or something? I'm starving, and I bet you are, too."

Maddie tried to remember when she'd last eaten. She'd had a

chocolate chip cookie at eleven a.m. Was that it? Yes, because she'd planned on grabbing food after the rally from that bakery that she liked near the school. She pulled her phone out of her pocket.

"I am starving, but I don't think pizza is a good idea. You were pretty sick in the hospital. I don't think you'll be able to keep pizza down. How about soup instead?"

Theo made a face.

"You know how I feel about soup. I like food I can chew. I don't like drinking my food. I have teeth for a reason!"

She patted his knee.

"I know, you've said this numerous times. But let's try you on some easy soup before you graduate to more substantial food."

Maddie's phone buzzed just as there was a knock at the door.

I'm outside, I picked up a few things

Maddie looked up from her phone at Theo.

"It's your brother at the door."

What the "few things" Ben would have picked up for Theo might be, she had no idea, but she hoped at least one of them was useful.

She opened the door to Ben holding two stuffed grocery bags.

"Hi," he said. "I drove by the grocery store, and I didn't know what kinds of supplies he had here, and since it seems like he'll be stuck here for a while, I figured I'd get him some stuff."

Ben walked through the open door and past Maddie before she could say anything.

"Hey, man," he said to Theo as he walked past the living room doorway. "You're already looking better outside that hospital room."

Theo and Maddie shrugged at each other and followed Ben to the kitchen.

"I know you hate soup," Ben said as Theo walked into the kitchen, "but Mom told me to get you soup, so I got you lots of it." Maddie shot a triumphant glance at Theo. He shook his head as Ben pulled a dozen cans of soup out of the bags.

"Please tell me you got me something edible in there, too."

Ben nodded.

"I also got you four different kinds of crackers."

Theo leaned against the wall and put his head in his hands.

"You're all conspiring against me! Do you really have nothing but soup and crackers in those bags?"

"I got you good stuff, too, but number one, this is only for when you've stopped throwing up, okay? For, like, a whole day." Ben paused with his hand in the grocery bag until Theo nodded. "And number two, do not tell Mom I got this. She'll kill me."

Ben pulled a stack of frozen pizzas out of the bag and held them in the air.

"But you have to eat all the soup first."

Theo folded his arms over his chest.

"I only threw up once, okay?"

Maddie grimaced.

"They told us you'd still forget things. No, you threw up at least three times."

Theo looked hard at her.

"Really? Are you sure? I don't . . ."

Ben held his finger up.

"Oh, that reminds me." He pulled eight bottles of ginger beer out of the bag. "I know there are people who like this stuff. I think it's disgusting, but I keep it around for hangovers, so I assume it's good for other kinds of nausea, too." He looked at Maddie. "Make him drink it."

She picked up a bottle and twisted off the top.

"Drink this." She handed it to Theo.

"If I'd known that getting hit over the head would make me end up being bossed around by the two of you, I would have reconsidered that choice." He took a sip of the ginger beer and shrugged. "It's not bad."

"Okay." Ben dropped the bags on the floor and turned to walk out of the kitchen. "Maddie will kill me if I stay too long, and I know you need your rest, but . . ." He shrugged. "I figured maybe at least some of this would be useful."

Despite how bro-y and careless he seemed, Ben clearly loved his older brother a lot.

Theo clapped his brother on the shoulder as he walked by, and Ben stopped.

"It's all useful. Thanks for coming by, Benny."

"No problem, Teddy," Ben said.

The two brothers walked together toward the door, and Maddie trailed after them.

Maddie pulled her keys out of her pocket and followed Ben out the door.

"I'm going to get your hospital bag out of my car," she called back to Theo.

Ben followed her to her car and stood there while she popped open the trunk.

"Hey. Thanks for taking such good care of my brother. It means a lot."

She was glad her face was hidden as she reached into the trunk of her car.

"Oh, it's no problem. I was there when he fell, and I just figured—"

Ben put his hand on her shoulder.

"You were there all day, and I bet you won't get any sleep tonight. It's not no problem. Thank you."

Maddie took a deep breath and composed her face before she pulled the bag out and shut the trunk.

"You're welcome. And thank you for bringing the food by."

Ben laughed on the way to his car.

"He's already so mad he has to eat soup. I'll come by tomorrow. Text me if you need anything."

Maddie turned to walk back up to Theo's apartment.

"I will."

Once she got inside, she watched Theo walk back to the couch and sit down. He was still slow, but it looked like his balance was coming back.

"I'm going to make you the soup now," she said. "Which one do you want?"

He made a face.

"If I have to have soup, I don't even care what kind it is. Can I have a grilled cheese sandwich with it?"

She turned to walk to the kitchen.

"Yes, if your imagination is good enough to think some of those crackers are a grilled cheese sandwich."

After he ate half the bowl of soup and a pile of crackers, she patted him on the knee.

"Okay, time to get you into bed."

Theo leered at her, and she rolled her eyes.

"If you are even *thinking* there will be any of that, you are very much mistaken. No exercise for two weeks, and that includes sex!"

His mouth dropped open.

"Are you serious?"

She nodded.

"Look, I'm not any happier about it than you are." She stood up and reached out her hand. "I feel like you blocked out the nurse saying that on purpose."

He took her hand and stood up.

"Two weeks. Good God."

After he fell asleep, Maddie prepared herself for a long night. The nurse had told her to watch him for dizziness or if he stopped being lucid, and she was worried that the nausea would come back, especially with all the crackers he'd eaten. She knew she needed to stay awake in order to be able to help him to the bathroom, especially if he got sick.

She took off the sundress she'd been wearing all day and was now ready to burn, and changed into the yoga pants and T-shirt she'd left there a few weeks ago. She wanted to take a shower, but she wasn't ready to leave him alone for that long.

Maddie sat gently on the other side of Theo's bed, checked to make sure she hadn't woken him up, and then settled herself more comfortably. She leaned her head back against the headboard and turned to look at Theo. He seemed like he was sleeping peacefully, thank God.

She might never forget that moment when he got hit and dropped to the ground. She didn't think she'd ever been so scared. Or felt so helpless. She'd spent all day holding that fear at bay, keeping it together so Theo wouldn't see how scared she was, so she could talk to the doctors and Alexa and Drew and Ben and not let her panic and fear out, acting as calm as possible, not letting herself feel anything. It had been so awful. She brushed her hand against her face to wipe away the tears that ran down her cheeks. This time she didn't try to hold the tears back, and just let herself cry, as silently as she could, until they finally dried up.

She got up to go wash her face, and when she looked in the mirror, she was even more relieved she hadn't cried while she was at the hospital, because she had mascara all over her face. She used one of the makeup wipes she kept in a corner of the bathroom cabinet and splashed cold water on her skin to attempt to pull herself back together.

When she got back in bed with Theo—this time with a box of tissues next to her, just in case—she contemplated what to do all night while she watched him. She stuck her phone in to charge, and stared at the screen.

She plugged her headphones in and checked all her streaming video apps to see what she was in the mood for. Oh hell with it, she was emotional anyway tonight; she might as well lean in to it. *Say Yes to the Dress* it was.

After every episode, she looked up from her phone and over at Theo to check on him, but each time, he was still sleeping soundly.

But after the fourth episode, she looked over at him as she mopped the tears from her eyes, and he was looking back at her.

"You okay?" he asked.

She nodded and grabbed another tissue. This was so embarrassing.

"Fine," she said as soon as she could talk. "It's just that this show . . ." He would laugh at her as soon as she told him the show, but she felt like she needed to explain her tears. "You're going to think this is so stupid, but it's *Say Yes to the Dress*, and . . ."

Theo smiled.

"The show Alexa said always makes you cry."

Maddie nodded.

"She always makes fun of me for it, but, like, this one was with a woman with cancer, and all her friends helped her find the perfect dress, and then at the end during the credits it said it's in memory of her, and . . ." The tears started flowing again. She couldn't help it. Hadn't she cried enough tonight? Obviously not.

Theo took her hand. He rubbed his thumb back and forth across the back of her hand until the tears stopped.

"I'm supposed to be taking care of you; you're not supposed to be making me feel better," she said. "Speaking of, are you okay? Why are you awake? Do you need anything?"

He shook his head.

"Just you."

She leaned over and kissed him. As soon as he pulled her closer, she sat back up.

"None of that, remember?" She was reminding herself as much as him. "Go back to sleep. I'm here."

He fell asleep again a few moments later, still holding on to Maddie's hand. She'd had enough crying for the night, so she switched over to her favorite soothing British mystery series. Somewhere in between the hot vicar discovering the murder and solving it, she fell asleep.

She woke up with a jerk from a dream about watching Theo getting chased around and around a track, with everyone but her laughing. She got up to go to the bathroom and try to shake the sick, trapped feeling of the dream away.

When she slid back in bed next to Theo, he stirred.

"Maddie?" he said in a thick voice. His eyes were still closed.

"I'm here. Are you okay?"

He reached out for her hand, just like he'd done at the hospital, and she slid her fingers in his.

"Mmmhmm. Thank you for taking care of me."

She stroked his head with her free hand.

"I just want you to be okay."

He closed his eyes and smiled.

"I love you," he said.

"I love you, too," Maddie said.

She froze.

Why had he said that?

Why had she said that?

She could tell by his regular breathing that he was back asleep within seconds.

She didn't think she'd ever sleep again.

Chapter Eighteen

WHEN THEO WOKE UP THE NEXT MORNING, HE WINCED. HIS HEAD HURT like hell.

He turned over and opened his eyes. Maddie was awake in bed next to him.

Oh. The rally. The rally he'd devoted so much time to this summer so it would be perfect. The rally that had been a disaster because of him.

He sat up and rubbed his head.

"Please tell me I just had a horrible nightmare and that's why my head hurts."

Maddie looked as exhausted as he felt.

"Did you forget again? Yesterday, at the rally—"

He sighed and reached for his glasses.

"No, I remembered. I was just hoping I'd remembered wrong." He put his hand over his eyes. "Am I allowed to take something for my headache? And am I allowed to have coffee? Please say yes."

Maddie swung her legs out of bed and stood up.

"You can have both Tylenol and coffee. I'll be right back."

Theo pulled himself out of bed and to the bathroom. He caught a glimpse of himself in the mirror and shuddered. He had a vague memory of being happy last night on the way home from the hospital; he couldn't for the life of him figure out why now. He'd worked so hard on that rally, and he'd done everything wrong. And now the whole world knew it.

He stumbled into the kitchen. Maddie was grinding coffee beans. The noise assaulted him.

"Do you need help with the coffee?" he asked.

She shook her head.

"You should be lying down. I can handle this."

He walked toward the cabinet.

"I'm not an invalid. I can help." He turned away from the window; the sun streaming through the windows hurt his eyes. Maddie just looked at him.

"Yeah, okay, fine, I probably need a little more rest in a darkened room. But I hate to just leave you here to make the coffee for me."

She filled up his electric kettle and set it on to boil.

"You can leave me here. Go to the living room if you want a change of scenery from your bedroom. I closed the shades."

When he got into the living room, he saw his plastic hospital bag sitting by the couch and opened it. He pulled out his destroyed clothes and shook his head. He held up the shirt, neatly cut in half right next to the buttons, and sighed. He'd loved that shirt. And that tie. He knew emergency workers had to do what they had to do, but he wished they could have at least just untied the tie.

What else was in here? Oh, there was his phone! Maybe he had an email or something telling him what happened at the rally after he'd gotten hit over the head. Had they continued? Had anyone else been hurt? He could look up press coverage from yesterday; that would give him more information.

What if there were pictures of him knocked out on the ground? There must be video. How humiliating.

He plugged the phone into the charger he kept in his living room and unlocked it.

He didn't think he'd ever had that many new text messages in his life. He even had more new emails than that day his boss had accidentally sworn on live TV. They were from everyone he'd worked with in the past ten years, and possibly everyone he'd ever met. He felt like such a phony for getting so much sympathy—this whole thing was all his fault. He was the one who'd made sure the rally was in Berkeley, and he'd been so eager to pretend the likelihood of a big protest away, he hadn't at all adequately prepared for one. He'd barely even briefed the police chief, when that should have been one of his top priorities. An actual plan could have stopped these guys long before they got violent and fucked everything up.

This must have been deadly to the campaign. This was definitely deadly to Theo's hopes of moving up the political ladder.

He couldn't concentrate very well on the screen; he hated that he couldn't think clearly. He gave up and forwarded any email that seemed important to his assistant. He switched over to his bulging text messages. He opened the series of texts from his mom, one of which read in part "If you EVER do this to me again . . ." when he heard Maddie's footsteps and looked up.

"Oh thank God, coffee," he said.

She looked down at the phone in his hands.

"WHAT do you think you're doing?" she asked.

He looked back down at the phone.

"Looking at my mom's texts. She seems like she's ready to kill me, but I get the impression that Ben managed to talk her down some."

Maddie set the coffee down on the table and snatched the phone out of his hands.

"You're not supposed to be looking at your phone! Did you not remember what I said about no screens?"

He actually hadn't remembered that part.

He narrowed his eyes at her.

"No screens? What do you mean, 'screens'?" He reached for his phone, but she stepped out of the way.

"No phone. No computer and no TV, either. No screens and no reading."

He picked up the coffee and took a sip. He needed some caffeine to help him deal with this.

"You're serious? But how am I supposed to do my job? Aside from everything else, I need to know, on a scale from one to one hundred, just how much I ruined things for my boss, the children of California, and also me, Theo Stephens." He thought for a second. "Maybe not in that order."

She sat down next to him.

"You can't look any of those things up, and I hate to break it to you, but you won't be doing your job at all for a week or so. Maybe two."

He dropped his head into his hands.

"A week? Two? But I have to fix this. Or at least, do what I can to fix it. I want to go back in time and hit myself on the head for not preparing for something like this. I was so obsessed with making everything perfect, I didn't think about the things I couldn't control. If I had, I would have planned for them!"

Maddie took a sip from her own cup of coffee and kept his phone firmly in her grasp.

"They kept going with the rally afterward. Alexa said everything stayed mostly on track."

Now that she said that, he had a vague memory of someone telling him that in the hospital.

"Okay." He tried to think about what that would be like, how the rally would be after he'd been knocked to the ground, but somehow he couldn't picture it. Why couldn't he think? "Maybe if I just read one article? Or you could read them to me?"

Maddie shook her head.

"You can talk to Alexa. She'll give you an update. You already look worse than you did when you woke up. I can't imagine the news will make you feel better."

He sighed.

"Okay, fine, I won't look at it. Can you just let me charge it? I want to be able to answer when my mom calls, and I'm sure she will today. And I can't talk to Alexa without a charged phone."

She pursed her lips but handed the phone back to him. He stuck it in the charger and put it facedown on the end table.

"I made toast," Maddie said. "Can I trust you in here while I go get it?"

She was right that he felt worse than he did when he woke up. Maybe some of that was from his phone.

Such betrayal from the device he'd loved so much.

"I promise. I won't even touch it."

When she came back a few minutes later with toast for both of them, he picked up a piece.

"Thank you for taking care of me," he said.

She stared at him with a frozen look on her face.

"You're welcome," she said finally.

He ate two slices of toast and closed his eyes. Maybe he would just rest his eyes for a minute; it was so bright in here.

Maddie was only halfway through a piece of toast when she realized Theo was sound asleep on her shoulder.

Did he remember what he'd said? He must not remember.

Or maybe he was just pretending to not remember?

Why had he said that to her?

Why had she said that to him?

How the hell was she supposed to sit here with him all day and know that he'd said that to her and she'd said that to him and just pretend neither of them had said anything to each other?

He couldn't have meant it. Just like she absolutely didn't mean it. They'd agreed months ago—this thing was just up until the wedding, just to get it out of their systems, then they'd be done with each other. Sure, they'd grown to like each other, but not . . . that thing they'd said the night before.

She looked down at him. He was frowning in his sleep. She smoothed his brow, and he sighed and cuddled closer to her but didn't wake up.

She turned away from him and picked up her phone. She needed to check her own texts and emails. She'd ignored everything in her life that didn't have to do with Theo since she'd walked into the rally yesterday.

Thank goodness he was more lucid than the day before, but she was still worried about the effects of the concussion on his brain.

The doctors had all seemed so relaxed about it, but a traumatic brain injury could affect him for years. She had to pay attention all day today to see if he slurred his words or seemed out of it. And he kept making light of the whole thing, which made her want to throttle him even more.

She took a deep breath and forced her mind away from Theo and back to herself. She'd been on pins and needles for the past week about the job at the TV station, but she hadn't even thought about it since the day before. They'd told her she'd hear something "within the next few weeks," which meant she'd been on high alert every time she'd picked up her phone all week, but . . . no, still nothing. No calls, no emails. She let out a sigh. She'd forgotten how bad it was to wait to hear back from a job she wanted. It was like everything bad about dating, but even more high pressure. One of the great things about having her own business was that she hadn't had to deal with that particular stress in years.

Speaking of her business, she'd better check her calendar and reply to her clients unless she wanted to lose a bunch of them.

In the next hour, she sent two quick "Family emergency, I need to reschedule" texts to her afternoon clients, replied to emails from five more, and uploaded the picture to Instagram that she'd meant to post the day before. As all the likes and comments popped up on her photo, she shook her head. She'd managed somehow to cultivate a cool, hip, glamorous brand for herself, but look at her now. In old yoga pants, no bra, her hair wild, and walking a tightrope of anxiety on this couch.

Finally, Theo stirred and sat up.

"Hey." He rubbed his neck. "Sorry about that. I didn't really intend to fall asleep."

He looked so pathetic that she felt bad for all of her frustration with him.

"It's okay, the doctor said you'd sleep a lot in the next few days. Are you hungry?"

He shook his head and then nodded.

"Actually, yeah. Did Ben . . . bring food here last night? Did that really happen?"

Oh, so he could remember that his brother came by, but not that he'd told her he loved her.

"Yeah, Ben came over with soup and stuff." She laughed at the face he made at that. "I know, but you kept getting sick yesterday, remember?"

He yawned as he stood up.

"I don't really remember that, but I believe you. Fine, I'll go make some soup."

She pulled herself off the couch and stifled her own yawn.

"No, I'll do it. You're still too shaky to be carrying hot liquids around."

He smiled his thanks to her and followed her down the hallway as far as the bathroom.

When she came back to the living room with soup and crackers for both of them, he was staring at the back of his phone, still face-down on the coffee table.

"This is your nightmare, isn't it?" She handed him the mug with soup and set the crackers on the table.

"All my answers are in there!" He reached into the box of crackers, took one, and snapped it in half before eating it. "I can't remember when the last time was that I went this long without checking my phone. This is painful."

She laughed at the look on his face. His phone addiction had always sort of charmed her, because she was almost as addicted to hers. She knew how she would feel if someone took her phone away.

She almost told him she'd google for news about the rally and read any articles to him, but she stopped herself. She had no idea what they would say, and she didn't want to upset him further.

"Here." She took pity on him and handed him his phone. "You can't read anything, but call Alexa; she'll update you."

She really wanted to text Alexa and tell her to reassure him, and have the two of them join forces to get Theo to relax about the rally and his job and whatever else was stressing him out so he could heal. But she couldn't do that, because Alexa couldn't know she was at Theo's apartment. It was one thing for her to have followed the ambulance to the hospital; she could play that off as watching over her best friend's best friend. But it was very different for her to be at his house the next morning.

"Oh thank God." He immediately clicked on his favorites and scrolled to Alexa's name. Was her name in there? She couldn't tell.

"Hey! . . . Yes, yes, I feel a lot better. What's going on at work? What happened with the rally? What is the mayor saying?"

When he got off the phone, he still looked troubled.

"She said the rally kept going and no one else was hurt, and while the press did write a lot about the protestors, everything will be fine, but I don't know if I believe her." He reached for a cracker and frowned again. "Because if the press wrote a lot about the protestors, that means they didn't write a lot about the campaign; they have only so much space for a story. So this means we didn't get the press we wanted, and people don't know what this ballot initiative is all about, or why it's so important."

She forced herself to not smooth out his brow again.

"There's nothing you can do about it right now. Eat your soup. It's going to get cold."

He shuddered.

"If there's one thing I hate more than soup, it's . . ."

She nodded.

"I know, I know, it's cold soup. We went over this about gazpacho in July."

He gave her a half smile and reached for the mug of soup.

She forced herself to look away from him.

Why had he said he loved her? Was it true? Did he really feel that way? Why couldn't she stop thinking about this?

And if it was true, why wasn't he acting like it this morning? Why hadn't he acted like it at any other time?

Okay, fine, last night when they'd gotten home from the hospital, he'd seemed really happy to have her there, that was true. But that was probably because he was just high from being alive, and had nothing to do with her.

Maybe what he'd said last night had nothing to do with her at all.

"Okay." He looked up from the soup. "What if you just looked up the articles in the *Chronicle* and the *L.A. Times*, and then counted the paragraphs that are about the protestors and me getting injured versus the number of paragraphs that are about the campaign, and then I'll . . ."

"Oh my God, will you please shut the fuck up about the rally?" She couldn't handle this anymore. "Why are you obsessing about this? You just got off the phone with Alexa, and she told you it would be fine, so can we please talk about something, anything else?"

His face fell, and he turned away from her.

"Sure. No problem."

Oh Lord, now he was mad at her. She felt bad for yelling at him, but there was seriously only so much she could take. She couldn't sit here and listen to him stress for one more second about the damn rally, like it was the most important thing in the world.

"At least the wedding is in a month. You won't have to deal with me bossing you around for that much longer," she said, in an attempt to lighten the mood. He didn't reply. Okay, fine.

They sat there for a while, her on her phone, scrolling through Instagram and not seeing anything, him eating crackers, until she finally couldn't handle the silence anymore.

"If you lie down and promise not to look at the TV, I'll turn something on so we have some entertainment, at least."

She picked up the remote and moved to the far end of the couch.

He shrugged and lay down. Oh great, was he still mad at her for not wanting to endlessly discuss the rally? Whatever, he'd get over it.

She found her favorite season of *The Great British Baking Show* and hit play. It was the next best thing to *Say Yes to the Dress* to give her a cathartic cry. When the theme song came on, she looked over at Theo. He didn't look at her, but she thought she saw him smile.

A few hours later, Ben walked in. He looked at the empty mug next to Theo, who had been asleep on and off ever since she'd turned on the TV.

"I can't believe he actually ate soup."

Theo sat up, and Maddie turned off the TV.

"Hey, man. The soup was disgusting, but thanks for the crackers."

Ben plopped down on the easy chair and looked at his brother, then her.

"You both look terrible. Maddie, did you get any sleep last night?"

She brushed that away.

"A little. I'm fine."

Ben shook his head.

"I know what 'fine' means. I speak woman. Go home and take a shower and get some rest. Eat something that isn't soup. You can't take care of him if you're this exhausted."

Maddie looked at Ben, and then over at Theo. She didn't want to leave, but Ben was right. She'd never be able to fall asleep here, not when she was vibrating with anxiety like this. She had no idea if she'd be able to fall asleep at home, either, but she should try. Otherwise she'd be a basket case tonight.

"Okay, but what if he—"

"Starts slurring or acting like he can't understand me? I know, I'll call 911. I did pay attention yesterday. Go home. You need a break."

She stood up.

"Don't let him watch TV. Or touch his phone."

She wanted to kiss Theo good-bye, but she hesitated to do it in front of his brother. Sure, Ben probably knew what was going on, but as long as no one said it out loud, she could pretend no one but she and Theo knew.

"Okay. Thanks, Ben."

Theo closed his eyes again before she walked out the door.

Theo woke up on the couch again. He didn't even remember falling asleep. Again. He had a feeling this was going to keep happening.

He turned over and sat up. What was baseball doing on his

TV? Why would Maddie have turned on baseball? He turned to ask her that question and saw Ben sitting in Maddie's chair.

"What are you doing here?" he asked his brother. "Where's Maddie?"

Ben tore his eyes off the TV.

"Oh, you're awake. Welcome back to the world of the living. You've been out cold for a while. Maddie left hours ago, remember? We sent her home to get some rest?"

He had a vague memory of that. He was both glad and resentful Maddie had left. Glad because he was getting sick of her telling him what to do all day. Don't look at your phone, Theo! Stare at the wall so I can watch TV, Theo! Eat this gross soup, Theo! Stop talking about the biggest professional crisis you've ever had, Theo!

And he was resentful because he somehow didn't know how to function without her there.

"Oh, right." He stood up and grabbed on to the arm of the couch as a wave of dizziness hit him. "I'll be back."

He made his way to the bathroom. He hated this. All of this: the protestors who had shown up at the rally; the specific protestor who had hit him over the head; the entire concept of concussions; the phone calls he hadn't made that would have doubled the number of police officers at the rally; that he'd failed at something he'd worked so hard at; the way Maddie had acted this morning; that Maddie had left.

Had Maddie just been pretending all summer when he'd talked to her about the rally and why it was so important to him? He'd thought she cared. About the campaign, and about him.

From the way she'd acted this morning, it seemed like she couldn't wait to be done with him.

He realized on his way back into the living room that he was hungry again. The last thing he wanted was more soup, but Ben probably wouldn't let him eat anything else.

"What's the least gross of the soups you brought me?" Theo asked. "Maddie made me eat . . . what's it called? . . . the noodle one. I can't wait to eat real food again."

Ben turned off the TV and stood up.

"I can't believe you ate chicken noodle soup. I'll heat you up something else. I know better than to let you walk down that hallway holding a bowl."

"Hey, I can walk almost normally now!" he shouted after Ben. Wait. He didn't know why he was arguing this. His little brother was waiting on him; he needed to enjoy this as long as it lasted.

After not too long, Ben came back with a bowl of some hot yellowish liquid and another box of crackers. He sat down next to Theo on the couch and plunked the bowl in front of him. Theo looked at it and sighed. At least he'd brought more crackers.

"Here." Ben handed Theo a spoon. "Eat. I promise it's not terrible."

Theo broke open the crackers, dipped one into the soup, and sniffed it.

"Concussions are the worst," he said. He bit into the cracker and shrugged, then took a few cautious bites of the soup. It tasted better than he'd expected, but he wanted food he could chew. The doctor had probably told them previously when he would be safe from yesterday's nausea, but he barely remembered anything the doctor had said. And Maddie wasn't here to tell him.

"Did the doctor say anything about when I can go back to normal food?" he asked Ben. Ben shrugged, like Theo knew he would.

"Maddie will know. You can ask her if she comes back tonight."

It wasn't until Ben said "if" that Theo had even considered the possibility of Maddie not coming home tonight. What if she'd been so sick of taking care of him she decided to stay at her house? What if she fell asleep and slept until morning?

He pushed back the panic that had risen in his chest. Maybe she'd finally realized what an obsessive stress case he was at all times, and had taken the opportunity when Ben had arrived to flee forever.

It would be fine. He would be fine. He could take care of himself. He'd survived this long without Maddie; he could survive this without her.

He turned to Ben to tell him to find that concussion fact sheet or whatever, and found Ben staring at him with a big smile on his face.

"Freaked out at the idea of her not coming back, huh? What's going on between you and Maddie anyway? From what you told me, I thought she was just some girl you were fucking. But then I got to the hospital yesterday and she was ordering everyone around like she was in charge. Hell, I let her order me around, because it seemed like she *was* in charge. That's how girlfriends act, dude."

Shit. He did not need Ben going around calling Maddie his girlfriend. He opened his mouth to deny it, but Ben just kept talking.

"You're obviously in love with her. Any asshole can see that in the way you look at her." Ben grinned. "I approve. And not just because she's so hot, but that helps. She has sister-in-law material written all over her."

Oh no. Now Ben was the one who was all excited and talking about how he and Maddie were meant to be together, the thing Maddie always said Alexa would be the one to do, the reason why she was so intent on keeping them a secret.

But that probably wasn't the real reason she didn't want to tell Alexa about them. It was probably that she always knew he was too uptight, too anxious, too dull for her.

He couldn't handle the idea of Ben knowing what Maddie really thought of him. Or of Ben knowing how hard he'd fallen for Maddie, while she was just counting the days until the wedding so she'd be done with him.

He needed to disabuse Ben of the notion that Maddie was his girlfriend, or Ben's future sister-in-law, or that Theo had fallen in love with her. Immediately.

It might help to disabuse himself of that notion at the same time.

"Look, Maddie's cool, but there's no *there* there. When I first met her, I thought she was just some superficial, bitchy hot girl, who only cared about status and looks and money, and didn't care about anything important. She's still that same shallow person I thought she was, no matter how long she stayed at the hospital yesterday."

The front door slammed.

"Oh really?" Maddie appeared in the doorway. "I'm just some superficial bitch?"

Note to self: next time he was giving his brother some bullshit reasons why he wasn't falling for someone, make sure it was in a place the someone didn't have the key to.

He stood up to face her. She had a pizza box in her hands and looked beautiful and well rested and furious.

Had she heard what Ben had said, about how he was obviously falling in love with her? Part of him hoped she had; maybe it would make her less mad about what she'd just heard. But another part really hoped she hadn't. He knew what her response to that would be.

Ben got up and slipped out of the room. He wanted to shout after his brother to stay here with him, but instead he watched him go.

"You think I'm just some superficial bitch?" she asked again. "Really?"

Okay, he had to explain why he'd said that to Ben. But he couldn't tell her what Ben had said, about how he was clearly falling in love with her.

A joke. He should turn it into a joke.

"Sometimes you sure as hell seem like it," he said. "Hell, you seemed more upset that my clothes got ruined than about anything else that happened yesterday."

That didn't come out like he'd meant it as a joke. Shit. He opened his mouth to try again, but Maddie jumped in before he could.

"After everything we talked about, after everything I told you, and that's what you think of me?"

He couldn't tell her what he really thought of her, or how he really felt about her. It was enough that Ben had figured it out. Her words and actions for the past few months had told him she didn't feel the same way. He had too much pride to let her ever know how he felt.

All of his anger, at Maddie and at himself for caring so much about her, came pouring out.

"We all know what matters and what doesn't matter to you. You'll hold my hand alone in the hospital, you'll come over to my apartment anytime, but as soon as anyone else is around, you jump back. It's clear Maddie Forest has a rep to uphold, and I'm not good enough for her. Why bother to pretend otherwise?"

Theo knew he shouldn't be saying any of this to her, that he was angry and lashing out, but he couldn't stop himself.

She looked at him like her face was made of stone.

"Why would someone like you ever be good enough for me? Someone like you, who hides in corners at parties, bores a crowd to tears at the drop of a hat, only dances alone, doesn't listen to anything but the sound of his own voice. Why do you think I wanted to keep this a secret? You don't think I'd want anyone to know I was sleeping with you, do you?"

That had maybe been an even harder hit than the one that had knocked him out the day before.

Maddie opened the pizza box. Shit. She'd gotten him roasted garlic pizza. It smelled so good.

"When I first met you, I thought you were the biggest asshole I'd ever met. I sure as hell was right about that."

She turned the pizza box over, and the entire pizza dropped facedown onto the floor.

"Do me a favor, Theo."

She dropped the box on top of the pizza.

"Never speak to me again."

She turned and walked out. This time, she didn't even slam the door.

Maddie's hands shook so much she could barely get her key in the ignition. She couldn't sit here in her car; she didn't want Theo or his brother to see how upset she was. She took a deep breath to help pull herself together, turned the key to start the car, and drove away as fast as she could.

How could he say something like that about her? How could he even think something like that about her? She thought he knew her.

She'd thought he'd seen her for who she really was, not just what she looked like or the Maddie she showed to the world, but the person she was inside. She'd thought he'd seen the real Maddie, and liked her, cheered for her, believed in her. But in the end, he was just who she'd thought he'd been in the first place: the kind of guy who would judge her for what she looked like and what she dressed like and would never bother to get to know the real person underneath.

She'd told him so much. About her struggles, about her goals for herself, about why she was the person she was. Had he ever listened to her? Or had he just been waiting for his turn to talk?

She'd known their relationship was too good to be true, she'd known no actual relationships were that comfortable and easy, she'd known they were heading for a bad ending. She'd been right all along.

That didn't make her feel any better.

She looked around and realized where she was; she'd driven straight to Alexa's house.

She shook her head and made a U-turn in the middle of the street to go back home. She couldn't tell Alexa about any of this, especially not now.

She walked into her unnaturally clean house and dropped her bags on the floor. She'd been keeping her house as clean as it was humanly possible for her to keep it ever since Theo had come over that first time. He'd been coming over often enough since then that it just made sense for her to clean up on a regular basis instead of cleaning in a frenzy whenever they had plans.

It was time for this nonsense to end.

She raced around her house, reverse cleaning. She knocked books off shelves, threw clothes out of the hamper and out of the dresser and onto the floor, tossed shopping bags from their hiding place in her bathroom closet to the middle of her living room, kicked empty boxes out of the recycling pile. Finally, she spun around in a circle to admire her handiwork and smiled.

And then she sat down in the middle of her living room floor, surrounded by all of her stuff, and sobbed.

Chapter Nineteen

THEO SHUT OFF THE PODCAST IN THE MIDDLE OF A SENTENCE. IF HE listened to one more fucking podcast, he might go wander the streets of Berkeley and yell in the ear of anyone who could listen about mattresses and food delivery boxes and razor delivery clubs and all the other stuff that every damn podcast advertised and he was now almost convinced he needed.

He couldn't remember a more miserable week of his life, and it was only Wednesday. His head still hurt, he still couldn't think straight, he was worried about his job, he couldn't read, or exercise, or work, and he couldn't stop thinking about Maddie.

He hadn't heard from her since she'd walked out of his apartment that night, not that he'd expected to. He hated himself for every terrible and untrue thing he'd said to her that day. He wanted to blame the concussion for what he'd said, but he knew that wasn't the biggest reason. It was that he'd been trying to save face with his little brother, and had ended up looking like a great big asshole instead.

How the hell had he managed to let himself fall in love with Maddie Forest? Because obviously, Ben—damn him—had been right about that.

But then, how could he help himself falling in love with her? She was so funny, and smart, and genuine, and caring. They'd had such a great summer together—sitting on his couch or her couch; giggling like teenagers about keeping their secret; having sex in every possible place in his apartment; venting and commiserating about their work and their families; laughing and talking and listening and being quiet together.

The problem was, he'd just been riding this wave with Maddie without looking ahead or thinking about where he was going, and now he'd been thrown back onto the rocky, cold shore, all alone.

See, this was the other problem with getting a concussion right before a breakup—he had way too much time to wallow, so he sat around and thought of increasingly more maudlin metaphors.

He needed to pull himself together. Maybe he should eat something. He still had like three or four of those frozen pizzas Ben had brought him, but between the ones they'd eaten and the pizzas they'd ordered, he was getting kind of sick of pizza.

He glanced over at Ben, who was at the desk in the corner, in front of his laptop. Ben had refused to leave him alone and had told his job he'd be working from home all week. After he'd listened to Ben's incessant chatter for two straight days, he'd forced Ben to play the quiet game, which had worked a hell of a lot better now than when they were kids. Maybe it was that Ben had more willpower now, or that the beer he gave Ben as a reward was a bigger draw than the play money he'd tried to give him twenty-five years ago.

His phone rang. Alexa. She'd been by once over the weekend

to check in on him and had looked surprised at finding him and Ben alone. She hadn't asked about Maddie, though, thank God.

"Bless you for calling. I'm so bored."

She laughed.

"Then I guess the answer is yes to whether you want me to bring you dinner?"

Oh thank God. For the food, and the company to keep him from yelling at the walls, or his brother.

"Absolutely. Anything that isn't pizza."

Ben caught his eye and pointed to himself with both hands. He sighed.

"Lex, Ben wants you to know he's here, too."

She laughed.

"I'll bring enough for both of you. Chinese work? I'll be there in half an hour."

When he got off the phone, he pointed at Ben.

"Remember, say nothing to Alexa about the whole Maddie thing, no matter how much you want to get her on your side. Alexa doesn't know anything about this."

One of the other reasons he'd threatened to tape his brother's mouth shut was that Ben kept telling him he needed to make up with Maddie. Maddie had made her feelings about him crystal clear right before she'd walked out of his door; what would the point even be of him trying to make up with her? She never wanted to hear from him again.

And after the awful things he'd said to her, he didn't blame her.

"I'm just saying, *I'm* the asshole," Ben said. "Why are you acting like me? You're supposed to be the smart one. Be smart here! Talk to her, text her, write her a letter to apologize and tell her how you feel, something."

Theo stood up. At least he wasn't dizzy anymore.

"We've been over this."

"I know we've been over this, but obviously we need to go over it again!" Ben said. "You always do this. One fight with a woman and you give up, even when you can make a save! I never cared before because I never liked any of the other women you've dated, but I liked Maddie!"

He should have kicked Ben out days ago.

"It doesn't matter how much you liked Maddie; this is about me, not you."

Ben smirked at him.

"Well, YOU liked Maddie a hell of a lot, and we both know that, so stop trying to pretend otherwise."

Theo had no real comeback for that. Unbeknownst to Ben, he *had* called Maddie. Twice. But she hadn't answered. He hadn't left a message either time, but he knew she would have seen his missed calls on her phone. But she hadn't responded in any way. She never wanted to hear from him again, like she'd said. Now he hated that he'd even tried.

"Just . . . for the love of God, please don't say anything to Alexa."

Ben rolled his eyes.

"I won't say anything," Ben said. "Even though I know she's on my side, whether she knows it or not. But I will tell her to talk some sense into you with all of your doomsday scenarios about your job and the campaign."

He didn't want to talk to Alexa about that, either. Part of him knew it might be irrational to be afraid for his job after the disaster of the rally, but another part of him felt like he needed to email his resignation in by the end of this week, before he got fired. He had

been the one to disregard what everyone had said about the protests, he had been the one who had derailed the rally, he had been
the one to take this victory away from his boss. Shouldn't he be the
one who had to pay for it?

Maybe whatever food Alexa brought would distract Ben enough
he wouldn't say anything about that, either.

Ben looked him over.

"Go change. Alexa can't see you looking like this."

Theo looked down at himself. He was in the sweatpants he'd
had on since Sunday, a food-stained T-shirt, and socks with holes
in them. Ben had a point.

Just as he walked back into the living room, after a fast shower
and with clean sweatpants on, Theo heard the doorbell rang.

"Come on in," he said as he opened the door. She had multiple
packages in her arms. Ben jumped to grab them from her.

"You look better, but you still look terrible," she said as she
walked in the door. "Hey, Ben, how's he doing?"

"Thanks, Lex, good to see you, too," Theo said. "*He* is doing
much better, thanks for asking."

She grinned at him and followed Ben down the hallway to the
kitchen.

"The mayor told me to say hi. He wanted to come and check
on you himself, but I managed to talk him out of that. He said he
wanted to see with his own eyes that you were better, since the last
time he saw you, you were on the ground being worked over by the
paramedics. I said I'd drop this off for you."

Theo winced as he opened the box she pushed toward him.
Great, a bouquet of fruit, just what he needed.

The whole reason he'd wanted the rally in Berkeley in the first
place was to show all of California the great things they were doing

there, that his boss deserved a statewide stage, and okay, fine, that he, Theo Stephens, was an asset to any politician or campaign. Now when anyone thought of him, they'd just think of him getting worked over by paramedics in the back of his own rally.

He sighed.

"Lex, I need to talk to you about something."

Alexa patted his arm and nodded.

"I've been waiting for this."

Ben grabbed a take-out container.

"Talk some sense into him, please, Alexa," Ben said. "He's been freaking out for days." Ben picked up some chopsticks and melted out of the room. The jerk had probably taken all the potstickers.

Theo sighed and looked at Alexa.

"I don't know how I'm going to face the mayor. Or anyone else in the office, for that matter, after the disaster I made of the rally. I don't know if my job can survive this."

Alexa opened another take-out container and pushed it toward him. Ahh, the potstickers. He picked one up and bit into it.

"Of course your job can survive this. What are you even talking about? I wasn't at the rally, so refresh me on this: did you hit yourself over the head?"

He should have known Alexa would make light of this to try to make him feel better.

"No, of course I didn't, but I should have known this was going to happen. I should have planned for this. And I didn't, so it's all my fault."

Alexa picked up a potsticker.

"Theo, I adore you, but you always have had a hero complex. In the same way you can't save the world single-handedly, you can't destroy the world single-handedly, either. This self-flagellation has got to end. You're taking way more responsibility for this than you need to—this wasn't all about you, Theo, and you know it."

He dropped his half-eaten potsticker on the counter. He'd thought he could depend on Alexa to know the deal here. Had she not listened to him all summer when he kept talking about all the conference calls about this very topic, and how he'd single-handedly gotten the campaign to have the rally in Berkeley, despite all the worries about protests?

No, of course she hadn't. Because Maddie had been the one he'd told all that to.

"It's not self-flagellation; it's reality. This is on me. Everyone told me they were worried about protests, but I blew them all off. I barely even talked to the police chief about the rally, other than to make sure he knew it was going on. I could have prepared for this. I could have prevented it! If I'd taken any of their worries seriously, we could have kept the rally from being disturbed in the first place."

Alexa reached for a potsticker.

"Hey, do you know whose job it is to plan for things like this? The chief of police! Who, by the way, is also mortified about what happened and has sent his apologies to you."

Okay, she had a point there, but it was still his job, too.

Alexa took a can of sparkling water out of his fridge. One of the ones he kept around for Maddie.

"But most important," she said, "you've been doing this for a long time. Everyone knows you and trusts you. One bad judgment call isn't going to destroy your reputation forever. Especially since this was a group effort. You always freak out like this."

He sighed. She was determined to try to make him feel better, wasn't she?

The problem was, Alexa cared about him too much. She was too worried about him recovering well from his injury, and had probably listened to Drew talk about how he needed peace and relaxation and a calm mind or something like that.

Damn it, where was his no-bullshit friend? The one who would tell him the truth, damn his feelings?

Maddie. That friend was Maddie.

Alexa patted him on the shoulder.

"It's not that I'm telling you to get over yourself, but also, get over yourself. Bad things happen; we all fuck up sometimes. We get up and move on. Get better, come back to work, apologize to everyone you need to apologize to, don't make this a bigger deal than it needs to be, and move on to the next thing." She took another potsticker. "Okay?"

All of what she said sounded right, but it felt dangerous to believe her.

"Okay," he said. What else could he say?

He wished he could ask Alexa for advice about Maddie. She knew Maddie better than anyone else, and he knew she'd be honest with him about that. But if he told Alexa the secret Maddie had been so adamant to keep from her, Maddie's revenge might reach biblical proportions.

"Also, stop eating all of my potstickers," he said.

"Delivery tax." She picked up her purse. "I've got to get home. You still think you'll be back at work Monday?"

He nodded.

"God, I hope so. And . . . thanks, Lex."

She gave him a quick hug.

"Anytime. About anything. I promise, everything is going to be okay." She waved at his brother on the way out the door. "Bye, Ben, see you soon."

"See?" Ben said, after the door closed. "I heard her! She agrees with me that you're freaking out for nothing. You should have talked to her about Maddie. I bet she would agree with me there, too!"

Theo sat down on the couch and dropped his head into his hands. He needed to get back to work soon, just so he didn't kill his brother.

Maddie was just about to walk out of her house to go to her mom's place when her phone rang. She glanced down at it. Some 415 number. Not Theo. She hated that she still hoped it was him every time her phone rang.

He'd called twice, the day after their fight, when she was still so mad at him there was no way she could have done anything but scream into the phone. Good thing she'd been with clients both times and had her phone on do not disturb.

Why did she even want him to call again? She never wanted to hear from him again, remember? Was it because she wanted to be able to yell at him like she'd done in her head for the past week? She had no idea.

Why had he even called her those times? Had he been calling to apologize? She'd hoped it had just been the concussion that had made him say those things to her, but if that was it, wouldn't he have left a message, or texted her, or called again?

She didn't even know if he was okay. Alexa had mentioned offhand that he was doing better, but she didn't know what that really meant: back at work better? Staying awake for more than an hour better? Could hold down lunch better? Had he even gone back to the doctor?

Not only was she still worried about him, but she felt so guilty about what she'd said to him. She'd said those things just to hurt him like he'd hurt her, and she was pretty sure she'd succeeded, but now she felt like the biggest asshole in the world for being that cruel to someone who'd gotten out of the hospital less than twenty-four hours before.

But if he didn't care enough about her feelings to call her to apologize for what he'd said, she had to make herself not care about his feelings, either.

Wait. That phone number calling her. Wasn't that the number of the TV station? *Focus, Maddie.*

She dropped the garment bag full of dresses for her mom on the couch and took a deep breath.

"This is Maddie."

"Hi, Maddie. This is Allen Barnes, over at KPTZ. How are you?"

Alexa had told her that if you smiled on the phone, it made you sound more friendly and warm, so she tried to smile.

How the fuck was someone supposed to smile at someone on the phone? Especially when she was this nervous?

"I'm great!" she said. Wait, was that too effusive? Should she have just said, *I'm doing well, thank you, how are you?* Why was he calling her in the first place? Couldn't they cut the preamble and just get to it?

"Good, good, that's wonderful to hear. It's great to talk to you again. Maddie, everyone at the station really enjoyed working with you, but unfortunately we've decided to go in a different direction for the show. But I certainly hope you . . ."

Maddie didn't listen to the rest of what he said. She said words like "thank you" and "wonderful opportunity" and "all my best" as she sank down on the couch. Finally, she heard him say good-bye, so she put her phone down.

She didn't get the job. She hadn't realized just how much she'd wanted it until this moment.

She put her head in her hands and took a few deep breaths.

When she opened her eyes, she saw the garment bag with dresses for her mom to wear to Alexa's wedding hanging over the side of the couch. Thank God her mom was already expecting her.

She got in her car and drove to the tiny two-bedroom house in East Oakland her mom had managed to buy about ten years ago.

Her mom opened the door, already talking.

"Hey, girl, I made those meatballs you like, but did you bring . . ." She took a look at Maddie and pulled her into the house.

"What's wrong?"

Maddie sank down on the couch. It was an old one her mom had had since Maddie was a teenager. She curled up in the corner and pulled a blanket around her shoulders. It felt comforting, to be around stuff that had been in her life for so long.

"I didn't get the job." It hurt to say it out loud. "They just called to tell me."

Her mom sat down on the couch next to her and wrapped the blanket around both of them.

"Oh, baby, I'm so sorry," she said. "I know how much you wanted it."

Maddie covered her eyes.

"I did want it. Going through this process . . . it really made me think about how much I want to help people who really need me, where I can really make a difference in their lives. I didn't realize how much I wanted this until I had the opportunity, and now it's gone."

Maddie buried her head in her mom's shoulder and smelled the perfume she'd been wearing for thirty years.

"I ruined it. I knew what they wanted, I knew how to *be* what they wanted, so why didn't I just give it to them? I could have been bitchy Maddie. Hell, I'm bitchy Maddie all the damn time; being her comes naturally to me. Then I would have had the show. Instead, I threw it away for stupid reasons."

Her mom pulled away until Maddie looked up at her.

"No. That's not true. You wouldn't have had your own respect, and that's what matters the most. If I've taught you anything, you know I've taught you that."

Finally, the tears came.

"Does that really matter the most, though? I see people out there in the world all day every day who do things to hurt people, who take and take and never give; who don't care about what they do and how they do it as long as they win. What's the point anymore of trying to do the right thing?"

Her mom didn't even answer; she just handed Maddie tissues from the box on the coffee table. Finally, Maddie sat up.

"I know. I know. You don't have to tell me. I don't want to be one of those people. I hate those people. Those are the people you've worked your entire life against. But why do they keep succeeding and people like us keep losing?"

Her mom got up and brought her a glass of water.

"Like you said, I've been working my entire life against people like this. And they do win. A lot. But the only thing we can do is keep on fighting and keep on helping people who need us. At least, that's the only thing that makes life worthwhile for me."

Maddie shook her head.

"I don't know what's wrong with me. I'm so overwrought about this stupid job. It's just one job, it's just a TV thing, it's just about fashion, not about, like, the downfall of society."

Her mom stroked her hair.

"Have you talked to Alexa about it?"

She shook her head.

"No, I just found out when I was on my way over here. I'll call her later."

Her mom nodded.

"Did you talk to Theo about it?"

Why would her mom ask that?

"Why would I talk to Theo about this?"

Vivian had a very smug look on her face.

"Maddie, please. I haven't been your mother for thirty-four years for nothing. Momma knows everything. How's he doing, anyway, after the concussion at the rally?"

Maddie burst into tears. Again.

"I don't know! We had a fight the next day and I haven't seen him since and he said terrible things to me and I said terrible things to him. I'm so worried about him and mad at him and I feel so bad about what I said to him and I don't know what to do!"

Her mom pulled her back down against her chest. Maddie had spent what felt like years crying into her mom's comfortable bosom. About mean girls, and cruel teachers, and stupid boys, and bad bosses. Vivian just let her keep crying.

"How did you know something was going on between the two of us? Not even Alexa knows."

Her mom laughed at her as she got up to put the teakettle on.

"Oh please. I have ears! You used every opportunity possible to bring up his name, you had this smile on your face whenever you talked about him, and I could even hear you smiling about him over the phone!"

Huh, Alexa was right about that phone smiling thing.

"Come on," her mom said. "Tell me what happened."

Maddie confessed all, or almost all. She skipped over all the sex, though she was pretty sure her mom knew exactly what she was skipping.

And she didn't tell her about the I love yous. Her mom didn't need to know that part.

"Well," she said, "it's over now. It's probably for the best. Maybe he said all that because of the concussion, but it wouldn't have lasted much longer anyway. I always knew we were too different, and this thing between us was too good to be true; anything like that can't last very long. I'm going to have to see him at the wedding, which . . ." She sighed. "I'll worry about that later."

Her mom bustled around taking mugs down from the cabinet and getting tea bags out.

"It sounds like you had some strong feelings for him, which I thought was the case."

Of course her mom would think that.

"No, that's not it. I just got used to being around him, that's all. And the end left a bad taste in my mouth. I'll get over it."

She should be over this. She couldn't believe she'd cried again about Theo.

"You remember when your aunt Janet had that car accident, and the two of us got so mad at each other because of something silly?"

Maddie sighed.

"Yeah, Mom, I remember, but this isn't . . ."

"I'm just saying, emotions get high at times like that." Vivian poured boiling water into their mugs. "Everyone is stressed and at a breaking point, and sometimes people say things they don't mean. Maybe you both did that."

"That's not what it was, Mom." Maddie reached for her mug. "I don't want to talk about Theo anymore, okay?"

Vivian sat down next to her.

"Okay. Then let's talk about the job."

Maddie picked up the mug and went to the kitchen to add more sugar. Her mom never put enough sugar in her tea.

"What's the point? I didn't get the job, the end."

Her mom shook her head.

"No, not the end. This wasn't your only opportunity. Now did you want to be on TV, or did you want to help women who need you?"

Maddie threw up her arms.

"I wanted to help women who need me on TV!"

She and her mom both burst out laughing.

"Okay, but seriously," Vivian said. "There are other ways for you to do this kind of work. I know a million places you can volunteer to help women in this way. You can do whole seminars; you can help people dig through all the clothes that get donated to shelters to find outfits for job interviews—remember like you used to do for me at thrift stores?"

Why had something like that never occurred to her?

"Of course I remember." She sat back on the couch and tucked her feet under the blanket. "Tell me all your ideas."

Chapter Twenty

WHEN THEO WALKED BACK INTO CITY HALL MONDAY MORNING, IT FELT like it had been months since he'd been there, not a week and a half. Apparently, it felt like that to other people, too: two people from the counsel's office hugged him as he walked into the building, the security guard who did like him gave him a high five in the lobby, and there were "Welcome back!" balloons in his office.

It was all so nice, except how it made him feel like a piece of shit. Didn't they all know the concussion had been his fault in the first place? That he'd ruined the kickoff rally for a major statewide initiative because of his own hubris?

Didn't they all know he was the biggest asshole Maddie had ever met?

On the plus side, he'd been able to think more clearly over the past few days and had realized it was possible that his anxiety about losing his job over the rally was not completely rational, even though he still felt terrible about ruining the rally. The mayor liked him; he'd done great work there—Alexa had maybe even been right about all that. At least, he hoped so.

Everything with Maddie, however, seemed just as dire. He missed her so fucking much he felt pathetic. He constantly wanted to pick up the phone and text her something ridiculous Ben had said, or tell her something he knew she'd think was funny, or see when she was coming over. But he knew she didn't want to hear from him.

Alexa walked into his office holding two cups of coffee.

"This was your doing, wasn't it?" he asked her, gesturing to the balloons in the corner.

She set his coffee on his desk and shook her head.

"Nope. I guess there are more people in this building who care about you than you knew."

He got up to give her a tight hug.

"We missed you around here, you know," she said.

He'd missed them, too. He was so glad to be back at work. He knew he wasn't anywhere near a hundred percent well, but not working for so long had made him jittery. And he was so glad to be out of the house and have something to do other than miss Maddie. He needed to apologize for what he'd said to her, but the only way he could explain why he'd said what he'd said to Ben was to tell her the truth. And he couldn't admit that he'd fallen in love with her.

"Are you sure you're okay to be back here?" Alexa asked.

He nodded, even though it hurt his head.

"One more day in my apartment and I would have started climbing the walls, Lex. Or murdered my little brother. I'm probably not going to be in great form for the first week, but I had to come back."

He couldn't tell her he also needed the distraction from thinking about Maddie.

"Okay, but go home early, at least today, okay? See you at staff meeting."

Theo finished his coffee and then walked over to the mayor's office. He might as well get this part over with as soon as possible.

The mayor's secretary jumped up and gave him a hug as soon as she saw him.

"Theo! I was so worried about you! Did you get the banana bread I sent over?"

He hugged her back.

"I did, and I was so grateful for it. Thank you. I ate it for breakfast every day last week." He pointed at the mayor's office door. "Is he in there?"

She nodded and glanced down at the phone on her desk.

"Yes, and he's off the phone. Go on in."

Theo knocked on the door and walked in when the mayor boomed out, "Come in!"

"You're back!" The mayor grinned as Theo walked through the door. "I knew the bastards couldn't keep you down for long."

Theo returned his boss's vigorous handshake.

"I'm back. I may not be up to speed for a few days, but I couldn't handle being at home another day."

Maybe everything really was okay? The mayor seemed happy to see him.

"Someday, someone needs to teach you how to take a break," the mayor said as he sat back down at his desk.

Theo sat down, too, and took a deep breath. No matter how relaxed his boss was, he still had to say this.

"Sir, I just want to say that I'm sorry about what happened with the rally. I'm the one who pushed to have it in Berkeley, and I blew off the people who predicted we'd have issues with protestors. I should have done a much better job on contingency plans. I know it hurt the campaign, and I take—"

The mayor's laugh rang out.

"Please don't tell me you take full responsibility for some violent protestors; the chief of police was in here telling me the same thing, and he's not even the one who got hit over the head. He feels awful about what happened to you, by the way."

Alexa had told him the chief of police sent him an apology, but he hadn't really believed her.

"I appreciate that, but I really should have—"

"No more apologies! You should have talked to him, yes. He should have staffed the rally better, absolutely. But it's over and done with, and both of you will do better in the future. And yeah, I'm not going to lie to you and say we got great press out of it, but a lot more people know there's a ballot initiative for universal pre-K on the November ballot than they did two weeks ago, that's for sure."

Theo hoped his face didn't show how relieved he felt.

"Well, I'm glad my concussion could help the cause." He stood up. "See you at staff meeting."

On his way back to his office, he ran into ten more people, all of whom hugged him and asked him how he was doing. After a while, he wished he had a little card he could hand everyone. "FEELING MUCH BETTER, THANK YOU. STILL HAVE A HEADACHE, CAN'T READ MUCH FOR A WHILE, BUT HAPPY TO BE BACK AT WORK."

He poked his head into Alexa's office. She had a bakery box sitting on the edge of her desk.

"What's in that box?"

She glanced up from her computer.

"Oh, just leftover cake. Drew and I did a cake tasting this weekend, and I have some leftovers to share."

Cake tasting. For her wedding. Shit.

"I'm the worst person in the world. I can't believe you've spent
the past two weeks doing my job and your job when it's less than
three weeks before your wedding. No wonder you need me to pull
myself together."

She laughed at him.

"You're exaggerating again. You aren't the worst person in the
world; let's reserve that label for the guy who hit you over the head,
causing me to have to do my job and part of your job for the past
week and a half."

He plopped down in the chair in front of her desk.

"Okay, fine, I'm the worst bridesman in the world. I'm sorry. I
should have been more helpful, Lex."

She rolled her eyes at him.

"You had a concussion—give me a break. Plus, I don't really
know what you could have done. I mean yes, I had to do a wedding
dress fitting while I was on conference calls the entire time, so keep
your fingers crossed that I told them the right stuff to fix and the
dress doesn't come out a size too small or with brand-new ruffles
around the bottom or whatever. But other than that, this wedding
thing hasn't been as stressful as everyone says. It'll be fine."

He reached for the box.

"I want to see this cake."

But when he popped the box top open, it was row after row of
his favorite chocolate chip cookies.

"It's not cake, come on. Who does a cake tasting less than a
month before the wedding? I can't believe you bought that. We

had the cake even before I had the dress. You didn't think I'd get you cookies to welcome you back?"

He grabbed a cookie as he stood up.

"Thanks. You're the best."

She grinned.

"I know. Everything went okay when you went to talk to the boss?"

He hadn't even told her he was going to do that.

"Yeah. Just like you said." He shook his head. "I always thought I had to be perfect, I could never make a misstep, or everything would come crashing down, but I guess I was wrong about that? I could have been fucking up for years!"

She laughed and reached for a cookie.

"See? It's never as bad as you think, Teddy."

He thought about that on his way back to his office. Was it as bad as he thought with Maddie, too?

He sighed. No, that was different. He'd proved himself to his boss. The only thing he'd proved to Maddie was how right she'd been about him all along. He never should have said those things to her. He'd been hurt and scared and lashing out, he realized now, but why did he have to say the handful of things he knew would hurt her the most?

He sat down at his desk.

Maybe if he apologized to Maddie, it would make him feel a little bit less like a piece of shit?

His phone rang. Oh thank God, he had work to do.

Maddie drove over to Alexa's house with a bottle of wine in her purse. It was two weeks and a day before the wedding, and Alexa had called her in a panic twenty minutes ago. She was pretty sure Alexa was starting to lose it. Honestly, Maddie was impressed Alexa hadn't lost it until now.

Hell, Maddie was starting to lose it, too. In two weeks she would have to see Theo again, be in close quarters with Theo again, and she wasn't sure how she was going to handle it. She'd tried hard for the past week to pretend he didn't exist, that the two of them had never existed, but she'd failed miserably at that. No matter how much she told herself they were doomed anyway, he'd never respected her, she'd been too good for him, none of it helped her feel better.

"Hey!" Alexa answered her front door with a glazed look in her eyes, her hair falling out of the messy bun on the top of her head, and what looked like red nail polish on her cheek.

"Hey," Maddie said, as she looked her friend up and down. "What was it you needed help with?"

Alexa pulled her inside and shut the door.

"Thank God you're here."

Maddie followed her to the living room, which had tiny pots of paint, ribbons, and other weird objects strewn all over the floor. Was that a bowl full of dirt?

"Have you taken up . . . crafting?"

Alexa plopped down on the floor and motioned for her to follow.

"The better question is, why didn't I take up crafting years ago? I'm trying to make our fucking wedding favors, because my mom says we have to have wedding favors, and I've already had one million fights with my mom about this stupid wedding, and I couldn't even deal with fighting her about this, so I said yes, of course we're having favors, I've already taken care of that, so now I have to take care of the fucking favors!!!"

Maddie slowly pulled the bottle of wine out of her purse and got up to get some wineglasses.

"Okay, so what are we making?"

Alexa picked up a tiny glass container and scooped some dirt into it with a spoon.

"Mom showed me a long time ago this thing in *Martha Stewart Weddings* about people giving terrariums as wedding favors, and she said it was so cute and you know how much I love Martha and how I still think about that amazing shawl she wore when she got out of jail, but OH MY GOD, I wish the woman never existed right about now, because I bought little things to put the dirt and the plants in, but the plants all look stupid and I think they're dying and you need to help me, Maddie."

Maddie took the half-made terrarium out of Alexa's hand and put the full wineglass in its place.

"First, drink some of that."

Alexa took a gulp of wine and closed her eyes while she swallowed.

"Okay, that's a little better. Now what?"

Maddie took out her phone.

"Now I order us pizza. Pepperoni and black olive?"

Alexa nodded.

"Even better. Now what?"

Maddie picked up one of the glass whatchamacallits.

"Now let's make some fucking terrariums."

They sat there for the next hour, drinking wine, scooping dirt into tiny bowls, and decorating the dirt with tiny plants.

"Thank you so much for coming to help me, Mads. How are you feeling about the whole job thing? I'm still furious at them for not hiring you."

Maddie grinned. Nothing like a ride or die friend.

"Oh, my client Maya is, too. She called me yelling the day she found out. I thought she was going to quit her job. Instead, I just got her to promise to do a seminar for the series I'm planning with that women's organization you hooked me up with. I'm going to do styling sessions for women there twice a month, and we're going to pull in other local women to help out and do events and give them job search advice."

Alexa narrowed her eyes.

"You know I'm in, too, right?"

Maddie laughed.

"Obviously. That wasn't even a question." She took a sip of wine. "But really, I'm doing okay. I'm proud of my audition, I gave them the best of me, and if that's not what they wanted, I wouldn't have been happy doing the show anyway. But I'm really glad I had the opportunity; it helped me realize one of the things that was missing in my life. And I'm excited for this new plan."

Alexa got up and brought back another bottle of wine.

"I am, too. And I'm really proud of you."

They smiled at each other as they clinked glasses.

Maddie picked up one of her completed terrariums and turned it around to look at it from all sides.

"Lex, I have to tell you something." She paused and looked up at Alexa. "I think we're going to get a very bad grade on this science project."

Alexa giggled.

"This is like old times, isn't it?"

Maddie looked at her best friend, the joyful smile on her face just the same as the one the first day they'd met, and she couldn't stop tears from coming to her eyes.

"It is just like old times. Oh, Lex"—her voice caught—"I'm going to miss you."

Alexa pushed aside all the plant life on the floor and plopped down next to Maddie.

"What do you mean, you're going to miss me? I'm not going anywhere! I'm not getting married and moving to Married People Land! I'm still going to be Alexa Monroe, I'll still be right here, I'll still be your best friend, husband or no husband!"

Maddie tried to stop her tears from falling, but there was no stopping them now.

"I know, but still, it'll be different! I'm so happy for you, and I even think Drew is almost worthy of you, but it's like when we graduated from high school and I didn't know if we would be the same people when we saw each other again. What if you're a different person after you get married?"

Maddie shook her head and wiped her eyes with the bottom of her shirt.

"Sorry, you're trying to do these damn favors and I'm sitting here crying all over you. I'm just weirdly emotional this week."

Alexa put her arm around Maddie.

"I am ALSO weirdly emotional this week. I almost sobbed over poor Theo when he came back to work on Monday."

Theo was back at work already? That seemed too early, from all the reading she'd done.

"Oh, he's back at work? Um, how's he doing?" Maddie picked up her own wineglass and sipped the remainder slowly.

"A lot better. He's far from a hundred percent, but he definitely looks better than he did the weekend after, when he looked depressed and was in a daze the whole time, and could barely put a sentence together."

Theo had looked depressed and in a daze the weekend after? Huh.

"Yeah, I bet that weekend was really hard for him. But can he
handle being back at work?"

Alexa nodded.

"He says he still has a constant headache, and he gets a lot of
printouts of emails and memos in very large fonts now, but he said
being at home got really boring, especially since he couldn't read
or watch TV. He still looks off, though."

She really shouldn't ask. She shouldn't be having this conversation at all, actually.

"He looks off how?"

Alexa dropped a handful of succulent leaves in some dirt.

"Not sure. Just sad, I think." Alexa shrugged. "Maybe I'm just
imagining it. Or maybe it's because he's had a headache for over
two weeks straight. I'd look depressed all the time if I'd had a headache for that long, too."

There was a knock on the door, and Maddie jumped up.

"I bet that's our pizza. I'll get it."

God, she wished she could talk to Alexa about Theo. But even
if she'd been ready to tell Alexa the secret she'd been keeping from
her for so long, she couldn't tell her now, just weeks before her wedding, the one she and Theo were both in. She couldn't throw chaos
into the middle of her best friend's wedding like that. She needed
to get her mind away from Theo and back to Alexa.

Drew came home an hour later and found them sprawled on
the floor with dirt everywhere.

"You're home early!" Alexa jumped up and ran to kiss Drew.
He dropped his bag on the floor and wrapped his arms around her.
They were still so happy, so excited to greet each other, even when

they'd just seen each other that morning. Maddie turned away from them with tears in her eyes. She wanted to be that happy.

Just a few weeks ago, when she'd walked into Theo's apartment, he'd picked her up and spun her around until they'd fallen together on the couch and laughed so hard they could barely speak. She'd been that happy when she was with Theo.

She was in love with him. She'd been in love with him for weeks. Maybe even months.

She couldn't believe she'd fallen in love with fucking Theo Stephens. This might be the stupidest thing she'd ever done in her life, and that included that time she'd worn a white romper to an outdoor festival. He was pompous and full of himself and constantly had a stick up his ass.

But he'd also talked her down from a crisis, wiped her tears when she'd cried both from joy and sorrow, laughed with her for hours, spent days working with parents to help them feel comfortable speaking at the rally, stopped to talk to every dog he saw, and taught her how to moonwalk.

She loved him, spreadsheets and all. She'd meant it when she'd said she loved him in the middle of the night. Part of her had known that all along.

Had he meant it when he said he loved her?

Oh God, what was she going to do?

She looked up. Alexa and Drew were still murmuring to each other. She wasn't going to do anything. At least, not until after the wedding. She could wait two weeks and two days to have this crisis; she couldn't ruin her best friend's wedding with her nonsense.

Plus, she loved him, okay, fine, but she was still furious and hurt by what he'd said to her when they'd fought. But maybe he hadn't meant what he said to her, just like she hadn't meant what she'd said to him?

But then when he'd told Ben she was still that same shallow person he'd always thought she was, he hadn't known she'd been listening. Why would he lie to Ben about that? She didn't know what to think.

Nothing, that's what to think. Didn't she *just* say she was going to wait to have this emotional crisis until after Alexa's wedding?

Drew walked over and looked at their terrariums, all lined up on the floor.

"Did you guys . . . make these?" he asked.

Alexa and Maddie both burst out laughing.

"Look how hard he's trying to pretend they don't look ridiculous." Alexa stared down at the terrariums and the smile dropped from her face. Maddie could see the glaze coming back into her eyes. "Oh my God, these are terrible. We can't give these out at our wedding. What was I thinking? My mother will kill me if I don't have favors, and it's two weeks and a day before the wedding. What are we going to do?"

Maddie put her hand on Alexa's shoulder.

"Don't worry, I've taken care of it. I know someone through a local women's small business group who makes custom wineglasses for weddings. I texted her as soon as I saw you sitting here with piles of dirt and dead plants. She texted me back ten minutes ago: she'll make a hundred of them with your names and your wedding date on them. They'll be done in a week. Call it a wedding present."

Alexa threw her arms around Maddie.

"What would I do without you?"

Drew stood behind Alexa and mouthed, "Thank you," to Maddie. She winked at him.

If only she could solve all her problems this easily.

Chapter Twenty-one

MADDIE GOT DRESSED FOR THE REHEARSAL LIKE SHE WAS PREPARING for battle. She felt ridiculous as soon as she thought that—nothing about the first time she'd see Theo in weeks could be compared to a battle. But as she put on her favorite bra, slipped on the pale pink dress that made her boobs look great, blew out her hair, and spent a full forty-five minutes on her "no makeup" makeup look, it felt like she was putting on the right armor in order to face him.

She'd spent all morning doing last-minute errands with Alexa and Olivia, but between how much nervous energy Alexa had and how stressed about seeing Theo tonight she was, she'd felt so anxious the whole time she'd wanted to jump out of her skin. She'd been glad Olivia had invoked big sister bossiness and had dropped Alexa off to get an hour and a half massage right after lunch.

"Nope, you're all done. Now it's relaxation time," Olivia had said when Alexa had tried to say she didn't have time for that. "The only thing you have to do after this is get dressed for tonight.

And don't worry about Mom. I made her a hair appointment this afternoon, and I told her hairdresser I'd pay her double if she made it take twice as long."

Alexa gasped.

"She'll be at the hair salon for at least four hours! Maybe five!"

Olivia had an evil grin on her face.

"She'll be done just in time to get dressed and get herself to the rehearsal. I gave Dad all the directions and told them we'd meet them there. Now, go."

Instead of a massage, Maddie had gone to a very hard yoga class. The good thing about strenuous exercise when she was anxious about something was that when it was hard enough, it took all her brainpower to hold the pose, or lift herself that way, or run to the next block, and pushed away all the space that held her worries.

She slipped on her strappy sandals and looked at herself in the mirror one more time before leaving the house. Okay. She could do this.

She parked her car outside the Rose Garden, and another car immediately pulled up behind her. Please let the first person she saw not be Theo, please let the first person she saw not be Theo.

She took a deep breath, grabbed her clutch, and got out of the car. She forced herself not to turn around to check who was getting out of the cars behind her.

"Maddie!"

Now she turned around with a grin.

"Carlos!"

He stood next to the car behind hers, along with a black woman in a pale blue dress.

She waited for them to catch up to her, and gave Carlos a big hug. Thank God. What a good person to see first.

"Maddie, I'd love for you to meet my girlfriend, Nik. Nik, this is Maddie. She's Alexa's best friend and one of the bridesmaids." Carlos paused. "Wait, aren't you actually the only bridesmaid? Since Olivia is the maid of honor, and Theo is a bridesman?"

Maybe it would have been better to see Theo first, just to get it over with. Maybe then every mention of his name wouldn't hit her so hard.

She reached out to shake Nik's hand.

"Nice to meet you, Nik. I've heard a lot about you from Alexa and Drew. They were both stunned that someone as great as you would want to date this guy."

"Hey!" Carlos put his arms around both of them as they walked down the stairs to the garden. "I come up to Northern California, like, twice a year, and this is the kind of abuse I get? What kind of gratitude is this?"

Maddie and Nik both laughed.

"I'm already excited about this wedding if it means people are going to make fun of Carlos all weekend," Nik said. "And since we flew up here, he has to drive a rented sedan, which is just hilarious."

He shook his head in disgust.

"I haven't driven an automatic in years. It's going to take me weeks to recover."

They walked toward the group clustered around the back of the garden, as Carlos complained about the rental car. Theo was already there; Maddie had seen him the second they'd walked in. He hadn't turned around to look at her.

There was a flurry of hugging and introductions and more hugging. In the midst of all of that, she turned around and found herself face-to-face with Theo. She forced a smile.

"Hi, Theo," she said.

"Hey, Maddie," he said. "You look beautiful."

She tried not to let that melt everything inside her, but it took a lot of effort. Maybe he hadn't meant what he said about her. He couldn't have meant it, could he?

Of course he could have.

"Thank you, Theo," she said. "How are you feeling?"

She could hear how stiff and hostile she sounded.

"A lot better. Thanks for asking." He nodded at her and turned away to go greet Alexa's parents.

Well, that had been a disaster. Was this just how it was going to be between them forever now?

She glanced at him throughout the rehearsal. She couldn't stop herself. He laughed and chatted with Alexa's mom, with Carlos, with Alexa's cousin, like nothing was wrong, like he was totally fine having to stand next to her for the entire ceremony, so close she could feel his body heat as the sun went down and the air got cooler.

This was her revenge for telling Alexa all smug that time she should just talk to Drew and tell him how she felt. Why do people even say that? Why had she even said that? "Just talk to him," like that's so easy to do. Didn't they understand how hard, how impossible that was? Why hadn't she understood that until now?

She knew she'd always wonder how he felt about her if she didn't find out for sure. She knew she'd always wonder if he'd meant the terrible things he said that day.

But what if he had meant them?

She wanted to punch the Maddie who'd said, "Just talk to him!" to Alexa right in the face.

"Okay!" The minister clapped his hands. "All done with the rehearsal, but no kissing, you two, not until tomorrow!"

Alexa and Drew were holding hands and looking so happy the minister's bad jokes didn't even seem to register with them. Drew still looked at Alexa like he couldn't believe his luck. Maddie wanted that. She looked over at Theo again, but he was looking down at the roses growing along the walkway.

They all walked to their cars to head to the rehearsal dinner, and Maddie found herself wishing she could fall in line with Theo, in the way Nik fell in line with Carlos, and Molly fell in line with Josh. She walked faster to catch up with Olivia.

"Do we think the flower girls will manage tomorrow, or do we think they'll have a meltdown?" she asked Olivia.

Olivia shook her head.

"It's about fifty-fifty, but luckily, I think my mom is the only one who really cares. Alexa is just happy their dresses fit." She slowed down as they approached the stairs. "Hey, can I get a ride with you over to the dinner? I rode over here with Alexa and Drew, since I'm staying at their place, but I want to let the lovebirds have this car ride to themselves, since it's the last time they'll get to themselves before tomorrow is over."

Maddie was relieved she would have someone to talk to on the way over to the dinner, instead of just obsessing about Theo and if he'd meant what he'd said in the middle of that night.

"Of course. Is your mom still furious Alexa refused to stay in a hotel tonight and Drew's staying in a hotel instead?"

Olivia laughed as they approached Maddie's car.

"Oh, totally, but what she doesn't know is that was the compromise. Alexa didn't want them to spend this night apart at all, but I managed to get her to concede that to Mom. And I agree with her that it seems way easier to get ready for your wedding around all your own stuff. I can only imagine how many things she would have forgotten this morning if she was packing everything to go to a hotel."

"Yeah." Maddie pulled out of her parking spot and found herself right behind Theo's car at the stoplight. He was bopping his head to music in that way she'd always made fun of him for. She sighed.

"I'm so happy Alexa has found someone who loves her so much," Maddie said.

Olivia handed her a tissue. She hadn't even realized she'd started crying.

"So am I," Olivia said.

Maddie hated him. Again. Still. He'd been so relieved she'd said hi to him, and then she'd had that frozen look on her face and steely tone in her voice after he'd responded. She really never wanted him to talk to her again, didn't she?

He probably shouldn't have started with "You look beautiful," but he couldn't help it. He'd missed her so much. He'd wanted to apologize to her, but he couldn't do that in the middle of the wedding rehearsal. He didn't want to put her on the spot like that in public. He'd even taken Ben's terrible advice and written her a stupid letter and put it in his pocket, but there was no way he could give it to her there. Or maybe ever.

He was happy for Alexa, he really was, but watching her face full of love and excitement for Drew and their new life together while standing next to the woman he loved and who hated him was brutal.

He pulled into a parking spot near the restaurant where the rehearsal dinner was and leaned his head on his steering wheel for a few seconds. He'd spent hours working on that letter, and had finally given up on making it perfect and just folded up the last version he'd written, even though it was way too maudlin and rambling. Oh God, she'd probably laugh at it.

At least the rehearsal was over. He just had to endure the rest of dinner tonight, and then all day tomorrow, and he wouldn't have to stand near Maddie anymore and pretend away his feelings for her, while trying to be around her as much as possible, just for the glory of seeing her and smelling her and hearing her laugh.

He sighed and got out of his car.

He ran into Carlos and Nik on the way into the restaurant.

"Hey, man. Is Drew ready for tomorrow?"

Carlos laughed and reached for Nik's hand. Theo looked away. People always got extra touchy-feely on wedding weekends. Unfortunately, all public displays of affection just made him bitter right now. He'd never gotten to do that with Maddie. And never would.

"He's more than ready. He told me a few months ago that he couldn't wait to marry her, and even though the past month or so has been frantic with all the wedding planning, he still feels that way more than ever." Carlos raised his eyebrows at him. "What about you? What's going on with you and that one over there?" He nodded toward Maddie, standing over by the bar with Olivia.

Theo shook his head.

"First of all, you don't know anything about that. Second . . . not great. There was a whole . . ." He shook his head. "I fucked up, in more ways than one. I probably never should have started the whole thing. Feelings are the worst."

Carlos looked at Nik and they both laughed.

"I agree with you one hundred percent," Nik said. "Carlos, go get us some drinks. Theo and I can stand here in the corner and not talk about feelings."

He and Nik stood in companionable silence as they watched a stream of people come in and Alexa and Drew greet them all. Appetizers circulated, and soon they had napkins full of tiny cheeseburgers and puff-pastry-and-Brie triangles.

"If these appetizers are any signal of what the food at this wedding is going to be like, we're in for a treat," Nik said after finishing everything in her napkin.

Theo nodded.

"If there's one thing I know about Alexa's wedding, it's that the food is going to be great."

Carlos headed back toward them, three glasses of rosé in his hands, but people stopped him to say hi after every few steps he took.

Nik turned to Theo with a fond smile on her face.

"Carlos has never been able to stop himself from socializing."

Theo tore his eyes away from Maddie to look where she was pointing.

Nik shook her head at him.

"Oh no. I don't even know you, but I can tell you have it bad."

Theo sighed.

"It's that obvious, huh? I need to put on my game face for the rest of the night and tomorrow. Alexa and Drew don't know about any of this. It's complicated."

Carlos finally reached them, just then. Nik took her glass of rosé and winked at Carlos.

"You've got to get some of those tiny cheeseburgers," she said to Carlos. "They're amazing."

Carlos grinned.

"Oh, I had three before I even got to the bar." He took her hand. "Come on, I have some people I want you to meet."

Nik turned back to Theo before she walked away.

"It's always complicated. The complications don't matter."

Theo just smiled and nodded at her. Like she would know. People in happy relationships always said things like "the complications don't matter" when they had no idea what the problems were.

He endured the rest of the rehearsal dinner with a practiced smile on his face. He ate the food, he joined in on the toasts, he even made a toast of his own that got people laughing, and he snuck glances at Maddie the whole time. He hadn't seen her for weeks; it was like he was starved for the sight of her. He was thrilled when she got up to give a toast. It gave him an excuse to look at her the whole time. She didn't look at him once. Every time the letter in his pocket crackled, he winced.

This was going to be the worst wedding ever.

Chapter Twenty-two

MADDIE GOT TO ALEXA'S HOUSE AT NINE A.M. ON THE MORNING OF THE wedding. She had her dress over her shoulder, a duffel bag holding her shoes, makeup, and other necessities in one hand, and a bakery bag in the other. Today was going to be brutal; she needed as many good snacks as she could get.

Hell, last night had been brutal. She had to stand there and smile at the world and watch Theo chat with every woman who walked by him except for her, and today was going to be even worse.

She just had to take a deep breath, concentrate on Alexa, and get herself through it.

"Welcome to the madhouse." Olivia opened the front door and ushered her in.

"Oh no." Maddie handed the bakery bag to Olivia. "How is she?"

Olivia smiled and shook her head.

"You'll see."

They walked into the living room, where Maddie draped her plastic-encased dress over a chair and dumped her bag on the floor. She followed Olivia into the kitchen, and her eyes widened.

"Maddie!" Alexa gave her a hug. "You're finally here! Fantastic. Do you want some coffee? I have lots of coffee!"

Maddie looked around at the trays full of cookies that blanketed the kitchen.

"Sure, I'll take some coffee. Um . . . where did all of these cookies come from?"

Alexa picked up a cookie and handed it to Maddie.

"Wasn't it a great idea? I woke up early and couldn't go back to sleep, and I realized that we still had a bunch of eggs and butter in the fridge, and since we're going to be gone for the next two weeks, the thing that made the most sense was to turn all of that into cookies! That way, we'll all have stuff to snack on later today, and we can take cookies with us on our honeymoon. I just took the last batch out of the oven when you walked in!"

Olivia mouthed, "She's lost it," over Alexa's head. Maddie tried not to grin and instead picked up a cookie.

"Yeah, um, that was a great idea. But the wedding isn't until five. Aren't you going to be exhausted later if you've been up baking for so long? Do you want to take a nap in a little while, or . . . ?"

Alexa picked up a cup and poured herself more coffee.

"I'll be fine! I feel great! What do you have there?"

Maddie took the box out of the bakery bag.

"Oh, well, you always say how important it is for brides to eat on the day of their wedding so they don't start drinking champagne on an empty stomach and then get drunk really fast, so I brought some doughnuts to start us off." She looked around the room. "But I didn't realize there would be so many cookies."

Alexa opened the doughnut box and grabbed one.

"You're an angel, thank you—we definitely needed both doughnuts and cookies, didn't we, Olivia?"

Olivia poured herself more coffee.

"Sure, yes, definitely, we needed doughnuts as well as the cookies."

They stood in the kitchen drinking coffee and eating doughnuts, while Alexa talked a mile a minute.

Alexa's phone buzzed, and she glanced at it.

"Ooh, you know what we need now? Champagne! How could I have forgotten this? Maddie, can you go in the big closet in the guest room and get some champagne? I bought some specifically for today and forgot it in there. It's in the box on the second shelf in the back. I'm going to grab some more treats."

Maddie walked into the guest room and opened the closet door. God only knew what other kinds of "treats" Alexa had up her sleeve. People warned you about bridezilla, but never about caffeinated-zilla. She must have had at least four cups of coffee, two cookies, and a doughnut already. What was going to happen later today with all of that caffeine and sugar in her system? She guessed they were going to find out.

Maddie went deep into the back of the closet, around all the random crap Alexa and Drew had stored back there: an old bike helmet; a few tote bags she knew she'd told Alexa to throw away; and piles of wedding presents. She turned on the closet light and let out a sigh. The last time she'd been in there, it was with Theo, at the engagement party.

She tried to put those memories out of her head and reached up to the second shelf for a box that looked like it could be holding champagne. When she heard the closet door close, she spun around. Theo stood there with his back to the door.

"Theo!" He stared back at her as she stared at him. "What are you doing here? I mean, in here, I mean, not here at Alexa's, I know you're supposed to be here."

Way to go, Maddie. Making a lot of sense.

"Um. I just got here, and Alexa sent me back to the closet to get some champagne. I didn't mean to close the door; it just shut behind me. I didn't know you were in here."

Maddie held up the box.

"She sent me back here to get champagne, too. I think it's in here. She didn't get a lot of sleep last night."

Theo nodded and turned around.

"Oh, okay, right." He tried to open the door, but it seemed stuck. "Alexa? Olivia? I think the door is stuck."

"The door isn't stuck. It's locked!" Alexa yelled from the other side of the door. "I've locked you both in until you figure your shit out!"

Maddie and Theo looked at each other, and then at the closed door.

"What do you mean?" Maddie tried. "I got the champagne."

"The champagne is in the refrigerator, not in the closet. You know me too well to think that I wouldn't stock my fridge with champagne bottles the night before my wedding. I can't believe both of you fell for that!"

Maddie and Theo looked at each other again.

"I think she knows," Maddie whispered.

"Of course I know!" Alexa yelled. "Everyone knew! I've had it with both of you! I can't believe the two of you thought I was so stupid that I wouldn't know that my two best friends have been banging for months. What kind of fool do you think I am? I've known since you were tearing each other's clothes off with your eyes at my engagement party! Did you really think I bought your nonsense? Two of the people who know me better than anyone in the world, and who I know better than anyone in the world, and you thought I wouldn't know what was going on? All your secret texting while I was right there? What were you thinking? You thought I didn't see you holding hands in the hospital? Or see that Theo suddenly stocks Maddie's favorite sparkling water in his fridge? Or that I wouldn't notice Theo's bag on the floor of your living room that time, when you kept glancing at the kitchen door? Come on. Theo, I made sure to project when I told Maddie we got the venue, just so I wouldn't have to tell you the whole story all over again."

Oops. Maddie looked at Theo and they both grinned, and then looked away.

"Um. Thanks?" Theo said.

"You're welcome!" Alexa yelled back. Boy, she sure was in a yelling mood. "I even got you both to come over here for margaritas that time to confirm my suspicions. You were both so giddy around each other that I knew I was right, and I figured one of you would break down and tell me eventually, but no!"

Alexa had known since then. Maddie shook her head. After all she'd done to keep this from Alexa, it had all been pointless.

"And you know, it was all fine and good when you two were doing your secret little thing that any person with half a brain could figure out, because you both seemed happier than I'd ever seen you—especially you, Madeleine."

Maddie looked down at the floor so she couldn't see if Theo was looking at her to see if that part about her being so happy was true. It probably was.

"But then it was clear you'd had a fight, by the way you were both moping around everywhere. And then you each came to me with your 'I need to talk about something' faces on, and I was sure that this was FINALLY the time when you would each tell me the secret and I could talk sense into both of you and you would both stop this bullshit and call each other, but noooo, neither of you gave me the opportunity to do that, so I had to just keep pretending I didn't know anything, and that almost broke me in the middle of planning a damn wedding. I hoped you'd figure your shit out by now, but after the way the two of you were staring longingly at each other last night, it's clear you haven't."

Maddie could hear Olivia in the background laughing hysterically. Alexa was still going.

"And I'm not going to have you two ruining my one fucking wedding by walking around with little rain clouds above your heads and being too scared to talk to each other, so you're staying in this fucking closet until you fucking make up, do you hear?"

Oh God. She really had lost it.

"Lex, we don't have time for this!" Maddie said. "We have to get you ready, and take pictures, and . . . everything."

"Oh, I have the time, believe me." She heard the distinctive pop from a bottle of champagne. "Thanks, Olivia! Can you believe they thought I fell for that? But if you're worried about time, here, I'll give you a head start: Maddie, I know you probably got hotheaded after Theo got hurt, because you were scared of how much you cared about him, and so you lashed out at him. Theo, I know you're probably too stubborn to deal with your bullshit—Ben is right about that! But who knows, maybe Maddie's also being stubborn, and Theo's also being a hothead—it could be either one! All I know is that I'm going to do a very expensive sheet mask and drink some fucking champagne right now. Make up while I'm gone."

Maddie needed to do something to get them out of this closet.

"Lex, we're sorry we didn't tell you, but really, there's nothing

to make up. We just had a deal that this would last until the wedding, and now it's the wedding and we're done, but we're fine,
there are no hard feelings." She glanced at Theo. "Right, Theo?"

Theo looked back at her for a long moment.

"No." He shook his head. "That's not true. We don't . . . I'm
not saying I want Alexa to keep us locked in here. I don't want you
to be forced to talk to me. But there's something I have to say."

"Bye, guys! Chat later!" Alexa yelled from the other side of the
closet door.

Theo looked down at the floor for a few seconds and then
straight at her.

"She's right. I've been too stubborn to deal with my bullshit.
Maddie, I'm sorry. I'm so, so sorry. That was fucked up, what I
said about you. I'm sorry I said it; it wasn't true. I've been sorry
since the moment it came out of my mouth. I've just been too much
of a freaked-out asshole to say so."

Was he just saying this because Alexa locked them in the closet
and so he felt like he had to say something? She wasn't sure.

He sighed.

"I even wrote you"—he pulled a piece of paper out of his
pocket—"a letter to tell you I was sorry, but it felt shitty to give it
to you in the middle of Alexa's wedding weekend. And, okay, fine,
I was scared. So I didn't."

Hope rose in her chest, and it scared her. She wanted to lunge
for that letter, but she stayed still.

"This isn't a justification for how I acted that day, I swear. But.
I started having . . ." He sighed. "Feelings for you. But you kept
talking about how we would be over after the wedding, and then
after the hospital you seemed so mad at me, and you kept saying
how you couldn't wait to be done with me. I was so hurt and angry

that you were so sick of me, and us. When Ben figured out how I felt about you, I needed to say something to save face. And maybe I needed to say it for myself, so I would stop caring about you so much. Call it my fucked-up male ego, or just call me a jackass. It's probably both of those things. But I'm sorry."

She was glad the lighting in the closet was dim. She didn't want him to know she was close to tears.

"I should have said all of this a long time ago." He gave her a small smile. "I guess I was just scared. Or stubborn, like Alexa said. Anyway, I'm really sorry, Maddie." He looked down at the floor. "You don't have to say anything. I'll talk to Alexa. I know she won't make you pretend just because of her wedding; she's not like that."

He turned around and was about to pound on the closet door, but Maddie grabbed his hand in time.

"No. Wait."

She let out a long sigh.

"Alexa was right about me, too. Seeing you collapse like that, being there in the hospital with you . . ." She had to pause before she went on. "It was so scary. I hated it. When we were there, everything in me was focused on making sure you were well, but when I had to bring you home, I was so panicked about whether you would be okay. And I couldn't tell anybody how I was feeling, and how scared I'd been, and why, because no one knew what was going on. And plus, I was so mad at you for acting like a hero to save me and not thinking about yourself, for getting hurt like that, for making me so scared."

She closed her eyes.

"And then that night . . . I'm so sorry about what I said about you the next day. I swear I didn't mean it. I feel horrible that I said it. I was just so hurt, because I'd started to . . ." She shook her head. She didn't want to go down that road. She couldn't tell him what he'd said. What she'd said back. What she'd wanted to believe. "Because I really thought you understood me, in a way so few people do."

He reached for her hand.

"I think I do. And I know I love you."

Oh no. He must remember now what he'd said that night. She dropped his hand and stepped back.

"You don't have to say that, just because you said it before."

He narrowed his eyes at her.

"What are you talking about? When did I say it before?"

Was he going to pretend he didn't remember now?

"In the middle of the night. I was up, watching you, and you woke up and reached for me, and then you told me you loved me." She wasn't going to say what she'd said back, though. "It's okay. You were half asleep, you had a concussion, you didn't know what you were saying."

He stepped toward her again and took a deep breath.

"All of that is true. But I'm wide-awake and mostly recovered now. Maddie, I love you."

"Are you sure you didn't remember? Are you sure you're not just saying that?" Now she wished the lighting in the closet was better so she could see his face clearly.

He laughed.

"No, I don't remember, and no, I'm not just saying that. I know it for sure. I've thought of nothing else for the past three weeks, I promise you."

She laughed, too.

"I'm sorry, it's just . . . you said it that night, and then . . . well, that's why I was so on edge the next day. I didn't know if you meant it. And I didn't know what to do with all those"—she waved her hands in the air—"feelings."

He took a deep breath.

"Well, I didn't remember, but it's true. I love you. I'v
since . . . Oh God, I guess I really realized it earlier that day
you showed up at the rally, and I was so happy to see you,
think I've loved you since that night I locked myself out an
showed up at your house, all angry and frustrated, and I felt bette
just seeing you." He looked down. "But—"

She jumped in before he could say anything else.

"I love you, too." His head shot up, and he stared at her as she
continued. "I said it back that night, when you told me you loved me.
And at first I wanted to take it back, because I didn't know that's
how I felt, and I didn't think I felt that way, and I hoped you wouldn't
remember. And then I was furious that you didn't remember."

He reached for her hand.

"Are you sure? Wait, scratch that; I'm not letting you go back
on that. I'm holding you to it."

She finally let her tears fall as she laughed.

"I'm sure. I really am. Also, I'm sorry about the secret thing and
how that made you feel. I swear, the reason I wanted it to stay a secret wasn't what I said that day. It was just . . . everything was so
great, you know? We had such a good time together, hiding out in
your apartment or at my house, eating takeout and watching TV
and talking, or reading, or just being silent. And you seemed to like
doing that with me, and you seemed to like me, just as I was, even
after all the stuff that happened about that job. I've never been that
comfortable with someone I was dating. I've never been able to relax. I've always felt like I had to put on a show about who I was and
look and be perfect all the time. But with you, it was different. So it
felt like if we weren't a secret anymore, it would ruin everything."

Theo reached for her other hand.

"Oh, Maddie."

She shook her head.

"No, let me finish. But then when I saw Alexa and Drew, and how happy they are together, it made me feel like I'd given up something that could give me that same kind of happiness. I felt like I'd finally been with someone who knew me and liked me and believed in me just the way I was, and I'd lost that. But I didn't know how to get it back."

Theo looked straight at her.

"I promise you, I like you just the way you are. I love you, just the way you are, your hot head and tender heart and messy house and all. I'm sorry I ever made you think otherwise."

She took a deep breath and smiled at him.

"I'm sorry, too. I love you, just the way you are, your garlic breath and great hugs and spreadsheets and all."

He wrapped her up in one of those great hugs, and she let herself cry on his chest. She was back in the circle of his arms. She'd missed this so much.

"Oh." She looked up at him. "I didn't get the job. But my mom and I already have a plan for the kind of pro bono work I can do. Want to hear all about it?"

He grinned.

"I'd love to."

She took advantage of their proximity to reach into his pocket.

"I need to see that letter."

He tried to snatch it back from her, but she turned around.

"Oh God, it's so embarrassing. I can't believe I . . ."

She ignored him and unfolded it as he tickled her.

"Tell me the truth, did you make a spreadsheet before you wrote this?"

He threw his hands in the air.

"Just to organize my thoughts!"

She laughed out loud. Then she started to read the letter.

Maddie—

~~You probably~~

    ~~This is going to be long but~~

    ~~I keep starting letters to you but they're all~~

    I love you.

    I was trying to come up with a way to ease into this letter, but every-thing was all too long and complicated and detailed (sound familiar?). So I decided to just cut to the chase for once in my life and start with the most important thing. Oh wait, here's the other really important thing.

    I'm sorry. I didn't mean any of what I said that morning.

    I've known for a long time that I was falling in love with you, and I kept trying to fight it. I was going to tell you (okay, I was getting close to telling you) that I wanted to keep our thing going, that I wanted to make it a real thing, the night we went out to dinner, but things got weird, and I didn't really think you wanted to hear it. (I have no idea if you want to hear it now, but I'm writing this anyway for some masochistic reason; I don't know why I ever listen to my fucking brother. Anyway. I'm sorry I'm rambling.)

    So every time you reminded me that the wedding was coming up and we didn't have much time left, it felt like a slap in the face. It felt like you couldn't wait to be done with me—that you couldn't wait to be done with us. Maybe you meant it that way, I don't know.

    But for some reason, in those last few weeks, I allowed myself to hope more, especially after you came home with me after I was in the hospital. It seemed like you cared, and that's what I wanted more than anything else.

And the thing is, before you left that morning, you brought up the wedding again. So when Ben asked me what was going on between the two of us, I was already hurt and angry, mostly at myself. And there was no way I could confess to my little brother—who has always been better with women than I have—that I'd fallen for a woman who didn't love me back.

So I lied about how I felt about you, I lied about what our relationship meant to me; I lied about who you are. I lied to make myself feel better, but instead it made me lose the best thing that has ever happened to me.

I have no idea how you feel about me. Maybe you never want to see me again. Maybe you threw this letter away without even reading it. Maybe you're reading it with other people and laughing at me (though I don't think you are). But all I know is I'd never forgive myself if I didn't tell you all of this.

All my love,
Theo

This was the best letter anyone had ever written. She spun around so she could look at him.

"I love you so much."

She grabbed him and kissed him hard.

They stayed like that for a while, as their bodies fit together like puzzle pieces, their whispers of "I love you" a constant refrain.

Finally, Theo looked up.

"I think we owe a certain someone a thank-you." He turned to the door. "Alexa!"

The closet door shot open.

Alexa stood there with a huge grin on her face and two champagne glasses in her hands.

"NOW we can get this party started."

Chapter Twenty-three

THE REST OF THE DAY UNTIL THEY LEFT TO GO TO THE WEDDING PASSED by in a blur for Theo. There was a lot of champagne, many, many snacks, constant hand-holding with Maddie, and an overwhelming amount of laughter.

"Okay, it's time to get her into the dress!" Olivia said, once the other three of them were all dressed and Alexa's parents had arrived at the house. She turned to Maddie and Theo after Alexa's mom rushed into the bedroom. "You two probably don't even remember what the dress looks like, after all of your secret texting while we were shopping."

Theo opened his mouth to object, until he realized that no, he did not remember what the dress looked like.

"I remember it looked great on her?" he said. Maddie laughed and kissed him.

Alexa's dad drove Alexa, her mom, and Olivia up to the Rose Garden, so Theo drove himself and Maddie.

He smiled reminiscently on the way to the wedding as he thought about the hour Alexa had napped and he and Maddie had disappeared back to their closet. Maddie swatted him on the knee.

"I can tell what you're thinking about, and you need to stop! We can't do that again for hours. Like, seven or eight, probably."

He looked over at her and grinned.

"Okay, but after that, we need to make up for lost time."

She grinned back.

"Agreed."

When he pulled into a parking spot, neither of them got out of the car right away. He lifted their intertwined hands and kissed hers.

"I'm so happy." Had that morning really happened? "I love you so much. I missed you so damn much."

She beamed at him. He couldn't believe that that look on her face was for him. But it was.

"I'm so happy, too," she said. "I think I'm going to have to give Alexa that KitchenAid mixer she registered for, just to thank her for this."

The day before, he'd been horrified that he'd have to stand next to Maddie throughout the ceremony. Now he was overjoyed. He spent the whole time watching her face. His thoughts were so intent on Maddie he was surprised when they pronounced Drew and Alexa husband and wife.

They'd practiced the processional, with first Alexa and Drew, and then Olivia and Carlos, and then Maddie and Dan, with him and Josh pulling up the rear. But there was no way he wasn't walking out of this wedding with Maddie on his arm. As they started to follow the bride and groom down the aisle, he tucked Maddie's arm in his, and winked at Dan, who grinned at him and stepped back. Ahh, he saw the news had spread to the groom's side of the wedding party.

Before the photos started, Maddie beckoned him over to the entrance of the Rose Garden, toward a woman who looked a lot like a twenty-year-older version of Maddie.

"Theo, I'd like you to meet my mom, Vivian Forest. Mom, this is Theo Stephens. You've, um, heard a lot about each other."

Maddie's mom had a huge smile on her face.

"Theo, it's so nice to finally meet you." She took his hand in both of hers. "I know you all have a million things to do today, but I look forward to getting to know you better."

He put his other hand over the top of theirs.

"So do I, Ms. Forest."

She shook her head.

"Vivian." She winked at him. "Now, I'm ready for some champagne. See you two over at the reception."

The photos were endless, but thankfully the photographer seemed very happy for Theo's hand to be in Maddie's the entire time. Alexa had a smug smile on her face whenever she looked at them, which . . . okay, fine, he would give that to her.

Olivia jumped in his car for a ride over to the reception and proceeded to tease them the entire ten-minute drive.

"Lex had already told me she knew something was up between the two of you, but I could not *believe* how bold you were at the bridal salon. You just sat there texting each other, with me just feet away. Did you somehow think you were getting away with that?"

He and Maddie looked at each other.

"We really did think that," he said. "But don't ask me to explain why. In retrospect, it makes no sense."

"My mom knew, too, even though I didn't tell her," Maddie said.

They had really thought they were so slick, and yet everyone around them had known. Hell, the mayor had probably even known!

"Ah, that explains why your mom and Alexa had matching Cheshire cat grins today."

He and Maddie smiled at each other.

At the end of the many toasts at the reception, he looked over at Maddie. Tears ran down her face. He leaned over and kissed her.

"I'm so lucky," he said.

She picked up her napkin and dabbed at her eyes.

"We both are."

Alexa poked Maddie in the shoulder.

"Hey, lovebirds. This is great and all, but I need you to help me bustle this dress so we can get the first dance over with."

After Maddie and Alexa disappeared to the bathroom, Nik grinned across the table at Theo.

"Looks like someone talked about their feelings, hmm?"

Theo laughed.

"It was as terrible as I thought it would be, but then . . . sometimes good things happen after you do it."

She smiled at Carlos, who put his arm around her.

"Hard agree," she said.

When Alexa came back to the table, with Maddie trailing behind her, she winked at him. He opened his mouth to ask her what she needed, but she held her finger up in front of her lips. Oh no, what was she going to do next?

Alexa picked up her bouquet and turned around to Maddie.

"Oh, hey, Mads, can you hold this for me?" She tossed it right at Maddie's chest. Maddie caught it, and then burst out laughing.

"You are the worst."

Alexa grinned.

"You mean I'm the best. Come on, Drew. It's time to dance."

Once the official first dances were over, the party really started. Someone—he knew it was Maddie—got the DJ to play NSYNC, and managed to convince Theo to show off his moonwalk, to much cheering. They all danced, and cried a little, to Prince. And then when "Crazy in Love" came on, he grabbed Maddie's hand and twirled her on the dance floor, next to Alexa and Drew, and Nik and Carlos.

When everyone around them shouted the words to the song, he leaned forward and whispered in Maddie's ear.

"Tomorrow, can we sit on the couch in our pajamas for the entire day?"

She beamed at him.

"Absolutely."

JASMINE GUILLORY

Discussion Questions

1. When Theo and Maddie initially meet, he judges her based on her career, something that people often do without realizing it. Have you experienced either side of this?

2. Drew and Alexa getting married is a big step for them, and it affects Theo and Maddie as well. Have you ever had a friendship change because of your friend's love life? If so, how did you handle it?

3. Maddie puts on a certain persona because she thinks that's what the potential TV job requires. Have you ever behaved in a way that isn't really you for the sake of a job?

4. In retrospect, do you think Maddie and Theo were bad at hiding their secret fling? Did the ending surprise you?

5. Have you ever disliked someone at first, only to become good friends (or significant others) in the end?

6. Both Maddie and Theo talk about how their mothers sacrificed a lot for them growing up, not thinking about their own needs and desires to provide for their children. Can you relate to this in any way?

7. Being a bridesmaid or groomsman comes with many obligations. Were you ever part of a wedding party? What was the experience like?

8. On the surface, Maddie and Theo are two very different people: Maddie is more casual and relaxed; Theo is a bit of a control freak and very organized. Do you think this is a case of "opposites attract" or are they more alike than they appear?

Photo by Andrea Scher

Jasmine Guillory is the *New York Times* bestselling author of *The Wedding Date*, *The Proposal*, and *The Wedding Party*. Her work has appeared in *Cosmopolitan*, *Real Simple*, OprahMagazine.com, and Shondaland.com. She lives in Oakland, California.

CONNECT ONLINE

jasmineguillory.com

🐦 thebestjasmine